Winding Wood

Stevie Henden

Copyright © 2025 Stevie Henden
All Right reserved

No part of this book may be reproduced without the prior written permission of the author

ISBN: 9798317070403

This book is dedicated to my beloved mother, a great story teller, who continues to love and support me from spirit. With all my love

With huge thanks and gratitude to :

Ivana Bajic-Hajdukovic for so diligently editing my manuscript and Mikel Enriquez for the wonderful cover artwork.

On the 18th of June 1944, a V1 Flying Bomb struck The Guards' Chapel in Birdcage Walk during the morning service. 121 Soldiers and Civilians died.
May they rest in peace

Prologue to Part One

The soft fragrances filling the air are always a surprise, as I never thought you had a sense of smell while dreaming. The crisp green aroma of freshly mown lawns is replaced by musky bluebells in the spring woods, the glorious old English roses, and their almost overpowering heady perfume. When I visit again, the breeze carries the musty, earthy flavours of crushed autumn leaves.

Not all the fragrances are of nature; here, the comforting warmth of a cup of tea served on the terrace; there, the ripe, lush tones of strawberries and cream in the high summer.

All these scents come back to me during my nocturnal wanderings. In my dreams, I float like a wraith, in and out of the abundant herbaceous borders, overseeing everything which unfolds in the garden. It's as if I conduct the growth of each season's plants in their rhythm. Sometimes, detached from my own body, I catch a glimpse of myself as a young child. Other times, noisy, unfamiliar children play in my garden. This leaves me a little confused. Such is the nature of dreams; people like to divine their meaning and draw guidance from them, but often, they stay enigmatic.

Beyond the lawn are the tennis courts. I'm saddened they are weed-ridden and unloved. How can this be? And amidst the greenery grow strange plants. Had there always been a bank of azaleas alongside the path which winds into the woodland? I am anxious, but familiar things reassure me as I glide over the garden again. The pond remains still, alive with dragonflies. The bronze sundial, a relic from when the house was first built, stands as a silent witness, and the greenhouse where Father grows his tomatoes continues to deliver its abundance.

Silently, I approach the entrance of the house. The mellow red brickwork extends a loving, warm hug around me, and the sturdy studded oak door is not a barrier or threat; it's a sign of welcome. This is my home, and once the door is shut behind me, I'll always be secure, safe, and loved. The long wood-panelled hall welcomes me in as an old friend. It's solid and reassuring, the heart of the house, and here is the throbbing of its regular beat. Stories to tell of happy times, children running shrieking around the minstrels' gallery, which encircles the hall. Their cries embed themselves into the fabric of the walls so that future generations can still experience their joy.

Sometimes, I explore one of the many rooms, but the one I visit most often is my bedroom, which sits opposite the top of the stairs. Without effort, I ascend the staircase and find the door shut tight to protect the secrets of girlhood. The door opens with no sound, pushed by an unseen hand, and I enter my room, its lead-lighted window overlooking the lawns and the walled Rose Garden beyond. My threadbare teddy propped up, guarding the bed, ready to welcome me back and everything just as I remember it. Warmth and love fill my soul as I rest, sitting at the dressing table, complete with its frothy pink frills. This is my castle, my lair, where I chose to be away from the troubles and noise of the outside world.

Yet often, my dream is cut short far too soon; I yearn for more; I must have time to contemplate, but I am pulled back into my waking body, and for that night at least, my dreams are over. I have accepted that I can never return to Winding Wood again, but if you believe in a higher power, they have enabled me to visit in my dreams, so I have the joy of seeing my home once more.

Part One
Like a fairy tale

Chapter One
A sudden chill
May 1989
East Sussex

Spring came late that year, with sharp frosts blackening the glorious pink-white blossom on the old magnolia flowering outside the sitting room. As the days got a little warmer, Emily's morning stroll around the garden revealed abundant vigorous green growth. The rhododendrons and azaleas glowed, vibrant and alive with colour, lately at the height of their glory. Even the herbaceous borders began to stir from their winter sleep. On good days, she loved the garden and house when she felt in a positive frame of mind.

 She meandered to the bottom of the lawn and almost into the woodland. She turned and looked at the house, as always appreciating its graceful beauty, a symbiotic part of the landscape. But then her eyes moved to the rows of fresh new red tiles on the roof, and she remembered the bill waiting on her desk. As usual, Pritchard & Bristow's of East Grinstead's estimate did not bear much semblance to the final total. Emily dreaded having to battle it out with the ever-bad-tempered Reg Bristow to try and reduce the cost. The house had become a lovely but ageing money pit.

 Winding Wood held the family tight in its arms like a beautiful but elderly and clingy courtesan; her charm still intrigued with a certain sparkle, yet she often demanded expensive treatments to retain her youthful appearance. However, the lipstick and powder did only so much to cover up a crumbling façade.

Whatever Emily's feelings were about this house, it would be difficult to consider leaving. Her mother, Bryony, had a greater attachment. She grew up here and insisted she would die here. It was her house, and the family lived in it rent-free, so she held the upper hand on any discussions about moving. And it was not going to happen any time soon.

When Emily's father, James, died, Bryony persuaded Emily and her husband, Joe, to move in with her; she feared widowhood alone and wanted to have her family close by. A shrewd woman, she judged that her son-in-law would never earn much, and they would be unable to afford to buy a house for themselves. At first, Joe resisted, but in time gave in. He had been seduced by Winding Woods' beauty. On agreeing, he said to Emily.

'But I won't be nagged into doing what she calls a "proper job." Your brother had to get away and work abroad to escape your mother doling out sage advice about how to run his life!' Emily laughed and replied.

'Joe, that's unfair; David loves Mum. The opportunity in Dubai was too good to turn down.' But she also accepted there was a grain of truth in what he said.

Bryony had strong opinions on artists' ability to make money, and to Emily's extreme irritation, she was proven right. In her first flushes of love, she believed Joe when he predicted his future success. In time, it dawned on her that he would only sell the occasional portrait, so Emily needed to earn as much money for the family as possible.

They all rubbed along together in this beautiful, ageing, and frustrating house. Almost eighty years old, it needed some TLC, but the family did not have enough money to do everything. The wiring dated from before the war and often blew, sometimes spitting out sparks spectacularly. The house had last been decorated thirty-odd years ago, and the place aged with an air of gentile decrepitude.

Chapter Two
Ghosts

By the time the family sat down to dinner that night, Elsie's wails and tears had been forgotten. Emily dismissed them as the overactive imagination of a sensitive child. Elsie often made up fairy stories. Emily enjoyed her tales of frogs and handsome princes, but this one sounded slightly different.

Joe rushed in, as late as ever, red and flustered from his journey home. The train to East Grinstead was delayed, and a long queue for taxis snaked outside. Joe always managed to find a reason for being late; he was that kind of person. Bryony maintained it went with his '*artistic*' temperament.

With Elsie in bed, Bryony, Joe and Emily sat down to eat Shepherd's pie in the panelled dining room and catch up on the day's news. They only ate in the room in the summer, as in wintertime, they used less of the house to keep the ever-larger heating bills at bay. It was, however, the most beautiful of the rooms, with tall, elegant French doors opening onto the expansive lawns which lead to the woods beyond. Emily decided to raise the thorny topic of how they would pay the roof repair bill.

'It's going to mean taking something out of savings, and we don't have much left.'

'There's nothing else for it. I'm sure things will be better soon,' replied Bryony, ever the optimist. She continued.

'Joe, how's the portrait commission going? I hope you'll be paid for it before long?'

Joe looked uncomfortable, went red and said.;

'Not well, I'm afraid. Sir Harold hated the first version. I've scrapped it and started again.'

'What a surprise,' Bryony muttered under her breath, and both Joe and Emily chose to ignore her, not wanting another sparring match about when Joe would bring some money in. Bryony went on.

But who would not be in love with Winding Wood, not far from the village of Forest Row, down a peaceful lane cut into the Ashdown Forest? Its homely appearance wove an alchemical beauty which held one in a magical web. Four acres of land gave the house peace and privacy, a combination of garden and deep old English woodlands, with the hint of a distant verdant hillside through gaps in the trees.

The family could not afford a gardener, so the garden was not what it used to be. However, the three of them kept as much going as possible; perhaps one day, they would have more money to work on the rest.

Later that day, Emily was in the kitchen making dinner. Four-year-old Elsie rushed in, howling. Emily scooped her up in her arms, suspecting she had fallen and grazed a knee. A mother's rapid assessment of her physical condition assured her there was nothing serious to worry about.

'Sweetheart, what's wrong, tell Mummy, have you hurt yourself?' It took several minutes to pry out of Elsie what happened. In between snotty sobs, further reassurance and hugs, she managed to stutter.

'Mummy, I'm scared. There's a lady in the playroom.'

'What do you mean, dear? No one else is in the house other than me and you.'

'There was a lady, Mummy I'm telling the truth.' Elsie started to howl again. When her sobs subsided, Emily decided to humour her rather than have Elsie think she did not believe her.

'Did you recognise the lady?'

'No, Mummy, but she's ever so pretty.'

'So why are you scared of her?'

'Because, when she hugged me, she made me feel funny inside and then…' Elsie sniffled.

'She wasn't there anymore.' An icy chill went through Emily, and she held Elsie close to her. She was not sure who was reassuring who.

---

v

'Pass the wine, Joe, dear! Well, at least you're earning a wage, Emily. Someone in the house must.' Bryony was right. She was doing well, and although income from her design work could be erratic, she earned enough for them to get by. Only the ever-demanding house challenged their finances.

Bryony often got the knife into Joe about his lack of income, and he was sensitive about it. For Emily, she thought it enough, him being fulfilled by creating beautiful art, a passion which ran deep in his soul. Emily decided to move the conversation to another subject.

'Something odd happened today. Elsie came to me in a terrible state. When she calmed down, I managed to get out of her that an apparition appeared in the playroom. It's nonsense, but I'm worried she might be upset about something and is making up stories.'

'What poppycock!' laughed Bryony. Emily agreed with her mother and never believed in anything otherworldly. Joe's views on these things tended to be somewhat more left-field and said.

'You're assuming she's lying; perhaps you should consider the possibility she's telling the truth.' Bryony snorted in derision.

'No, maybe not lying,' she replied. 'But sometimes children imagine things.' She lit a cigarette, a habit Emily did not find appealing but could say little about; this was her mother's house. Bryony continued.

'You must keep an eye on her, Emily. If she does this again, you might consider taking her to the doctor.'

'And pump her full of pills!' retorted Joe.

'That's not what I mean. She may need someone to talk to,' Bryony added.

'I think she just needs to be left alone to be a child!' Joe said, sounding cross. Emily felt the tension rising between the pair, so decided to interject.

'I don't believe in ghosts, but say for a moment let's pretend we all do, then who do we think would be haunting Winding Wood? This old house must have a lot of stories to tell.'

After Emily said this, she regretted it, remembering that her mother had lost two sisters. It was not a sensible trajectory to take the conversation into; in her naivety, she wanted there to be talk about Anne Boleyn or Charles the First sans head. Something like that. Bryony drew on her cigarette again, and a brief sad shadow crossed her face. Emily thought she would change the subject, but before she could, Joe said.

'C'mon, Bryony. What phantom presence may be haunting us?'

'It's all nonsense, of course, but if Winding Wood had ghosts, if such things existed, I would want them to be my dear sisters Grace and Florence. Poor Grace died before I was born, but as for Florence, it's been over forty years, but I still miss her. I wish ghosts were real and we could meet our loved ones again, but they're not. When we die, we die. We're burned, or we rot, and that's all there is to it. I've lived all my life in the shadow of my sisters. Your grandmother's grief became overwhelming, and in the process, I lost part of her. As for Grandpa, he never spoke of either of them again after they passed away.' Emily said.

'Granny and Grandpa suffered awful tragedies but also enjoyed happy times. After all, they started their married life living in Docklands and ended up here. Granny often says that the second half of their life became like a fairy tale.' Joe cut in.

'Doesn't Violet maintain she's psychic? I remember her telling us she had weird dreams about things that came true.' Emily replied.

'It's a load of nonsense. Granny has a very overactive imagination. I suspect she made those stories up to frighten the children!'

Bryony said, 'Such an amazing story - Violet Gosling, a factory worker and Thomas Thomson, an engraver; her transformation to doyenne of the Forest Row Women's Institute and his to be a linchpin of the Golf Club. It doesn't get better than that. I wonder if all those good things that happened helped soften their difficult memories?' Emily asked.

'Do you think they forgot? A mother never forgets a lost child.'

'No, that's not what I'm saying. I lived under the shadow of my dead sisters. Trust me, Mother's grief overwhelmed her; a part of her died with them. But it could be that their charmed later life gave her some solace.'

'I hope so', said Emily, looking pensive.

Chapter Three
The ice
Plaistow London
1913

Through the bone-chilling winter mist, Violet glimpsed the face of a woman she didn't quite recognise, yet who seemed hauntingly familiar. Her eyes held a sinister glint that made Violet shiver with a sense of déjà vu. The woman's skin was deathly pale, as white as a hard January frost, with a cadaverous blue tint that sent shivers down Violet's spine. The apparition drifted closer, her movements eerily smooth, and without warning, stretched out her arm. Her icy palm met Violet's cheek, sending a shock of cold that made her face ache. Then, tendrils of cold spread from her face and snaked unstoppably through her body, chilling and freezing as they spread until they reached her heart. Violet could feel the wicked woman's icy touch infiltrating every fibre of the life-bringing organ, yet she was powerless to resist, move, or push the deadly hand away. Her heart began to harden in her chest, the blood within it turning to ice, and she felt the excruciating process of dying begin.

Violet awoke from her dream, sweating and anxious. The most vivid of nightmares had interrupted the rhythm of her sleep. She reached for her husband's reassurance, but he grunted and turned over. She wished to drown out the memory, which almost had a taste and texture. The image of the ungodly ice-cold woman who started to kill her in her dream state must be purged. To calm herself, she tried to turn her thoughts to the things she daydreamed about; perhaps these images would be strong enough; they would rid her of the horrible shadow of her nightmare.

During her waking hours, Violet was very much the daydreamer. She pictured elegant clothes bought from a smart department store in Regent Street or summer holidays in the salty ozone of the seaside. She escaped the smoky confines of London's Docklands in her dreams to find a life where fresh air and quiet prevailed.

x

Sometimes, she imagined herself flying through the air, propelled over the muddy, poisoned waters of the Thames, to be deposited on a hillside overlooking the glorious sweep of the green Kentish Weald, which she once visited on a day trip. The gorgeous spot bathed in the velvet summer sunshine, the leaves around her alive with red admiral butterflies.

Other times, she fantasised about travelling to foreign countries. She had seen pictures of beautiful cities like Venice and exciting sights such as the mysterious Great Pyramids in an encyclopaedia. She thought it must be wonderful to be able to visit exotic places. The furthest she had ever been to Epping Forest, and once took the train to Southend for the day.

These were Violet's fantasies, her waking dreams, but as a practical woman, she understood there was no question what they were, and the lot she had been dealt in life was not as bad as for many. At seventeen, she considered herself fortunate to have married well and settled into life with her dear husband.

Violet dreamed of something else, far away from Plaistow, but she accepted that her life in the grimy East End was as it was. Household duties took up much of the time. Each day, she made breakfast for the family and then commenced sweeping, scrubbing, dusting, and washing. With all that done, clothes must be ironed, food bought, meals cooked, and fires lit. It never ceased day in and day out, trying to keep on top of the filth created by the clattering industry and foul-belching chimneys around them. Specks of muck and soot covered every surface, and when she cleaned, everything became grubby again a few hours later.

In the evenings, Violet tried to forget her daydreams and find contentment with her husband. Even though she only married Thomas the year before, it felt much longer. He would sit in a chair smoking his pipe and reading the Evening Standard. She would be baking, sewing, or knitting. She often glanced at his handsome profile, then sighed, so content she had such a fine man as a husband. Many evenings, they spoke little; Violet thought he liked it that way.

Not long after they married, another of Violet's dreams came true. She yearned to be a mother, and when she realised she was pregnant, she cried tears of joy, thinking,

'I'm a grown woman now!'

When baby Grace was born, she gurgled her way into the affections of the whole household. It did not matter that their cramped rented rooms became even more difficult to squeeze into; the joy of a fresh, new, young life overwhelmed any other concerns the family may have.

On one particular night, when Violet's vivid, frosty nightmare came to her again, she found the image and taste of her terrifying dream impossible to shift. The awful thoughts, which often came back to her, did once again.

'I sometimes sense when things are going to happen. I hope my nightmare never comes true!'

Violet remembered the time she had a bad dream just before an awful accident on the High Street, where a little boy was trampled by a horse and died. Violet knew that Thomas would be dismissive, brushing off her concerns as mere figments of her imagination. Scared, she looked to her mother for reassurance. Sophia, always the pillar of strength, tried to soothe her daughter's fears.

'Violet dear, I'm sure you think you're right, although I wonder if you've been reading over-imaginative books. I wouldn't tell people about this. They may have the wrong idea; many folk think foresight is an evil curse. Mark my words and try to focus on the housework.'

In the quiet of her room, Violet whispered a silent prayer, hoping that her nightmare would remain just that, a nightmare. She clung to the hope that her premonitions would not come true, that the horrors she envisioned would stay confined to her dreams. But the fear lingered, a shadow that refused to be dispelled, leaving her to face the night alone with her terrifying thoughts.

Chapter Four
A miasma of mothballs

'Mother, can you help me with Grace? I'm exhausted,' pleaded Violet. Looking after her two-month-old baby drained her. Before giving birth, she retained a youthful naivety with no concept whatsoever of how challenging motherhood would be. In her romanticised imagination, she dreamed of her happy children playing in the sun-filled park, faces peachy-clean, wearing immaculate white clothing, or sitting bouncing and giggling on her knee as she sang nursery rhymes. Nothing prepared her for the constant onslaught of crying, nappies, and the needy demands of an ever-hungry infant at her breast. It was a blessing that her mother, Sophia, raised six children and was on hand to give much-needed guidance and practical support.

The family's living conditions did not help Violet's stress levels. The dreary lodgings were no better or worse than those of millions of working-class city dwellers but soul-draining all the same. Unlike many of her neighbours, Violet aspired to something different. Not that there would be any sign of an escape to a hoped-for haven on the horizon. She dreamed of a wisteria-clad detached house with a pretty garden far away from the grime. But reality would come crashing back in, the harsh truth pressing its unwelcome message.

'This is how it'll always be.' Only in her daydreams did she fly off to the leafy surroundings she yearned for.

Thomas's job engraving with Westborough's was at least steady, but his pay was insufficient to borrow the money to buy somewhere to live, so they lodged with Mrs Ida Haddock. The house sulked in a narrow, miserable street in Plaistow, not far from the Royal Docks. Mrs Haddock, a portly, God-fearing widow, moved in a stately manner enveloped by a permanent miasma of mothballs. She lived downstairs, with Violet and her family crammed into three rooms above. Most of the neighbours were docking people, as had been Violet's father. For no good reason, she positioned herself a cut above them. She thought the women were coarse and despised the men as louche drunks.

The house could not be described as a slum, far from it. Mrs Haddock considered her lodgings to be a picture of respectability, but the condition of the place drained the energy from Violet. The faded, once-patterned carpet on the narrow stairway had bare patches showing through. Its nod to the Indian sub-continent somehow made it appear even drabber. At the top of the stairs lay a tiny landing which led to three mean rooms. The largest they used as a sitting room cum-kitchen, the window overlooking the dreary sooted brick backs of cramped London terraces. A table and chairs completed the furnishings along with a sink and gas cooker, the floor covered with turgid green lino.

On one wall hung a tin bath. Calls of nature involved going down the stairs, then outside along the side passage to the W.C. at the bottom of the tiny garden. In foul weather, the journey was epic, and even in the summer, the family chose to use chamber pots at night. Everything was brown: the woodwork brown, the curtain fabric brown and the miserable smog-laden London air penetrating every pore brown. It had been many years since anything had been done to the house, and everything decayed into faded and shabby old age.

Violet dreamed of fresh air, light and just a touch of luxury. In her fantasies, she imagined a proper kitchen rather than a makeshift affair erected on one side of the room. Perhaps a larder and a sofa instead of long, uncomfortable evenings spent on upright chairs before retiring to bed early. Her mother enjoyed the privilege of her own room; Violet, Thomas and the new baby shared the other. Frederick, Violet's youngest sibling, slept on a put-you-up.

'Give her to me, sweetheart,' Sophia encouraged, and Violet handed over the screaming child to her mother.

Violet poured them both a cup of tea and daydreamed, relieved of the baby's immediate burden for the moment. Her thoughts turned to the countryside, trees, fresh air, peace, and tranquillity. She had never experienced this herself, but her mother often talked of her own childhood, and hearing it made Violet yearn even more to escape from Docklands; Sophia told the same story over and over.

'We used to go to Germany to visit family in Bavaria. Mama and Papa sold all our possessions, and we left London, only to return and start again some months later. It was so beautiful; my family lived in a sweet little farmhouse with its own duck pond.'

Violet sighed, knowing her vision of green countryside, ingrained in her by her mother, would never be hers. She had a firm word with herself, understanding how grateful she should be for her life. Many were much worse off. She had a healthy baby and a loving family. She adored her handsome husband, and he always brought money home at the end of the week. Even then, his meagre pay packet didn't go far, and after paying the rent to Mrs Haddock and buying food, not much remained.

'Don't vex yourself, Vi; we'll make do,' Thomas would say, and they did. Just. That's how life had always been for Violet. At fourteen, her beloved father died, and being the oldest of the children who still lived at home, she had a duty to help her mother care for the family. So, she left school and got a job she loathed, working in a factory. The endless and soul-destroying process of ensuring lids fitted onto tins of paint made her desperate to do something else.

After she settled Grace in her cot, Sophia sat at the table with her daughter to enjoy a moment of respite.

'What time will Thomas be in?' asked her mother. 'We need to put the lamb on the stove.'

'Seven-thirty. He's not going to the boxing club tonight.'

'Why are you so glum Vi?'

'I'm exhausted. Grace keeps me up all hours of the night, so I'm not sleeping well.'

'You're no different from any other young mother. It's what us women have to do.'

'Yes, I know, I really do.'

'Count your blessings, my girl. Thomas is a good man, and you could've done a lot worse.'

Violet coloured a little, thinking momentarily of how entranced she had been by Thomas when they met. Friends told her Thomas was a catch; she was pretty and dark, and her slender figure turned young men's heads, but when someone complimented her, she never believed it.

Later, Thomas returned, harassed after the long day and crammed Tube journey from the City. He greeted Violet, asked what she had prepared for supper, sat down, and stuck his nose in the newspaper.

She made tea and got him his pipe and slippers. A quiet, self-contained man, he said little. Looking at his handsome profile, she once again reminded herself how lucky she was to marry him. Life may be challenging, but having found true love with a man like this was wonderful.

That night, Violet once again found herself ensnared in the clutches of the Ice Woman, as she so often did. She had hoped that growing up, marrying, and having a baby would somehow banish the dreadful nightmares, but it hadn't. This night was no different. She awoke with a shuddering gasp, momentarily disoriented and unsure if she was still dreaming. Her trembling hand reached her face, and to her immense relief, it was warm, unlike the icy caress from her nightmares.

As she lay there, trying to steady her racing heart and coax her mind back into sleep, the same question churned relentlessly in her thoughts. Why do I have this horrid dream, and who is the woman who looks so familiar?

The Ice Woman's visage, vivid and terrifying, loomed in her thoughts. The cold eyes stared back at her from the depths of her subconscious. Violet pondered who she was and why she returned to torment her night after night. The questions remained, gnawing at her as the dark hours of the night stretched on.

Chapter Five
Torpedo
1915

Violet scurried along the damp, malodorous street from the Underground station; the chilly summer drizzle and grey skies did nothing for her mood. Her ears rang with the appalling tragedy cried out by the newspaper boy, a banshee telegraph of misery and horror for all the East End to hear. Hands were clasped to mouths to suppress vocal expressions of shock.

'*Lusitania torpedoed! Terrible loss of Life!*'

A cold shudder passed deep through Violet's innards. She could not swim, and the thought of the victims struggling in the icy water of the North Atlantic terrified her. Violet pulled her coat a little tighter around her as if somehow to protect herself from the Kaiser's evil and hurried home to share the grim news with her mother.

With Thomas away at the army camp in Yorkshire, she had no one else to talk to. Little Grace, almost eighteen months old, gurgled a few words but nothing meaningful, and Violet did not mix much with the people in the street. At the front door, she encountered Mrs Haddock, who, on hearing the appalling fate of the Lusitania's human cargo, swayed as if she would faint, crossed herself and started to mutter the Lord's prayer under her breath. Upstairs, Sophia, just as shocked, sat down, face drained and pale, to take in the awful news.

'Dear Lord, those poor lost souls!' When will this terrible war end? How could anyone sink a liner full of women and children? It's wicked. I'll pray for them tonight, but that'll be of little help.' Violet added.

'I'm not sure how much more bad news I can bear.' Sophia agreed.

'The word from the front gets worse by the day. We were told the war would only go on for a few months. And poor Frederick. When I read his last letter, it broke my heart to learn how many friends he lost.'

Keen to enlist and do his bit for King and Country, Sophia's youngest son Frederick had been in France for a year, trapped in the endless clinging mud and shell-fire brutality of trench warfare. Sophia hoped her prayers would be enough to keep him alive. Violet went on.

'Those bloody Germans, they're evil monsters. How can they kill innocent women and children and still think themselves decent Christians?' Sophia's expression turned from shock to steely anger; she breathed deeply for a long moment to control herself and said.

'Violet, that's not true, your grandparents are German and good people. You can't condemn a whole nation because of the misdeeds of their rulers. You should know better than that. Remember, my brothers still bear their German surnames with pride.'

'I'm sorry, Mother. I should've thought about it before I spoke. This awful war keeps me on edge all the time. I worry so about Frederick. Every time I hear a knock on the door, I fear it'll be a telegram with dreadful news.'

'As do I. I wake in the night terrified we'll lose him, but we must count our blessings. Thomas is safe at Catterick. Thank goodness he was posted as a gym instructor, and he isn't at the front, too.' Violet replied.

'You're right, Mother, but so are the army fortunate in having him; he gained a lot of experience at the boxing club. I miss him terribly, and making ends meet on his army pay is even more difficult than before the war. What are we supposed to do?'

'We manage; we always do, Violet. You need to be strong for little Grace.' Violet smiled a thin smile; her mother was always right. They had no choice other than to cope, keep carrying on, and hope and pray they would not suffer the grievous loss of one of their loved ones. Earlier the same year, Mrs Haddock lost Ronald, her only son, at Neuve Chappelle, and the woman physically shrivelled before their eyes. The ebullient landlady, replaced by a silent weeping, grey ghost.

Grace came tottering over, giggling, and hugged Violet's legs. She learned to walk early and ran happily around the cramped lodgings, unaware of the world's brutal travails. Violet envied her innocence. She insisted there would never be a shortage of love in her household. In the moment of shared affection with her daughter, all of Violet's troubles disappeared.

Later that evening, Violet soothed Grace to sleep, and the women ate a meagre stew. Each time she went to the market, there were interminable queues, and they spent many hours finding provisions. Today, Violet managed to buy a little scrag end of lamb. They would eke this out for several meals, the mean amount of meat padded with potatoes.

There was an insistent knock on the door. Violet got up to find out who it was, a tight knot in her stomach; loud knocking in wartime did not presage good news. It was her Aunt Helena. From the deathly pale skin tone and shaking hands, it was evident she was in shock, and Violet feared the worst. They calmed her down with a cup of tea, and when Helena could speak, she stammered out.

'This morning, I went to Canning Town market to see if there were any vegetables. There's so little in the greengrocers now. I came across a group of women I recognised. They live on the street next to us. I went over to greet them and saw straight away something was wrong. They were angry. It didn't occur to me for one moment that they were upset with me.' Helena started crying.

'Go on,' encouraged Sophia.

'Their expressions were horrible, so cruel and hard. One of them shouted at me: "Murdering Hun! You Germans butcher women and children. Your evil U Boat captain slaughtered babies and their mothers. Filthy types like you should not be allowed to live amongst decent people. Go back home to your bloody Kaiser!" She walked up to me and spat in my face.'

'Oh, my good Lord!' exclaimed Violet, clasping her hand to her mouth.

'And there's worse to come,' Helena continued.

'Stones were thrown through our parlour window this afternoon whilst I was cleaning. Further down the street, a mob ransacked the German bakery, and the family returned to find their windows broken and possessions piled in a bonfire. I'm terrified this will happen to us, too.'

'That's terrible, Helena,' said Sophia and squeezed her sister-in-law's hand in reassurance, who replied.

'Charles and I are good members of the community. We go to church, we give to the poor, and we're respectable people, but we're treated like this just because he carries a German surname!' A grave sense of foreboding flooded over Violet; she said.

'How can people be so cruel to others because of the blood which runs in their veins?' Her mother glared at her but said nothing. She didn't need to. Violet blushed, recalling their earlier conversation.

Sophia talked to Helena, trying to calm her down. Sometimes, her sister-in-law got her emotions under control, then the dam would burst again, and she started to cry. It was quite late when she left for the bus ride home. Violet went with her.

'And come right back, dear,' implored Sophia, 'the streets are so dark.'

'I can take care of myself, Mother,' replied Violet.' But she was not as confident as she sounded.

Despite her bravado, she found herself anxious during the journey. Looking at her fellow passengers, she wondered if they would hate her if they suspected she too had German blood.

In an instant, Violet was overwhelmed by a wave of heat and dizziness. The bus seat beneath her jolted violently, sending her stomach into a nauseating spiral. For a gut-wrenching moment, reality blurred; she couldn't discern if she was awake or trapped in her usual nightmare. To her utter terror, she felt the chilling caress of icy fingers against her face. And then, just as suddenly, it vanished.

She snapped back to reality, desperately gripping the grab rail beside her. The conductor, his face etched with concern, hurried over and said.

'Are you alright, love? It looks like you've seen a ghost.'

Chapter Six
London in the time of plague
1918

London wept, heartbroken, in deep mourning for its dead. The battered and broken city lay dank and damp under the choking blanket of yellow-brown winter smog. The heady joie de vivre of summer 1914 long evaporated, never to return, and was replaced with an all-pervading funeral dirge—a sad hymn that resonated through every person.

Life drained from the fabric of the buildings and streets, from the people and the animals, emptied of the blood which leeched into the Flanders fields. Houses became unkempt, people dressed in shabby clothes, their pallor pale from years of shortages. Often, a bereaved widow or mother could be seen overcome with emotion. Most times, uninterested passers-by walked with their heads turned the other way in case the weeping woman tried to engage them in conversation. Or they glanced away in revulsion from discharged soldiers with disfiguring facial injuries or amputations. On other occasions, they would flinch, unsure of what they were seeing, when a man ranted and wept, his mind gone through shell shock. Embarrassed, they crossed to the other side of the road, fearing the awkwardness of having to acknowledge him.

As if the war was not horror enough, further misery beset the populace. A microscopic single strand of life, a simple virus wreaked brutal devastation across the whole planet, and London was no exception. When the Spanish flu first appeared the previous summer, it was no different from the normal variety. When the winter came, a more virulent mutation came back from the front, brought by soldiers who sickened and were transported to hospital. It distinguished itself by killing young, healthy people in large numbers.

London took on a ghostly, silent air as people stayed behind locked doors. When they ventured out with their faces covered it gave them the appearance of an alien species. A masked ball of frightened dancers moving in choreographed steps to avoid close contact with infected people. Sometimes, Violet thought Plaistow seemed beautiful, devoid of the usual irritating hustle and bustle. With streets free from horses and vehicles, a strange tranquillity fell over the East End. Other times, she found the atmosphere terrifying; this was not the familiar city she knew so well.

Violet, Sophia, and baby Grace managed to avoid catching the flu, but Thomas wrote to her from Catterick that he had been ill, although he had now recovered. She missed him all the time and hoped he would soon be discharged and come home. After all, with the war over, he could not be wanted at the camp.

In this atmosphere of terrible loss, Violet first met Edith Wilson. Violet had offered to help at the local orphanage for a few hours a week. The institution took in a number of new children who lost both their parents. Short of money and staff, they were glad to have the support of volunteers to take care of their charges.

On one of her regular visits, Violet found herself dealing with a projectile vomiting child; she cleaned her, and then the girl threw up again. She heard a kindly voice say: 'Do you need a hand?' Violet looked up. The woman was red-haired and pretty with a radiant smile; she liked her straight away.

'Bless you; would you find me the flannel and soap? I need to give her face a good wash!' The girl took the opportunity to vomit again, this time all over Violet's dress.

'Let me help! By the way, my name's Edith Wilson.'

'Pleased to meet you, I'm Violet Goldsmith.' The two women cleaned up the girl, and Violet sponged herself down.

'Do you live in Plaistow?' she enquired.

'Not far away, in West Ham. I feel I need to do something to help. My husband was killed in France, and I must keep myself busy. My neighbour looks after my little boy when I'm here. It's such a relief to get away and meet other people.'

'I'm so sorry. I lost my brother in the war. As to this awful illness, my husband Thomas fell ill, but I'm blessed it wasn't serious. I hope he'll be home soon. He's been away for four years, and I've only seen him a few times when he was on leave.'

Violet finished sponging vomit from her dress. Edith went on.

'It's been difficult for us women, such a struggle to feed our families, then there was the bombing…'

'I thought I'd try to be strong, Edith, and cope with all this, but then I lost my dear brother Frederick at the Somme. The awful day the telegram arrived, with the news he'd been killed, I wasn't sure if I could carry on anymore. I did, I had to for my child, but now this horrible illness. I worry so much about the future. The doctors don't have any treatments, and it seems as if the sickness will go on and on forever. Can we ever return to normal when so many people are dying? It's terrifying.'

'It's been difficult, but we'll get through it,' replied Edith.

'Maybe, but what comes next? Is it going to be any better for working people than what came before? Let me tell you something; I loathe living here. It's filthy. I dream of fresh air and green trees. Is that wrong of me? Should I accept my lot?'

'There's nothing wrong with dreams, Violet. Before the war, I had high hopes of studying to be a doctor. It's not easy for women; many barriers are put in our way. But I was determined. When the war broke out, I realised it was important I helped nurse those poor boys when they came back from France, broken both in body and mind. I think it's likely that my ambitions will never come true.'

'Gosh,' said Violet.' You must be clever to think of doing something like that!'

Edith smiled and said nothing.

Violet thought this woman was someone she would like to be friends with. The local women did not interest her. They talked about little other than what to cook for their husbands and what tactics they used to avoid their drunken advances. If she had not had to leave school, she would have done well. She was bright and inquisitive. Loss and duty stripped her of any chances.

In the coming weeks, Violet and Edith met at the orphanage several times. They chatted about their lives, and Violet came to see this was the first person who had ever taken an interest in her. She felt a little guilty even thinking this; she loved her husband, Thomas, and he was a good man. However, he had little time for the chatter of women. Edith proved to be a good listener, and Violet talked for hours about her family, dreams and concerns.

Once, when Violet was talking to Edith, a sudden flash of inner knowledge passed through her mind like a butterfly alighting on a summer flower, and then it went. A single crystal-clear moment of foretelling. But words poured from her mouth before she could stop them; she stared straight at her friend and said.

'One day, you'll tell my family something which will change everything, then in their eyes, I'll no longer exist.' Violet stopped speaking, horrified about what she had said. Bemused, Edith replied.

'Whatever are you talking about?' Violet covered her tracks and stuttered.

'I'm so sorry, dear; I was daydreaming and thinking out loud, ignore me. I'm being silly.'

Edith gave Violet an odd glance, and then they both forgot about the conversation and went back to discussing what they would make for supper that evening.

Chapter Seven
A savage blow
1921

Some days, Violet thought she would not cope. But whenever she felt like that, she stiffened her resolve and decided she was being self-indulgent. But at other times, the world fragmented into a million fragments of jagged glass around her, and she struggled to get out of bed in the morning until her mother insisted she did.

Losing Frederick in the war had been bad enough, but then, the previous winter, the grim reaper cast its cruel eyes on the Goldsmith household once more and deemed it was time for little Grace to die. Only seven years old, scarlet fever took her, and she died in Violet's arms after struggling with the illness for a week.

Violet wanted to scream and shout, and she berated God for his cruelty, but no one wanted to talk about it. Everywhere, grief hung like a tearful fog over London. Shattered families who lost all their sons in the war looked to a dark future with permanently devastated lives. Others, who could not cope looking after the mutilated men who survived, then came back broken from the front. And then there were those whose loved ones were taken by the flu. This was not a time to express raw emotion; if one did, the whole façade of civilised life might erode and crumble into dust.

As if the grief was not enough, Violet's awful dream continued to torment her, the icy woman making frequent nocturnal visits, deepening her agony further. Each time she awoke from the nightmares, drenched in sweat and trembling, the chilling presence of the Ice Woman lingered in her mind. Awake in the dead of night, Violet feared returning to sleep, her stomach churning and full of dread.

As she lay in the darkness, clutching her blankets tightly for a sense of security that never came, the same desperate questions echoed through her mind. Who is she, and what does she want? The Ice Woman's cold, emotionless eyes seemed to bore into her soul, and Violet could not shake the feeling that there was something deeply personal in this haunting. Thomas, trapped in grief for his little Grace, was unable to speak of any emotion. After her funeral, he told his wife he did not wish to speak of his lost child ever again, and he didn't. Violet yearned to be able to talk about her; this would keep her alive. Once she was not spoken about, she would be gone, and this must not be allowed to happen.

The one avenue Violet had to express herself was through her correspondence with Edith. It had saddened her when, a few months after their friendship blossomed, Edith told Violet she was remarrying, and they would be moving to York. Violet knew she would miss her friend and was jealous that she had the opportunity to escape from the London Docklands.

'Don't worry,' said Edith. 'We'll become pen pals! I'll write every week!'

Her latest letter arrived that morning. Violet left it until Thomas went to work and her mother was out shopping so she could savour the words with the privacy they deserved.

67, Harold Road
York
Yorkshire

21st May 1921

My Dearest Violet,

I hope you are finding life just a little easier than when you wrote your last letter. However, it is not for me to judge how long you will grieve for your little one. But please know that I, your dear friend, will always be here to listen when you need to talk about your terrible loss.

Only a mother can understand what losing a child is like, and even having two little ones myself, I cannot fathom the depth of your grieving, not having had to say farewell to any myself.

I hope that, in time, you and Thomas will be ready to have children again. None of them will replace Grace, and neither should they, but I pray that in the act of loving them, you find healing.

I hope you don't mind me sharing my happy news with you. Duncan's been promoted again. We think we may be able to afford a holiday in the Channel Islands next year - it would be such an adventure!

Please write soon and don't forget I'm always here to listen to you.
Your affectionate friend

Edith

1,Balaclava Lane
Plaistow
London

1st June 1921

Dear Edith,

Thank you so much for your letter and kind thoughts. They are appreciated. I am not sure I will ever get over Grace, but I keep going for the sake of Mother and Thomas. What else can I do?
    I now understand losing a child is the most grievous agony a mother can feel. It is impossible to describe the pain to anyone who has not experienced it. I can only tell you it is as if something ripped a ragged hole in my heart, and I suffer with physical agony as a result.
    Edith, I am so pleased to read your news. Do not be shy about sharing joyous things with me. Do not ever think that I am resentful because life is going well for you. I hope one day I will be able to tell you happy news of my own; it is just at the moment it seems like something good will never happen. Please forgive me for being such a burden.
    With all my warm thoughts as ever.

Violet

Chapter Eight
Seeking Solace
1925

With the last box unloaded, Violet relaxed a little, relieved the job of moving house was just about done. After years of being crammed into Mrs Haddock's fading lodgings, she persuaded Thomas they needed to rent something bigger.

Since Grace died, Violet refused to have any more children, fearing the same loss would strike them again. In time, her grief diminished enough for her to think about the future. Little Bryony came along the year before, and now Violet fell pregnant again. The expanding family could not be shoehorned into three rooms.

When the day came to leave for their larger abode, there were fond farewells. The Goldsmiths were only moving four streets away, but the bond with Mrs Haddock, forged through their losses in the mud on the Western Front, would not be quite as close. It was easy to pop downstairs for a quick chat. Having to arrange to visit put up a barrier.

Violet harangued Thomas to ask the bank to arrange a mortgage. He refused, insisting his meagre weekly pay packet would not be enough to cover the repayments.

'Anyway, Vi,' he said. 'What would happen if I lost my job? You know how hard things are.' She had no argument for that one. After much discussion, they met halfway; he agreed they would rent a bigger place—a house to themselves at last. Violet breathed a huge sigh of relief.

On one subject, Thomas still dug his heels in. She wanted to leave the East End she loathed and move further out into the new suburbs in Essex. It sounded so lovely when she read adverts in the Evening Standard, with Tudor-style semis lining tree-lined avenues. Her heart yearned for clean air and not needing to wipe layers of sooty dust off everything it clung to.

'I'm not leaving Plaistow Vi,' he insisted. 'All my friends are around here; it's my part of town. Where would I be without my mates at the boxing club?' Violet gave up and resigned herself to forever having to live in the grimy hinterland of the London Docklands.

Whenever Violet started to think negative thoughts, she spoke a firm word to herself: they were not poor, food was always on the table, and the children were healthy. So much more fortunate than many. Her husband was handsome, not drunk or brutal, and brought home steady money.

'I've nothing to complain about, and I love Thomas,' she said to a friend while shopping. 'He's a good man and does his best to provide for the family. I shouldn't nag him. He must think me a terrible scold.' The woman replied.

'Perhaps that's what women always have to do, hold our men to account.'

The Goldsmith's new home in Westmoreland Street was nothing remarkable. Just the same as hundreds of thousands of others, thrown up in haste and shoddily built, forty years earlier when burgeoning London grew like a blot of black ink spreading out on the surrounding green fields. Row after row of drab houses belched smoke from their chimneys, where only a few years before cows grazed and clear streams gurgled through lush meadows.

5, Westmoreland Street boasted a front room complete with bay window and slate fireplace. Violet thought the bay added a touch of class to the otherwise modest frontage. The next street had flat-fronted terraces, so she reigned superior in her domain. Behind it was a second reception room that served as a dining room. The kitchen lay beyond, opening onto a narrow garden. Upstairs, three bedrooms and the ultimate luxury: a bathroom with W.C. For Violet, this meant liberation. No longer having to empty foul-smelling chamber pots every morning, no more cold, damp trips to the bottom of the garden. The family had gone up several social rungs.

Her mother interrupted Violet's thoughts; she had not seen her entering the room.

'Violet, love. I've got something I want to tell you.'
'What is it, Mother?"

xxx

'Sit down, dear.' And the two women perched on up-turned packing chests.

'When you were at the shops yesterday, Mrs Haddock came for tea. It was clear that she was excited about something. She had a glow to her cheeks, which I've not seen since she lost her Ronald. She told me she visited a medium, who gave her a message from him in the afterlife and knowing he's not scared and in pain anymore, she feels so much better.'

'Don't you think that's a load of nonsense, Mother? These people are frauds trying to extort money from the vulnerable.'

'To be honest, when Mrs Haddock first mentioned it, I was sceptical, but when she described how the medium gave her information only Ronald knew, it convinced me. Oh, and the medium's very well known; she has an excellent reputation. She's called Ekatarina Zagorski. You must've read about her?'

'Goodness, yes! there was an article about her in the newspaper, but she must be expensive. How could we afford to pay for her?'

'I pawned your father's wedding ring.'

'Mother, that's such a generous thing to do. Can you bear to part with it?'

'Vi dearest, if just for one second I can hear something from my beloved Frederick and our darling little Grace and know they're safe in Heaven, it'll be worth every penny.'

Three days later, Violet and Sophia took the District line to Blackfriars, where they changed and caught the train to Crystal Palace. After winding through the grimy innards of the city, the train soon began the long climb through the wooded ridges of Honor Oak and Sydenham Hill, then beyond to the high-level station at Crystal Palace. The green trees and slopes of this part of South London a million miles away from the soulless, flat grey Thames hinterlands of Plaistow.

Finally, they burst out of a sooty-smelling tunnel into the daylight, and the two women alighted in the huge and almost empty terminus. An ornate glass roof soared over their heads, but the place appeared to be in a terrible state. Avaricious weeds grew through the wooden boarded platforms and Violet froze as she caught a glimpse of a large rat scurrying away at the sight of them. The station smelled of damp and soot. Sophia said.

'They say the Crystal Palace is in an awful condition. I used to visit with Father, but I haven't been for years. It would be so sad if it closed. I remember when we first came, I thought it was the most beautiful thing I'd ever seen, sparkling like a jewel on the hilltop.'

'It must've been wonderful! How do we get to Paxton Road from here, Mother?'

'Miss Zagorski gave me directions in her letter, it's only ten-minute away. She's Russian, I think that's so exotic! Not sure what she'll make of ordinary people like us. They say Virginia Woolf's one of her clients!' Violet mentally checked her appearance. She had put on her Sunday best, an apple green dress she sewed herself the previous year, and then she recalled, a little embarrassed, that her dark overcoat was old and faded. The outfit was topped by a cream cloche hat.

After pushing through a crowd of shoppers, they walked down the long Paxton Road, lined with tall London plane trees and ornate villas. A little pang struck Violet's heart; she would love to live somewhere like this. She sighed, knowing Thomas's pay would never stretch to it, so she would have to accept her lot. He worked hard and did his best, but for working folk like them, this was never going to happen. Her nerves jangled as they arrived at their destination. The gothic-style house, complete with a slate-clad turret, towered over them, and she thought.

'This isn't where people like us belong.' Not wanting to pass her anxiety onto her mother, she said nothing. Sophia said.

'This is it, Vi. The house is called "Winding Wood" - how beautiful and romantic!'

'It's a lovely name indeed; one day, if I live in a nice house, I shall name it after this one.'

———————

Chapter Nine
Ekatarina Zagorski

A neatly uniformed maid took Violet and Sophia's coats, then escorted them along the hall, through ornate carved double doors and into a grand reception room. She announced.

'Miss Zagorski, I have Mrs Goldsmith and Mrs Gosling for you. Violet perceived a certain judgment in the maid's voice, who did not consider them worthy of being presented to her esteemed mistress. The woman came to greet them. She was dark and slight, with her hair cut in a bob; Violet put her age in her thirties, immaculately dressed in a fashionable knee-length cream lace dress. She wished her own outfit was smarter and not homemade. In contrast to her haughty maid, Ekatarina Zagorski's greeting was warm and genuine.

'My dear ladies, you're most welcome in my home,' and extended her hand. Her handshake soft and warm, Violet immediately felt more relaxed. Miss Zagorski spoke in a gentle tone with just a hint of an accent. Violet remembered her mother said the medium was Russian. She had never met a Russian before; it seemed ever so exciting.

'Have you come from far? I hope your journey wasn't too arduous?'

'We took the train from London. It was quite quick,' replied Violet. She hoped Miss Zagorski had forgotten their Plaistow address.

'Please sit down.' The medium gestured to a brown leather Chesterfield sofa. The reception room stretched for thirty feet before opening into an airy conservatory full of huge tropical-looking plants. On one side of the room loomed a high black marble fireplace, and framed oil paintings adorned the walls. Violet decided it was '*sophisticated*.' She glimpsed something glinting on a table in the corner and peered to work it out. It was a scale model of the Crystal Palace, made from glass and lit from inside. She went over to it for a closer inspection and said.

'Oh, isn't it lovely!'

'Thank you, I had it made for me. The Palace is a most wonderful place that holds happy memories. There, some years ago, I first received a message from spirit that I should be working as a medium. It's somewhere where the walls between the worlds are thin.' Violet did not quite know what to say, so she replied.

'How charming,' and went to sit on the Chesterfield.

The maid returned pushing a trolley, displaying the trappings of afternoon tea. Finger sandwiches were followed by a coffee walnut cake, and then, to complete the feast, warm scones topped with cream and strawberry jam. Sophia said.

'Miss Zagorski, you're most hospitable. We were not expecting to be treated like this in your beautiful home. Thank you so very much. I have to say, it rather makes me feel like royalty.'

'It's nothing, Mrs Gosling. I don't usually put on this spread for my clients, but my guides told me you need a little fuss-making, and I know things have been tough. They said I have some special connection to you; they're not clear on what that is. I'm sure that all will be revealed in the future.' Violet jumped.

'How do you know anything about our business? I don't mean to be rude, but I don't believe my mother said anything about our loss.'

'Mrs Goldsmith, I'm a psychic, and my guides tell me much. Trust me, I only have your best interests at heart. You're two women who've endured the most grievous losses, and sometimes, the travails of everyday life don't allow you to be cared for and heal. It's my pleasure to offer you hospitality. I've not always been given consideration myself, so I like to be kind to strangers.' Violet replied.

'I'm sorry to hear that. I do hope you've not suffered bad experiences in London.'

'Far from it, I love this city, and people have been good to me. No, I endured terrible misfortune in Russia, which is why I left that ghastly, icy hell of a place, but I don't wish to speak of that.' Just then, the maid returned and ushered another two women into the room. The medium stood up and greeted them.

'Mrs Goldsmith and Mrs Gosling, may I introduce the Trout Sisters.'

'I am Ethel Trout,' beamed one of the thick-necked, sturdy, tweed-clad women.

'And I'm Mabel, the older one.'

'Only by five minutes,' replied Ethel, with an undertone of rancour.

'Come, let us go to where we'll hold our séance,' invited Miss Zagorski, and the group moved to a large round walnut table at the end of the reception room nearest to the conservatory. Violet and Sophia sat down, not knowing what to expect. The Trout sisters looked relaxed, and Violet assumed they were used to the procedure of seances. As if to echo her thoughts, Miss Zagorski said.

'You're blessed with the presence of three experienced mediums today, so it's my hope we'll be able to make a strong connection with your loved ones. Please hold hands.' Miss Zagorski quietly said a prayer, which Violet did not recognise, with lovely words about God, love and light. 'Nothing to fear here,' she thought.

She watched the medium. Her eyes were closed, now breathing deeply, and for a moment, a faint shadow crossed her face. When Violet peered, her features had changed a little; she spoke, and her voice, now a different timbre, with all traces of the Russian accent gone. The table shook, a gentle breeze blew from nowhere, and a pleasant warmth brushed Violet. Miss Zagorski said.

'There are people here today who've lost someone very close. It was such a grave loss. A terrible wound.' Violet thought this to be a vague generalisation. The medium continued, looking straight at Violet.

'I have a young man in uniform here who wishes to talk to you.' As this description covered millions of souls lost in the Great War, this did not help Violet recognise her brother. She wondered if the séance would get anywhere. She so much wanted to hear from Frederick and Grace, but could these unusual women do anything for them?

'He says to say, "Remember the river Thames."'

Confused, Violet and Sophia looked at each other. They had no idea what the medium was talking about. Violet thought the whole thing might be a fake. After more heavy breathing, Miss Zagorski continued.

'He's showing me a little beach with the Thames beyond.' Sophia and Violet started to cry, as they now understood exactly what the medium was referring to. It was years before when Violet and Frederick were small children, and their mother took them to play on the rivers' foreshore. The East End steamed rank and odorous on the July day; this had been the only way to find some relief.

'He says he loved Teddy!'

Sophia held a hanky to her mouth. When Frederick was little, she bought him a teddy bear, and her son refused to call him anything other than 'Teddy'. He took it to bed with him every night until it fell apart. Tears pricked at Violet's eyes, and she fought to hold back a sob.

Just then, the table shuddered, and the group's hands were pushed upwards as it rose by about six inches. After hovering for a few moments, it subsided to the floor with a soft thud as it landed. A tingle of excitement ran up Violet's back. Ekatarina spoke again.

'He's showing me a bunch of daffodils and he says to tell you to remember how special these were.'

Now Violet and Sophia had no doubts at all. During Frederick's last leave, before he returned to France for his final tour of duty, he collected the blooms from a nearby garden and dashed home with the owner chasing and shouting 'Thief!' after him. He gave them to his mother and sister, saying.

'Look how much I love you. I had to run fast so that Mr Hindwood didn't catch me!'

A wave of overwhelming love poured through Violet. Any remaining scepticism disappeared, and the knowledge Frederick was safe in the afterlife filled her with a sense of wonder and joy. Ekatarina continued.

'He wants to tell you it's beautiful here, and he loves you very much. Oh, and he also says there's a little girl with him. I can see her; she's got red hair in ringlets, and she's so pretty. What a tiny little thing. She's saying "Mummy, Mummy, I miss you so much. I love you!"' Violet wept uncontrollably as this was the exact description of her lost daughter, Grace.

Miss Zagorski slumped a little. The effort of getting the message from spirit had drained her energy. Her complexion had turned grey, and in the dim afternoon light of the reception room, Violet made out a faint white mist wisping around her head. She fell silent, and the women wondered if the séance was over.

Then, a sound took their attention; Ethel Trout breathed heavily, a rasp grating in her throat. Her extensive bosom heaved up and down, the beige cardigan pushed open by their buxom expansion. She began to speak, hesitantly at first, and then it came out in a gush.

'The story of Winding Wood will be told one day. The dark heart of the house of secrets will be revealed.' She stopped for a long moment, then started to shiver violently, and her teeth were chattering. She rasped.

'I'm so cold, it's freezing cold; why do I feel so cold?' Violet almost jumped out of her chair as she recalled her awful dreams. The medium slumped on the table with a thud. Her sister made a little mewling sound of concern, and the table gave one final twitch and then crashed to the floor with a bang. Miss Zagorski brought the séance to a close and ushered the four women back to where the maid laid out a fresh pot of tea. After two cups, Ethel Trout perked up and remembered nothing of what she said. Mable kept clucking around her.

'You shouldn't do trance, dear; I'm not sure it agrees with you. You came over most peculiar when working with that Aztec priestess last week. Your nerves can't take it anymore.' Sophia said.

'It was wonderful to hear the message from my dear Frederick and my granddaughter Grace. We miss them with all our hearts and are blessed to discover they're happy and safe in the afterlife. That knowledge comforts me, and I'm so grateful for what you've done for us.' Ekatarina Zagorski replied.

'You're welcome, Mrs Gosling. I'm honoured Spirit chose me to be a channel that can deliver messages from people's loved ones. Grief's a terrible emotion; if I can bring one moment of succour in the process, it makes me a happy woman.' Violet continued.

'But what about the message Miss Trout gave? I don't think that had anything to do with us.'

'What did she say? I recall nothing when I've been in a trance.' Violet repeated what the other medium said. Miss Zagorski replied.

'As she mentioned Winding Wood, the message must be for me, but I've no idea what it means. I'm unaware of any dark secrets. This is a happy place. I'm so sorry you've been disturbed like this.'

Not long afterwards, Violet and Sophia left for their train journey to Plaistow. On the way back to Blackfriars, Violet said.

'It's strange, but Miss Trout's message about Winding Wood unsettled me for some reason.' Sophia replied.

'I'm sure it means nothing; this can't have anything to do with us. Put it out of your mind and think about dear Frederick and Grace. I miss them every single moment of each day. The grief is like a physical pain which wants to burst out of my chest. I feel much better hearing his reassuring words.'

'Mother, I do know; the grief's not yours alone. The messages from Frederick and Grace were a great solace. It's of some help to have been told they're happy and that one day we'll be with them again.'

During the train journey home, Ethel Trout's strange and disturbing message continued to nag at Violet. She tried to dismiss it as irrelevant, but like her tongue wiggling a loose tooth, she couldn't ignore it. That night, she wrote the medium's words in her diary and then forgot all about them in the coming days.

Chapter Ten
On a hilltop in France

Violet stood alone in a thick black fog that penetrated her mouth and nose and burned her lungs. All around her, the air crackled with heat. The sky above was choked with oily smoke and glowing embers, swirling through a giant metal mass that groaned and screamed as it tore apart. Desperate people ran in every direction through the smog.

Their anguished cries filled the air. Flames licked at the steel, the orange glow of fire reflecting off twisted metal. Screams echoed, bodies clawing to escape the flames. Violet could not move, frozen in place, as the sky thickened with black smoke and horror.

She woke with a start, drenched in sweat, her heart pounding against her ribs. For a moment, she floated, lost in the hazy zone between sleep and wakefulness, the remnants of the nightmare clinging to her like the stifling, smoke-laden air of her dream. Violet sat up, her breath coming in gasps, her fingers gripping the sheets. The fiery images, still vivid and raw, lingered in her mind.

'It was just a dream,' she muttered, rubbing her temples. But the knot of dread refused to unravel, tightening and churning in her stomach. She turned to Thomas for comfort, and after grunting and muttering something unintelligible, he put his arm around her. Her anxiety subsided enough for her to find the balm of sleep once more.

The following day, Violet was still shaken and fearful. The dream left her anxious and disturbed in a way she could not explain. She spent the day in a haze, distracted, her mind repeatedly returning to the flames. She pushed the thought aside as best she could, focusing instead on the tasks at hand—tidying the house and making breakfast for the girls—but the image refused to fade.

One morning, a few weeks later, Thomas said to Violet.

'It says in the paper the R101 Airship will be flying over the East End on its maiden voyage to India. There'll be a clear view from the Isle of Dogs. Shall we go and watch it? What a wonderful thing for the girls to be able to see!'

There was an air of anticipation as they bundled into their coats, Bryony and Florence giggling as they tugged on their hats. They caught the bus from the corner of the road, which would take them to the Isle of Dogs. It was here that Thomas had read they would have the best view of the aerial behemoth as it flew over on the first leg of its long journey.

Violet tugged her coat tighter around her; the evening air was chilly, and it was drizzling, but like the rest of the family, she was excited about the spectacle they were about to witness. Thomas lifted Florence onto his shoulders so she would have a better view. Bryony clutched her mother's hand, shivering though she wore an excited smile. Violet's mind flickered to the dream again, and an uneasy sensation crept into her chest. She shook it off. This was something new and grand. The R101 was a symbol of progress; people looked to the future, to giant machines in the sky, and here she was, worrying over nightmares!

The sound of distant engines thrummed through the air, and the crowd stirred and craned their necks to see. Moments later, the lights of the airship appeared on the horizon.

'There it is!' Thomas exclaimed, pointing upward. Florence's eyes widened, and she clapped her hands in delight while Bryony gazed up in awe, her mouth dropped open.

The R101 was massive, its metallic frame shining against the darkening evening clouds. Even from a distance, its size was imposing, dwarfing the world below it. The children pointed up excitedly as it floated over the river, its sleek body gliding through the sky like a giant silver whale.

Violet decided the sight of the airship was hauntingly beautiful. She thought about the glamorous people who would be going on the adventure, how they would be dressed, and what they would eat. What a wonderful chance for them! Then, for a moment, she recalled her horrible flame-filled dream but dismissed it. She knew there was no way the R101 would be allowed to fly with its illustrious passenger list if they were in any danger.

The family stood, watching the airship disappear into the distance, its bulk swallowed by the rain and clouds. Bryony and Florence agreed they wished it could have stayed floating overhead, and Violet remained with a mixture of emotions and the edge of anxiety. Slowly, the crowd began to disperse, chatter filling the damp air as people discussed the marvel they had just witnessed.

The following day, Violet awoke to the sound of the radio crackling in the kitchen. Thomas stood hunched over it, his face pale and tense. The girls were still in bed, but Violet felt the tension in the air before she even asked.

'What is it?' she asked, stepping closer.

Thomas glanced up at her, his eyes wide with disbelief. 'It's the R101,' he said. 'It crashed.'

Violet stared at him, her mind reeling. 'What do you mean, crashed?'

'Over in France, near Beauvais. They say it went down in the night. Most of the passengers didn't make it.'

Violet's knees weakened. The dream, the burning wreckage, the screams, the twisted and broken metal—it had been more than a nightmare. Her hands trembled as she reached for the back of a chair to steady herself.

'It can't be,' she thought. But deep down, she knew. She had seen it.

Thomas continued, 'They're saying it caught fire. A lot of people didn't make it out. The whole thing went up in flames.' Violet sank into the chair, her mind racing. She dreamt of it days before it happened. She had somehow foreseen something terrible was going to happen. And now, it had.

For days after, Violet remained terrified. The tragedy in France was too awful to think about, and gnawing at her was a persistent, disturbing thought. It came to her now as she toiled over the week's laundry.

'But if I foresaw that terrible disaster, my horrid icy dream may come true too!' The weight of her worry hung heavily on her as she continued mangling the sheets. Her mind raced with possibilities, and the vivid images from her dreams that played out in her mind seemed all too real.

She reassured herself that the hard physical work that had left her hands chapped and raw would bring her back to earth. She clung to this thought, hoping it would anchor her firmly back in reality.

Chapter Eleven
Letters

67, Harold Road
York
Yorkshire

1st November 1930

Dear Violet,

    It was lovely to receive your letter, and I am pleased to read that the family is all well. Duncan and I visited London the other week, and we went to the theatre to see the new Noël Coward musical 'Cavalcade.' I loved it, although Duncan was rude about the lead and said he could not sing. I am so sorry we were not able to visit you. It was a last-minute trip, and there was not enough time to write and arrange to meet.

    Richard and Celia are both well. Celia is at Grammar School now! How quickly the years pass.

    I do worry about you, Violet, and I always want to be your supportive friend. You have told me a number of times about your dreams, and then you wrote that you thought you had a premonition about the R101 disaster. I do not wish to be harsh, but I am certain these things are in your imagination. I am sure you read about the R101's troubles on its test flights, and that planted the idea in your mind.

    You need to put such ideas behind you. There is no such thing as premonitions. I also suspect your nightmares have been triggered by the awful personal losses you have endured. You are a brave woman, but such tragedy can take its toll.

    I hope you value my words as they are written with love and concern for you.

Your affectionate friend

Edith

5, Westmoreland Street
Plaistow
Essex

28th November 1930

Dear Edith,
    Thank you so much for your letter. I am pleased to read that the family is well. I will be a little brief as I must go to London today. Thomas has been working overtime, and we are going to buy a gramophone! It is so exciting!
    I just wanted to say thank you for your kind words. I know you are right, and only fools believe dreams foretell something or that we can find out in advance what will happen. These are things which my mind has invented. Thank you for bringing me back to earth.

With much love

Violet

Chapter Twelve
A letter from America
1932

'Daddy, I've got a letter for you!' Bryony ran into the kitchen where her mother and father were eating breakfast. She loved to please her father. He often said she was his favourite, and she glowed each time he whispered it to her. She passed him the envelope, and in return, he gave her a peck on the cheek, then went to get ready to go to school.

The stamp was American, so Thomas thought the letter must be from his brother Albert, who emigrated when he was eighteen. He spread it out in front of him. Instead of his brother's usual scrawly handwriting, the letter was typed, and Thomas scrutinised it, wondering what it is was about. Watching from the other side of the table, Violet saw him pale and put his hand to his mouth.

'What is it, dear, bad news?'

'Yes, It's a letter from a solicitor in Pittsburgh. Albert was killed in an aeroplane accident three months ago!'

'That's awful, I'm sorry. I never met your brother, but from what you told me, he was a fine man.'

'He helped Mother look after me after Dad died. Although only five years older, he was like a father to me. But listen, there's more. I can't quite believe this, but the solicitors have advised me I'm the sole beneficiary of his will. They wrote that he made a great deal of money in his business and left it all to me. It's a huge amount, fifty thousand pounds!' Violet turned pale and fell back in her seat in stunned shock.

'Would that make us rich, Thomas?'

'I can't comprehend that amount of money. But yes, dear, I think we're extremely rich.'

After overcoming her shock, Violet soon became accustomed to the thought of being wealthy. In the following days, she floated through life on a warm, fluffy cloud. Never in one moment did she believe that one day, they would have so much money.

When she awoke some mornings, she reminded herself this was the truth and not some fantastical dream. One day, she would plan new wardrobes full of clothes purchased from the finest stores in Oxford Street. On others, she fantasised they were booking first-class cabins on a liner for a trip to the USA. Her life was going to alter beyond all recognition. She realised her good dreams were coming true.

With the chance to escape Plaistow, the East End dragged harder on Violet than before. She loathed the soot-layered, cramped mean terraces. She disliked the women at the market who, in her eyes, were *'coarse'*, and she hated the fact Docklands enjoyed so few trees. After a few days of wild fantasies about living in foreign cities, she decided to tell Thomas she wished to move somewhere leafy and clean. He responded sharply.

'You must be joking, Violet; I've lived in the East End all my life; my mates are around here. The boxing club means everything to me. It's not happening, and that's the end of the matter.' Violet's long experience with her husband taught her the best strategy to have her own way was not to confront him head-on but to make him think he had the idea himself, so she decided to leave the subject.

In time, it was Bryony who persuaded her father that they should leave Plaistow. Always a cheerful soul, she could light up the room with her humour and smile. She made it her mission to play little jokes on people and cause laughter. In her opinion, there was not enough of it around. After all, her mother often looked sad and sometimes she saw her crying for no reason. Then she would remember her lost sister, and even as a nine-year-old, she understood the long shadow which hung over the family. Grace was spoken of little; her father never mentioned her, and the hole which remained as a result could only be filled with more grief.

Bryony was a child who her mother rarely saw unhappy or weeping. The only time, since she was a baby, Violet spied any tears on her cheek had been when Ivy, her beloved school friend, died of measles. Still recovering from the illness herself, she watched the black-draped hearse with her friend's coffin go past from the front parlour window. After she'd stopped crying, in a typical Bryony way, she said to her mother.

'I'll go to Ivy's house tomorrow and take flowers for her mummy.'

'That's kind of you,' replied Violet. 'You're such a thoughtful girl.'

Whatever the situation, Bryony would try to make it better. Witnessing her parents' disagreement about where to live, she decided she didn't want to hear them having rows anymore. She made up her mind to speak to her grandmother for advice. She loved her dearly, and the old lady was always fussing over her when her mother rushed around, too busy with the housework to give her any attention. She asked.

'I don't like Mummy and Daddy arguing. What can I do to help Grandma?'

'Not sure you can, my sweetheart. I think that's for the adults to sort out.'

'I'm grown up! I'm eight years old.' Sophia laughed and hugged her and went on.

'If you want to help, why don't you tell Daddy how much you hate living here too? You know you're his favourite. He may listen to you.' Like her daughter, Sophia held a deep yearning for the countryside. She had visited her parents' old family home in their village in Germany and seen how lovely it was. Perhaps enough feminine pressure on Thomas would prevail.

Bryony picked her moment with care and, later that week, went with her father to his allotment. They often spent time together, talking for hours outside his ramshackle shed. Tonight was no different, and they chatted away, the sun going down into an orange horizon and the first stars glimmered in the sky.

'Daddy, I've something to ask you.'

'What is it, Bryony dear?'

'I'm so sad thinking about Ivy. I miss her every day. If I didn't live here in Plaistow, it would be easier as there'd be fewer things to remind me of her.'

'Did your mother put you up to this?'

'No, Daddy.' Bryony replied. 'But if we moved somewhere nicer, it would make us all happier. I'd stop being reminded of Ivy. Mummy would have trees and fields, and Granny might not nag you.' Thomas laughed.

'You're very persuasive, I'll think about it.' He kissed Bryony on the cheek and pondered if he could ever face leaving Plaistow, the boxing club and his drinking buddies.

Chapter Thirteen
Winding Wood
1932

Having thought long and hard, Thomas finally agreed to move to the country. This would make Violet happy and stop Sophia from nagging him, so he reluctantly decided it was best for his family. Violet wanted to leave Plaistow as soon as possible and buy a house far away from the East End. She feared the neighbours' jealousy if they got a whiff of the family's newfound wealth. She sensed they would not take it well. Those who climbed the social ladder were seen as class traitors.

Thomas and Violet talked for days about where they may live. The couple's experience of life was mainly limited to East London. Thomas suggested they consider Southend. Violet refused, insisting there were *'far too many cockneys'* in the town. Her aspirations soared much higher than that.

The answer came when Violet picked up the Evening Standard at the newsagents and browsed through the property section, and an advert caught her eye.

'*For Sale Freehold*

'*Crofton House, Forest Row Sussex*'

'*A glorious property built in 1905 and designed by the renowned architect Sir Roger Holroyd. Briefly: The house comprises five bedrooms, a bathroom, three reception rooms, and a kitchen with all modern appliances. Crofton House sits within four acres of land. Comprising gardens created by the acclaimed gardener Phyliss Fenn and three acres of woodland. Only two miles from Forest Row station, with its services to the West End and City. The house is vacant and ready for immediate possession. Three thousand pounds.*'

Forest Row lay far away on the other side of the river, deep in the country and a good distance from the loathed Plaistow. No one would recognise them, their previous life a distant memory. They would become newly middle class with no fear of anyone guessing their background. Violet circled the advert with a pencil and decided to tell Thomas to contact the estate agents. Whilst tiny, the picture of the house intrigued her. It looked pretty. She didn't like the name *Crofton House*, though. That would have to change.

Violet made careful plans; she was adamant they must not let the neighbours see them spending any money. Fancy new clothes would have spiteful tongues wagging. However, she insisted on one trip to Marshall & Snelgrove in Oxford Street to buy outfits suitable for viewing a property in Sussex. It would never do to arrive in their ordinary garb.

Even though Thomas protested, they travelled by train to Woodford twice weekly, where they took elocution lessons with the austere Mrs Ivy Wakerell. A most intimidating woman but an excellent teacher. Violet wanted to ensure the good folk in the salubrious home counties would not be able to use their cockney accents to pigeonhole them by class. At least some of the roughest East End edges would be rubbed off before they moved.

One damp September morning, Thomas and Violet set out, dressed in their new outfits. She mentioned to a neighbour they were going to a family wedding, so the smart clothes would not arouse suspicion. They caught the train from Victoria, which sped through the sooty London suburbs. After a steep climb to the North Downs, it steamed through a long tunnel and burst into the fresh air. After Oxted, the train meandered at a more leisurely pace until it arrived at Forest Row.

On the forecourt, a black taxi awaited the couple; it would not do to arrive at the property on foot. The agent would think they were not worthy. Violet brimmed over with excitement; she had only ridden in a taxi a few times. The cabby said over his shoulder.

'I hear you're looking at Crofton House. It's a lovely place. Mrs Hillman had to sell it. She lost her son in the war, and five years ago her husband died, and it's far too large for her. She moved to the South Coast to be close to her sister.'

Violet shrunk down in the back of the taxi, intimidated to learn from the driver that gossip flowed like water around the Sussex village. She decided to say as little as possible and, when she did, make sure she did not drop any Hs.

'I believe it's lovely,' she said, forcing a tense smile. Driving through Forest Row, Violet almost had to pinch herself. She could not believe how charming the village was after the dreary environs of their home. They drove along the main street, lined with a few shops, everything neat, tidy, and clean.

As they reached the outskirts, Violet noticed larger houses set in extensive gardens. Driving up a narrow road, tall trees arching over to make a green tunnel, then the taxi swerved off to the left up an unmade lane. Here, the few houses were detached, and she caught a glimpse of the golf course beyond.

For one moment, she thought she had died and gone to heaven. The taxi stopped, and Violet could not believe her eyes when she got her first sight of Crofton House nestling on a wide plot behind a copper beech hedge. The house sat in its garden, looking like it had always been there, the two in perfect balance. Mature oaks framed the property, and in the distance through the trees, the soft green line of hills highlighted the horizon beyond. The couple walked along the gravel drive to the house, taking in every detail.

Built of red brick, its two wings fanned out in a slight V shape. The central part, brought together by a prominent arched porch. Tall and ornate chimneys topped the roof, and the long, elegant windows completed the picturesque appearance. Violet thought it was beautiful. From that moment, she knew this would be their home. Then, she cast her eyes to the garden surrounding the house. She smiled; this was the garden of her good dreams. At the door stood a tall man wearing a trilby hat and a black bow tie, who must be Mr Jolly, the estate agent.

'Good morning, Mr and Mrs Goldsmith. Welcome to Crofton House; come in, and we'll start the tour. How was your journey from London?'

'We 'ad a very…' Violet was horrified. She dropped an H and coughed to cover up her mistake. 'So sorry, I have a slight chest. We had a pleasant trip, thank you. Forest Row is delightful. We'll be pleased to move out of the city.'

'What part do you live in?' Violet had already worked out their cover story. The dreaded East End could not be spoken of. She could not lie about their address, as Thomas had written to the agent but said.

'We've been having to stay in Plaistow for a few months as my elderly aunt is very sick and we have to look after her. It's such a dreadful place. She was forced to live there after her husband died. Normally, we live in Herne Hill. It's lovely, but in the last few years, it's getting so built up. Such a shame.' Mr Jolly tutted and said.

'The city is spreading a great deal.' Then gestured, 'This is the reception hall; it's my favourite room in the house!' After letting Violet and Thomas appreciate the hall, with its oak panelling and minstrels gallery, he said, 'let's go through to the drawing room.' Violet was unsure what a *drawing room* meant but almost let out an exclamation of surprise. It was large, with a beautiful ornate fireplace along one wall. All the furniture had been removed, and the sun shone through the French windows onto the polished parquet floor.

'This is lovely!' exclaimed Violet. And as Mr Jolly showed them around the rest of the house, she continued to express her gushing appreciation.

As the group entered the bedroom opposite the top of the stairs, Violet jumped, startled, as a bright burst of bluish light suddenly illuminated the room. It appeared like a photographer's flash gun, momentarily blinding her. When her vision cleared, she saw a young woman sitting on a bed, clearly distressed. The woman's face was hauntingly familiar, yet Violet couldn't place where she had seen her before. An air of sorrow and desperation clung to the woman, making Violet's heart ache with inexplicable empathy.

Just as quickly as it appeared, the image vanished, leaving the room empty and unfurnished again. The stark contrast between the ghostly apparition and the bare reality left Violet disoriented and shaken. Her breath caught in her throat, and she glanced around, half-expecting to see another flash.

Thomas and Mr Jolly were making small talk about the 'lovely view.' It was clear they had been undisturbed.

Her vision did nothing to put her off the house. She had been enchanted with it at first sight; there was no further discussion; the house would be theirs. She whispered to Thomas, who agreed. She insisted they should offer the full asking price. They shook on the deal with the estate agent, who looked somewhat surprised that the sale had been made without any of the usual haggling. On the train on the way home, Violet didn't stop talking about the virtues of the house.

'There'll be a bedroom for us, each of the girls, Mother, and a spare for guests. I never thought we'd have the opportunity to live in a place like this. It's like a fairy tale.'

'Neither did I,' agreed Thomas. Violet added.

'There's one thing: Crofton House is so dull. I want something more romantic that'll suit the house much better. Do you remember when I went to visit Ekatarina Zagorski, the medium? Her house was called Winding Wood. I shall write to the post office and ask them to change it. It'll be a reminder of the day when Mother and I heard reassurance that dear Frederick and Grace are happy in the afterlife. Every time I see the name, I shall think of them.'

Chapter Fourteen
Like a fairy tale
1933

One morning, Thomas travelled up to London, telling Violet he was meeting someone about their investments. Happy to spend her day by herself, she strolled around the garden, inspecting the new planting which she had established in the long herbaceous border running alongside the terrace. This was an important location, as being so close to the sitting room, the fragrance of the blossoms would drift through the open French doors in the summer. She sighed with deep satisfaction, pleased with the progress she had made. After a year's efforts, Winding Wood's garden was beginning to reflect her devoted care.

Gladys Hillman, the previous owner, had neglected it for many years, consumed by grief for Giles, her only son, lost in the war, then later the death of her husband. Before 1914, dahlias and lavender, hostas and phlox, and all manner of floral wonders proliferated.

With her beloved husband Peter, she took pride in showcasing the summer garden's glories to visitors. Designed by Phyllis Fenn, who had worked alongside William Morris, the fine borders once attracted horticultural societies eager to arrange visits.

After years of neglect, the garden degenerated into an overgrown, dejected memorial to a mother's grief. The tennis court was punctuated with bedraggled weeds and the sundial, Giles's last birthday gift to his mother before he proudly went off to France, became lost in a tangle of brambles. Only the lawn had been cut, while everything else fell into sad disrepair.

Violet threw herself into planning the garden's restoration with gusto. The woman, who once worked putting lids on tins of paint, had discovered a new confidence with the transformation of her life. A year later, she found no difficulty directing the men working to restore the borders, greenhouse, and sweeping lawns to their former beauty. When she first employed Arthur, the head gardener, he sucked his teeth and said.

'Mighty lot of work to do here, Mrs Goldsmith. Going to need some extra hands.'

Today, on her morning walk, Violet looked towards the woodland, squinting in the sun and envisioning the position for the pond she planned.

'It'll be so pretty,' she thought, 'and in the summer, there'll be newts and dragonflies. I must speak to the men about it so we can start work soon.' Violet thought her new life was like a rainbow-coloured fairy tale, a dream come true. Not in her wildest fantasies had she imagined somewhere as beautiful as this.

In Plaistow, she never had the chance to buy nice things for the home, but now she adorned her abode with fashionable furniture from Heals and had curtains and cushions made from Liberty fabrics. When a neighbour, Mrs Gladys Hatcher, first visited and inspected the drawing room with its pink and green floral print drapes, she commented.

'You have such good taste. You must have a lot of experience with this.' Violet smiled to herself. She had none whatsoever, but this adventure taught her she had an eye for beautiful things.

The room she loved above all others was the reception hall. Here, a metal-studded oak front door led into the panelled room, large enough to house a small settee, from which she made calls on the new telephone. A grand staircase curled up to the first floor, encircled on the upper level by a minstrels' gallery. She imagined sweeping down the stairs in an elegant evening gown to receive smart and entertaining house guests.

Winding Wood boasted all modern conveniences, including a kitchen equipped with every gadget imaginable and a scullery complete with a mangle. Violet was amazed when her daily woman first demonstrated the electric sweeper she called a 'Hoover'. She spent long, hard years on her hands and knees scrubbing and cleaning. Release from the daily dirge of housework was like a miracle. On another visit for tea, the neighbour who complimented Violet on her taste probed for information, extending her curiosity like an anteater's tongue seeking a juicy morsel.

'Your husband must've done well. What line did you say he's in?'

'He's no longer working. We inherited family money.' The neighbour looked relieved. Little did Violet suspect, but Mrs Hatcher needed to calculate if the Goldsmiths were the much-desired 'old money' or the 'ghastly nouveau riche.' Gossip travelled fast around Forest Row. Hungry for excitement, the locals devoured any titbit about the new residents at Winding Wood with gusto. Mrs Hatcher relayed.

'They're a good family. I understand they inherited a fortune.' The assembled group of steely-coiffed, judgmental W.I. doyens were delighted. The last time a house in Forest Row had sold, it had been bought by 'dreadful, common people who made their fortune running pubs.'

Violet spent the rest of the blissful summer day deadheading flowers, only interrupted by the sound of bees, songbirds, and the occasional hum of a distant car. Once, she saw a fragile little plane circling high above and squinted, trying to make it out against the strong sun. It seemed to wander without a care as it meandered back to a nearby airfield.

'One day, I would love to fly in an aircraft like that,' she thought.

The peace and quiet of Winding Wood's garden were a million miles away from Plaistow. Violet had come home. The long years of drudgery and penury were behind her, and the glorious setting and quintessentially English red-brick house was now her palace. Life was a good dream, and she intended it to stay that way.

Later, Violet called Arthur, the gardener, over to discuss another bed she wanted restored and planted. She laughed to herself.

'Perhaps in a previous life, I employed staff too. I'm well suited to it.' She picked some creamy-pink sweet peas to place in a cut-glass vase on the hall table. Their heady fragrance delighted her senses, like too much perfume dabbed by an ageing dowager. Just then, a car edged its way down the gravel drive. Snapping out of her pleasant thoughts, she realised Thomas had returned home. She went to greet him, excited to share her plans.

That evening, Florence was adamant that Violet should read to her in bed. While Bryony believed she was far too old for such things, her younger daughter, at almost seven, still delighted in fairy tales. Her current favourite was *'The Snow Queen'* and she demanded that it be read over and over again. Violet found the Queen terrifying and reminded her of her dreams. However, her insightful daughter insisted that the tale was about the battle between good and evil and that love would prevail. There was a particular quote she loved, and that night made Violet read the chapter with it again.

'The world may be frozen, but hope always thaws the coldest of hearts.' Florence interrupted her with a burst of excitement.

'See, Mummy, that's exactly what I've been saying about the story!' She exclaimed, her eyes shining.

Violet felt a surge of warmth wash over her as she looked at her daughter's earnest face. The wisdom of a child had the power to chase away the shadows of fear. Soon after, Florence's eyelids grew heavy, and she drifted off to sleep. Violet left her, switching on her night light as she went.

Chapter Fifteen
Mr Hitler
1933

Violet insisted that the Telegraph must be delivered to the house each day; otherwise, she was convinced the newsagent would pigeonhole them if they bought '*lower class*' papers. Thomas found the broadsheet wordy and boring, so on occasion; he drove to the newsagents in nearby Hartfield, where no one knew him, to covertly buy a Daily Mail or, if he was being particularly rebellious, the Daily Mirror. He kept these newspapers well hidden, especially the Mirror. He feared his mother-in-law would launch into long, angry rants about the evils of the Labour Party and how they were all about to be overrun by communists.

'And look what happened to the Tsars!' She finished during one rant. 'Our poor King and Queen must be terrified now that traitor Ramsay McDonald is Prime Minister.'

One beautiful, fresh summer morning, having purchased his forbidden Daily Mail, Thomas returned to Winding Wood and found himself a perch on a wooden bench at the bottom of the garden, on the fringes of the woodland. Relaxing in the warm sunshine, he glanced around and sighed with satisfaction, looking forward to his covert read.

He had not wanted to live here, but it could be much worse. While his heart stayed in the East End, he agreed to move to Sussex for a quiet life. His wife, mother-in-law, and children often ganged up on him. That was how it was, being the only man in the house, surrounded by always-chattering women. He smiled, lit his pipe, and decided life was good.

Today's newspaper headline wrote about Mr Hitler, the German leader, and the great things he was doing. Thomas thought Britain needed a firm prime minister like him to run the shambolic government.

The ongoing financial crisis had been draining the lifeblood out of the country. Fortunately for Violet and Thomas, an old friend from the boxing club, an accountant by trade who Thomas trusted to be discreet, had given wise advice on what to do with his inheritance. Thomas understood nothing of these things, but Manny Goldstein helped him to spread his fortune between gold, property, and investments. Thus, the ill headwinds of the recession did nothing to batter the family's wealth.

Later, Thomas went back into the house and thought he would ask Milly, the girl who came in to help Violet every day, to make him a cup of tea. Instead, he found his wife weeping at the kitchen table.

'Vi, whatever is it? I hope it's not bad news.' Violet composed herself and said.

'Do you remember I wrote to the hotel in Bournemouth to book our summer holiday?' Thomas nodded. 'This is the letter I got back.' She passed it to her husband.

Sea Horse Hotel
Cliff Parade
Bournemouth
Hampshire

25 June 1933

Dear Mrs Goldsmith,
We are in receipt of your letter dated 1st June.
Unfortunately, we are unable to make the booking for you as requested because we do not accept Jews.
Yours sincerely

Muriel Morrison

'That's ridiculous,' said Thomas. 'We're not Jewish!'

'But Goldsmith can often be taken as a Jewish name. This is horrible, and Thomas, I wonder if we should consider changing our surname. I've also been reading about how Mr Hitler is treating Jewish people in Germany, it's awful. What if it happened here?'

'I'm sure it won't,' assured Thomas. He thought about how he had been impressed earlier that day by what Adolf Hitler was doing but now was reminded there was another, darker side to the Nazi leader. He went on.

'It does seem like a lot of fuss changing our name. We'll need to engage a solicitor. I'm not sure it's worth the bother.' Violet remained troubled by the hotel owner's rejection and pressed the point.

'We need to think about the girls. We must do it for them.' Thomas pondered for a moment, then agreed.

'You're right, Bryony and Florence are our priority. But what name would we use? Perhaps Thomson, Mother's maiden name? I'll speak to the solicitors to find out what's involved, so don't fret, Vi. Mind you, we need to discuss how to deal with the nosey neighbours. If we don't explain, they'll think we're up to no good!'

Later that week, Violet visited Mrs Hatcher for tea at Hollybank House, only a pleasant ten-minute walk across the golf course. She told her about her inquiry to the hotel and the letter of rejection she received in return.

'They wrote that they don't accept bookings from Jews!' Violet dabbed her eyes with her handkerchief, still emotional about the subject.

'You're not…' Mrs Hatcher couldn't quite get the word 'Jewish' out.

'No! We're Church of England people, but our surname can sometimes be mistaken as such.' Mrs Hatcher's face betrayed her palpable relief.

'How terrible. Well, don't worry, dear. Once you've changed your name, I'm sure no one will ever make that mistake again. We had a Jewish family in Forest Row; they moved away a couple of years ago. I can't say anyone had much to do with them. They can be so…' She left her sentence unfinished and dabbed at her mouth with a hanky as if to wipe away some imagined food debris.

Winding Wood continued to transform into a haven of tranquillity as the summer blossomed around them. The garden flourished under Violet's watchful eye, and the house itself embraced the Thomson's new identity. With the burden of their old name lifted, the family stopped worrying about the ever-darkening situation far away in Germany.

One evening, as the sun set over the trees, casting a golden glow over the flower beds, Violet and Thomas sat together on the terrace. She drank sweet sherry and he, a glass of beer. They talked about their dreams for the future, the challenges they had faced, and the strength they found in each other. The air was filled with the scent of the blooms from the border below.

Violet looked at Thomas and smiled, feeling a deep sense of contentment. They had endured awful losses, but together, they built a new life full of love and optimism. As they watched the stars start to punctuate the darkening sky with little dots of light, Violet felt a surge of gratitude for the gift they had been given by Uncle Albert and the exciting chapters of their lives which lay ahead.

Chapter Sixteen
Fire!
1936

'Bryony, wake up!' Violet shook her daughter awake. 'We've just heard on the radio that the Crystal Palace is on fire! Quick, put your clothes on! Dad's going to drive us to the North Downs where we'll have a clear view. Hurry up!'

In a flurry of excitement and anticipation, the family soon found themselves in the car, navigating the meandering country lanes on the dark, crisp November night, heading towards the peak of the hills overlooking London. At first, Violet protested at the thought of the journey with Bryony, but Thomas insisted.

'None of us will ever see anything like this again! It won't take too long to drive there.' They left Florence behind with Gran, fearing the ten-year-old would be too frightened by the spectacle. Forty-five minutes later, Thomas pulled the Hillman into a little layby on the north-facing escarpment, providing an open vista across the South London suburbs. Once, on a sun-drenched summer day, the family had driven up there for a picnic. On that occasion, Violet said.

'This is my favourite view of the Crystal Palace. It's so beautiful. Look at the glass glistening in the sunshine!' The Palace lay on the next high ridge about eight miles north. On bright summer days, the enormous Victorian glasshouse glinted and sparkled like a jewel against the blue sky. Bryony had spun an intricate tale for her little sister Florence about a beautiful princess who lived in a Diamond-Crystal Palace atop a high mountain. Entranced, Florence listened with wide-eyed wonder, dreaming that one day, she might live in such a place and be a princess herself.

Once, when they lived in Plaistow, the family visited the Palace for a breathtaking fireworks display on bonfire night. Huddled together against the cold, they watched in awe as the enormous whirling Catherine wheels sputtered their brief, glorious life force, and the soaring rockets left optimistic, short-lived trails of gold in the sky. They whooped and cheered, agreeing these were the best fireworks they had ever seen.

As the family alighted from the car, Violet's eyes widened with astonishment. Their view, now unobstructed by roadside trees, presented a breathtaking and heartbreaking panoramic vista. What had once been the sparkling palace was now engulfed in flames from end to end, clearly in its agonising death throes. Instead of the sun glistening on the myriad glass panels, red and orange tongues of flame soared into the night sky. As parts of the building collapsed, towers of sparks and fire ascended into the ether.

There was a strange, mesmerising beauty to the scene, the sky and hillsides for miles around lit by the lurid, obscene glow. The family stood in silent mourning, watching as the building's life force ebbed away. The huge arched transept, the centrepiece of the structure, glowed against the dark night; then, it collapsed, throwing flames even higher into the air, and moments later, a massive crashing roar echoed out across the London suburbs and onwards into the countryside.

Spellbound, Violet found her mind taken elsewhere. She thought about the beautiful scale model of the Palace that had graced Ekatarina Zagorski's sitting room. Such a pretty, shining thing, crafted with the most intricate detail. She recalled the séance and the enormity of her grief for Frederick and Grace, then remembered Ethel Trout's strange words.

'*The story of Winding Wood will be told one day. The dark heart of the house of secrets will be revealed.*'

And for the first time, two pieces of jigsaw clicked together. Her house, named after the medium's home in Crystal Palace - was hers now the house of secrets?

Violet turned her attention back to the vista before her. Ribbons of fire could now be seen running down the hill below the palace.

'What are they?' she asked Thomas.

'I think it's molten glass,' he replied, and the scene, along with the flood of memories, became too much for Violet to bear, and she cried. Later, in the car on the way back to Forest Row, Bryony comforted her mother.

'Don't worry, Mummy. If people and animals go to heaven, then maybe buildings do too?'

'You're such a sweet girl, Bryony. What a nice thought. It would be lovely to believe it, wouldn't it? It's so kind of you to comfort me.'

The following day, over breakfast, the family listened to the radio. The BBC announced that the Palace had been destroyed. When Florence came down from her bedroom and heard the news, she burst into tears. Violet comforted her.

'I know you're sad about the poor Palace. It's such a shame. But perhaps it'll help me to explain something to you. One of the lessons you have to learn in life is nothing lasts forever; everything has its time. The important thing is that when things and people are gone, they're remembered. I was sad for many years for my brother, who was killed in the Great War, and your sister, Grace, who died before you were born. But over time, I've learned to remember how much I loved them.'

Violet reflected, with sadness, that it was all very well to sound wise and philosophical about loss, but often, the world around her morphed into a drab grey despite all the wonderful things she enjoyed in life. That is how it would always be. Part of Violet's soul died with Grace, and on some days, the pain overwhelmed her.

Thomas still never spoke of his lost daughter, and over the years, in the absence of her being remembered, she faded from reality until Violet could not recall the sound of her voice. But that's not what she would tell Florence. The sensitive child wanted to be told fairy stories, and everything in life had a happy ending, so this is what Violet always ensured she heard. The loss must be packaged into convenient and sanitised tales of fairies and mysterious unicorns soaring high over rainbows on white swan-feather wings. She consoled herself, thinking,

'At least I've kept my grief from my children. They'll never suffer as I have. They can live a life free from loss. Florence is a sensitive child, but I'm confident I can protect her. As for Bryony, she just breezes through life. Such a happy girl.' Aloud, she said.

'One day, when you have your children and grandchildren, you'll be able to tell them so many stories about our family but think how wonderful it'll be to tell them how you watched the Crystal Palace burning down. Won't it be exciting! Then, my darling, these things will never be forgotten.'

Chapter Seventeen
Letters

Winding Wood
Crofton Lane
Forest Row,
Sussex

September 30th, 1938

My dearest Edith,
   I hope this letter finds you in good health and spirits.
   The family are well, and Bryony got excellent results in her end-of-term exams this year. Thomas has a new car, and I must chide him for how fast he drives around the country lanes. However, I am writing to you with a heavy heart. Mr Chamberlain assures us we will have 'peace in our time'; I do hope he is right. Thomas is not so sure. He tells me how Mr Churchill has warned about Hitler and thinks we have not heard the end of it.
   Our dear Florence has been particularly affected by the recent turmoil. She is such a sensitive child. Even at only twelve years old, her delicate nature makes her acutely aware of the tension which hangs in the air. I worry about her so much as she absorbs the world's troubles like a sponge. Despite her anxiety, Florence is a beam of sunshine in our lives. She is loved by all who meet her, and her kindness and compassion never cease to amaze me. She possesses a vivid imagination and is becoming a talented artist. She spends hours in the garden, painting flowers and sketching the birds who visit us.
   You have been so firm with me whenever I've spoken to you about my bad dreams. I agreed with you that they couldn't possibly foretell anything, how could they? Yet, they continue to haunt me, these nightmares that return far too often. When I dream of the freezing cold, I wake up feeling as if the ice has seeped into my very soul. If only I could rid myself of this vision, this torment that leaves me feeling vulnerable and alone. Each night, I dread the moment my head hits the pillow, knowing that sleep often brings me back to that cold, desolate place. The weight of it is almost too much to bear.
   With all my love
   Violet

Beachcombers
High Street
Salcombe
Devon

5th October 1938

My dearest Violet,
        Thank you for your letter and heartfelt words. It troubles me greatly that your nightmares continue to haunt you so. I was reflecting on your worries, and I recalled that some years ago, you told me you had visited a medium who gave you an odd message about the dark heart of the house of secrets or some other nonsense. I fear dark thoughts were put into your head. These people are manipulative frauds, and I fear this is the cause of your troubles. They prey on people at their time of greatest need, and by unsettling them, hope you will go back over and over. Please promise me you will not go down this foolish avenue again.

        All is well in Salcombe. We are so pleased we decided to move down here. Duncan took up sailing this summer, and we had many jolly trips up the River Dart. The scenery is so pretty.

        Violet, your strength continues to inspire me. You have faced so much in your life, yet you remain a pillar of compassion for those around you. Let us hope brighter days will come and peace will prevail! Who knows? The world may be uncertain, but the love and support we share will always be a constant.

        With all my love

Edith

Chapter Eighteen
Florence & Sophia
1938

The soft glow of late afternoon sunlight filled the sitting room, streaming through the windows and casting long shadows. Florence sat cross-legged on the floor, sketching, alone with her thoughts.

She was a shy and unusual girl with a warm, affectionate manner, which attracted people strongly to her. Her gentle nature made her a beloved member of the family, even though her anxiety often found her taught and fearful. At twelve years old, there was no doubt she would become a beautiful young woman. Her expressive brown eyes spoke so much of her inner emotions, and Violet thought her lustrous reddish-tinged brown hair and rosy complexion reminded her of a painting she had once seen on a visit to the National Gallery in London.

Florence was one of those people who looked at life from an unusual angle. She could be filled with joy, seeing beauty in the moment, whereas other people's mood would be deflated. A disappointing grey summer's day would inspire her to paint the busy grey clouds; a bone-chilling January afternoon encouraged her to walk in the winter-barren woodlands and find a tangle of fallen logs, then she would return to the house and draw it. Violet was horrified when she discovered her then ten-year-old daughter was reading the gruesome Edgar Allan Poe horror stories in bed at night. Her favourite was *'The Pit and the Pendulum'* and she sulked for several days when her mother confiscated the books as 'unsuitable.' Florence could not understand the fuss and said she found the stories interesting rather than scary.

At other times, Florence would be riven with anxiety at the slightest thing. Thomas and Violet stopped her listening to the radio, as the BBC news often had her in paroxysms of nervousness. Any indication of something wrong in the family found her crying in her room. On one occasion, Violet had been complaining of a stomach ache. It was nothing more than having eaten a large Sunday roast, yet Florence had to be consoled, hysterical and convinced her mother was about to die.

If Violet had to choose one special quality about her youngest, it was her overwhelmingly loving nature. Unlike Bryony, who rolled through life beaming sunshine all around her, Florence shone with a reserved but no less intense love. It did not matter what people did or said; she poured out love and affection in return. There were times when Bryony was quite mean, as older sisters often are, but then Florence would pick her a bunch of flowers from the garden or tell her she would share one of her favourite dolls. Once, Violet said to Sophia.

'Florence is a remarkable girl. I've never heard one angry word come out of her mouth. When she was made, God poured a huge amount of love into her.' Sophia replied.

'It's the way you've brought her up, dear. She's a credit to you.'

'Maybe,' smiled Violet.

Today, Florence was sketching her grandmother. The old woman sat in her high-backed chair, reading Daphne Du Maurier's' latest novel *'Rebecca'*. Putting it down on the side table, she said.

'That's a good place to stop. It's such a wonderful story! Would you be a darling and make me a cup of tea, Florence? My hips are hurting badly.' Sophia's arthritis had been painful of late, and she was spending more and more time in her chair. Florence smiled, went to the kitchen, and returned with a tray and two cups of tea. As Sophia leaned forward to take the brew, she winced with pain.

Florence sat on the floor beside her grandmother and looked up at her with concern. She hated seeing her in pain and felt that there was nothing she could do to help.

'Is there anything else I can get for you, Grandma?' she asked. Sophia took a sip of tea.

'Just having you here is enough, Florence,' she replied, reaching out to pat her granddaughter's hand. 'You're such a kind girl.'

Florence blushed at the compliment; she twisted her hands nervously in her lap.

'I wish I could do more. I'm so useless sometimes.'

'You do more than you realise, my dear,' she said gently. 'Your kindness brings light into this house. You have a gift for finding beauty everywhere.' Florence's eyes filled with tears; she struggled with self-doubt, and hearing such lovely words from someone she looked up to meant the world to her.

'Thank you, Grandma,' she said. 'I wish I were more confident like Bryony. I never know what to say, and I always think I've done the wrong thing.'

They sat in silence for a while, the only sound the gentle ticking of the clock on the mantelpiece.

'Florence, I want you to promise me something.'

'What is it, Grandma?' Florence asked.

'I want you to promise you'll never let your fears hold you back,' Sophia said firmly. 'You have so much potential to offer the world. Don't allow your worries to keep you from living your life to the fullest.' Florence swallowed hard.

'I'll try my best, Grandma,' she said, her voice trembling. Sophia reached out and took her granddaughter's hand in hers, giving it a reassuring squeeze.

That's all I ask,' she said softly. 'Just promise me you'll try.

Chapter Nineteen
Bluebirds over the White Cliffs
1939

Bryony and the rest of the family huddled around the radio in the sitting room, listening intently to Neville Chamberlain's ominous words crackling across the airwaves. The grim news was expected, but it struck a chill in Bryony's heart all the same. Her mother's complexion faded to white, and her father, seated beside her, his face ashen and silent, squeezed her hand. Bryony looked at him with pleading eyes, seeking reassurance, but it was difficult for him to offer any. Her grandmother sat in her high-backed chair on the other side of the room, a hanky clasped to her mouth, her shoulders shaking with dry sobs.

It was only a few minutes later when the air raid siren wailed. Its haunting sound pierced the silence, soaring up and down in an ear-splitting cacophony, heralding the imminent arrival of massed Nazi bombers. The Thomsons had read Home Office leaflets about bombing and gas attacks. Now, hearing the first alert, they were terrified, fearing the oncoming onslaught from the skies.

Florence began crying, and Bryony tried to comfort her, but without success. For a moment, she became frustrated. It seemed to the fifteen-year-old Bryony that all she ever did was calm her anxious sister. She loved Florence deeply and quickly decided she was being mean and would do what she could to help. Her mother implored.

'Girls, the air raid shelter! Now! And you too, Mother!' Sophia complained.

'Must I? I can't bear the thought of being underground!' Violet insisted, hurrying her truculent mother towards the safety of the shelter. The family made their way through the open French doors, scanning the skies for approaching enemy planes.

Thomas had employed a local builder to construct a shelter in the garden. He encouraged each of his brood down the concrete stairwell, the last being Gran, some way behind, still muttering curses. Then, giving one final glance to the skies, he entered the gloomy underground room and pulled the heavy metal blast door closed behind him.

Florence was beside herself and would not be comforted. Her temperament was totally at odds with her sister's. Bryony's mission in life was to make everything better. From an early age, she had set up a hospital for her dolls, nursed each one back to health after suffering a debilitating but curable illness. Later, she insisted on having a menagerie of pets: cats, hamsters, goldfish, and once a gerbil. When one of them died, she conducted a mournful funeral service in the garden, to which she insisted all the family attended. They sang *'All Things Bright and Beautiful,'* and Bryony spoke of her beloved pet's life and how it was now happy in heaven.

'We're all going to be killed by bombs!' wailed Florence. Bryony put her arm around her, held her tight, and soothed her.

'Look at this shelter Daddy built for us. It's so strong. I'm sure we'll be safe down here.' Florence wailed even louder in response.

'But it smells horrid, and I think I saw a spider!' Bryony held her sister tight to her, and then her mind wandered off into a train of thought, oblivious to the bombs about to rain down on them.

'It's just so unfair. I want a boyfriend. Will they all be going off to fight? What am I supposed to do? I want to be married and have children!' She recalled her grandmother telling her that after the last war, there had been a shortage of young men to marry, so many having been lost in the carnage. Then, her mind wandered again, and she daydreamed of the exact husband she wanted.

He would be fair-haired with blue eyes, tallish but not over six feet, and slender. He would have a steady job in the City, so they did not need to worry about money, and there would be three children. She did not want him to be too glamorous or adventurous; perhaps a well-paid civil servant or banker would do, for the thing which Bryony craved more than anything else in the world was normality and security. Not some gung-ho type who would climb mountains or take risks gambling on the stock market.

Bryony's attention turned back to Florence, thinking that she should help her mother keep her sister calm during the rain of bombs about to fall on the house. Then she thought.

'Or will it be gas? That sounds terrifying! I don't want to choke to death down here!'

Before long, the air-raid siren wailed again, but this time with a monotone indicating the all-clear.

'What's happening, Dad?' asked Bryony.

'I think it's been a false alarm.' Bryony followed her father out of the shelter, gripping onto Florence's hand behind her. She stood, confused, at the top of the stairs, blinking in the bright sunshine. Bryony said.

'There, Florence, I told you it would be alright.' And Florence looked up to her big sister with her loving brown eyes and said.

'Thank you for looking after me,' even though her sister had done nothing. Bryony replied.

'I always will, Florence. I promise you I'll look after you forever.' The two returned to the house, Florence's arm linked through Bryony's.

As they walked, Bryony told Florence all about *'Gone with the Wind'* which she was reading.

'But you mustn't tell Mummy; she'd disapprove because Scarlet O'Hara is divorced, and she'll confiscate the book. They giggled and spent the rest of the day together, sharing secrets that only sisters would tell each other.

———————————

Chapter Twenty
George
1944

The brutal, dreary war years dragged by, and on some days, Violet wasn't sure how she would cope. But she did; she had to, for Thomas and the girls. She did not often read the paper, fearing the worst news, and in any case, she thought the nation was only being fed heavily censored information. So, what was the point? Much better to go on stretching out limited rations and repairing the family's clothes. When she spent hours engrossed in sewing, all else faded away, and for a moment, the horrors were forgotten. That's how she preferred to handle it.

Of course, it was impossible to distance herself. People talked, and she heard tales of tragedies and heartbreaks. She resolved that she would not cry; she could not afford the luxury of emotional displays, no matter how bad the news. In any case, had she not endured enough loss in her life?

The thing which broke her years of resolve to shed no tears was hearing about the destruction of Canterbury during a German revenge raid. She had visited once with Thomas and found its ancient streets beautiful. All the news of human tragedy touched her but did not bring an overflowing of emotion, yet this did. The images of the glorious stained glass in Canterbury Cathedral were fixed in her mind. She prayed it survived the fearsome rain of explosives and firebombs. Many years later, she got to revisit Canterbury, and once more, she cried when she saw that the wonderful medieval windows had miraculously escaped blast and fire.

When Bryony left to join the Land Army, Violet felt a pang of loss. Her brood was leaving the family nest, and now, only Florence was still at home. Winding Wood fell into a subdued quiet without the bubbly and cheerful Bryony. In her gloomier moods, Violet often thought that her life was only ever defined by the absence of those she loved.

It was her youngest daughter, Florence, who concerned her most. Like Bryony, she had grown up to be a beautiful and talented young woman but endured periods of dark depression. On one occasion, they took her to a psychiatrist in Harley Street. He got little out of her and told her parents.

'She seems so distant, as if she's somewhere else. I wonder if you have any problems at home?' Violet reacted as if she had been stung. Bristling, she sat up straight in the chair and said.

'We have a happy family life and live in a beautiful house. My children have everything they could want.' Violet spoke with a mixture of pride and defensiveness, then decided any further consultations were a waste of time and that, in due course, Florence would improve, given their love and support.

Florence's mood changed for the better when she started going out with George, her first boyfriend. It was clear from the glow in both her and George's eyes that they were keen on each other. Violet hoped nothing would go wrong, fearing the devastating effect on her sensitive daughter, should the man turn out to be no good for her. On a more practical level, she worried Florence would allow him to have sex with her. She resolved to speak to her about the facts of life and how respectable young women must behave.

One summer afternoon, Florence rushed into the sitting room at Winding Wood, flushed with youthful excitement. Her eyes shone bright and sparkling. Violet was unused to seeing her so animated. This was new, and she felt happy for her. She hoped her daughter was growing out of her teenage sensitivities at last.

'Mummy! George has asked me to go to church in London with him next weekend! It's a military service. One of his friends is in the regiment and has invited us. The soldiers will be so dashing and handsome in their uniforms.'

'How lovely dear,' replied Violet, overcoming a mother's natural concerns, and she was pleased with her daughter's choice of boyfriend. George was the son of Sir Arthur Warren, the industrial magnate, and Violet thought this match might see her daughter married and taken care of. When Florence first asked her mother if she could go to a dance with George, Violet enquired why he was not in the forces. Her daughter reassured her it was because he ran the factory for his father. Before the war, the production line had been making cars; now, it was turned over to building Spitfires.

'Where's the service?' Violet inquired. 'It does sound very exciting.'

'It's the Guards' Chapel in Birdcage Walk.'

At that point, Violet experienced the most horrible sensation. An insistent oily black torrent was drowning her, and her knees began to buckle. The room around her spun as if she had been drinking, and a wave of nausea rose up her throat. She collapsed to the floor and came to a minute later with Florence's concerned face looming over her.

'Mummy, are you okay? You gave me a terrible scare!' After a few moments, Violet managed to stutter out.

'It's nothing dear, just my time of life. Can you make me a cup of tea, please, with sugar?'

Violet felt something awful was about to happen, but she pulled herself together, dismissed the thought, and decided she was being silly. Edith had been so firm with her that any type of foretelling was impossible, and she did not want to spoil Florence's occasion. After sipping the tea, Violet chatted with her daughter again.

'I'm happy you've met George. He seems like a nice young man. I hope he isn't making any inappropriate advances to you?' Florence blushed, fully aware of what her mother referred to but too embarrassed to discuss it. She shook her head, giving Violet the answer she wanted.

'I think he may be the one, Mummy. He treats me well. I'm so shy, but he's gentle and reassuring, and I feel more confident when we're together.'

'Well, that sounds like true love to me, darling.' Florence blushed again. 'I hope so, and I'm excited about the service next weekend!'

The following Sunday came, and after breakfast, George arrived in his open-top car to pick up Florence for their drive to London. She waved to her mother, her face lit up with excitement.

'Bye-bye, Mummy, we'll be back this evening!'

'Don't worry, Mrs Thomson. I'll take good care of your daughter,' George added.

As they drove off, a little chill went through Violet. She dismissed the sensation as the breeze and went back indoors.

Just after seven pm, the phone rang, and Violet answered it. It was Sir Arthur Warren. When he started to speak, Violet's stomach churned. He spoke in the tone of voice of someone who was about to deliver bad news.

'Mrs Thomson, I'm going to have to ask you to brace yourself for the most awful news,' he began, his voice heavy with dread. 'One of my contacts at the Air Ministry just called me. I'm so sorry to tell you that the Guards' Chapel was hit by a flying bomb during the morning service. It seems that most of the congregation were killed. We've heard nothing from George and fear the worst.'

The words echoed in Violet's mind, a relentless tide of despair washing over her. Her hand trembled as she clutched the phone, the gravity of the news sinking in. The world around her slowed, the edges of her vision blurring as if shrouded in a dark, suffocating fog. She could barely breathe, each word cutting through her heart like a knife. Her strength drained, and her legs gave way beneath her, then she dropped the phone and collapsed to the floor. Sir Arthur's voice could still be heard coming out of the earpiece.

'Mrs Thomson, are you there? Mrs Thomson...'

Three days later, Violet forced herself out of bed, her head muzzy and swimming from the sedative the doctor had prescribed. She put on her slippers and shuffled to Florence's room. Her face was devoid of emotion; only the dark, hollow-eyed shock etched deeply into her features betrayed the storm of grief within.

As she stepped into the room, her eyes scanned the familiar surroundings. The battered old bear sat forlornly on the bed. Florence's china trinkets were neatly arranged on the mantelpiece, each one a cherished memory now tinged with sorrow. On the bedside table, Violet's gaze fell upon a slightly battered book. It was the copy of *'The Snow Queen'* she used to read to her daughter. A cold chill passed through her as she picked it up, her fingers trembling.

The memories flooded back, each one a dagger to her heart. She could almost hear Florence's sweet voice, excitedly discussing the story's meaning. The weight of the loss was too much to bear, and Violet felt an overwhelming wave of anguish. She could take no more.

With a heavy heart, she placed the book back on the table. She left the room, locked the door behind her, and made a solemn decision: no one would be allowed to enter it again. The room would remain a sanctuary of memories, forever sealed from the outside world.

Part two
From darkness to the storm

"It has been said that time heals all wounds, I don't agree. The wounds remain. In time, the mind, protecting its sanity, covers them with scar tissue, and the pain lessens, but is never gone."
— Rose Fitzgerald Kennedy

Chapter one
Letters

Winding Wood
Crofton Lane
Forest Row
Sussex

15th January 1947

Dearest Edith,
I trust my letter finds you well amidst the chills of this relentless winter, which has proven to be the harshest I can remember. It feels like the Snow Queen from the fairy tale has come for a long visit! The coal shortages have made it an ordeal just to keep warm, but we are fortunate to have woodlands next to the house so we can gather logs for the fireplace in the sitting room.

Winding Wood is in a terrible state. The roof is still covered with a tarpaulin from when a parachute mine came down nearby in 1941, and the wind howls through the gaps. The house wears its battle wounds with a certain stoicism, yet I am so sad about its neglected condition. The paint is peeling, and the decay of years of disrepair is everywhere.

I must admit that since losing Florence, my spirits have been in perpetual mourning. Her absence has left a scar on my heart, and it's a struggle to find joy in the everyday. I worked hard for so many years to recover from Grace, but now this! It's too grievous a blow to bear. However, Thomas is my rock, and Bryony continues to be as caring and loving as ever. She is engaged to a nice boy called James Marshall and I hope they'll be married soon. Goodness knows we need some happy news, and it would be wonderful to hear children playing at Winding Wood again.

Our lovely garden is desolate; much of it had been turned over to growing vegetables during the war. Seeing the neglected beds and overgrown paths fills me with a deep sense of loss. It was a place of beauty, and now it serves as a reminder of what the country has sacrificed. I will try and restore it when it becomes possible. Much demanding work lies ahead. My priority will be the walled garden where we always grew the most beautiful roses.

How are things with you, dear Edith? I hope you are faring better in these trying times. I await the day we can sit together and be happy in each other's company. Until then, please take care of yourself.
With all my love,

Violet

> Beachcombers
> High Street
> Salcombe
> Devon

23rd February 1947

My dearest Violet,

Your letter brought a tear to my eye. I cannot begin to comprehend what it was like to lose Florence; now you have lost two children, your grief is awful to contemplate. I can only imagine the depth of your sorrow, and I wish I were there to comfort you in person.

Even now, three years later, I thank God we've been blessed as both my boys returned from the war alive and uninjured. It's a small miracle.

You're fortunate to have logs to burn at Winding Wood; here in Salcombe, the fuel situation worsens by the day. Neighbours have resorted to taking a log or piece of coal when visiting friends; it's seen as good manners!

Duncan has decided to venture into business and has purchased a toy shop on Salcombe High Street. Given the times, it's a bold move, but he has had his fill of working for other people. When his mother died, she left him some money, just enough to buy the freehold.

You are always welcome here, and I encourage you to visit one day. A change of scenery might do you some good; Devon is so charming. It would warm my heart to have you here with us, even if just for a short while.

Take care, dear friend, and hold onto the hope that better days are ahead.

You are always in my thoughts and prayers.

With all my love,

Edith

Chapter Two
Commies at the Door
1950

Over the years, life at Winding Wood slowly returned to a semblance of normality. The blast-damaged house was repaired after years of temporary patch-ups. The day workmen removed the tarpaulin from the shattered roof and replaced it with proper tiles felt like a marking point to Violet; the end of one era and the beginning of another. Perhaps it would be an easier time for everyone.

Eventually, the house was redecorated, covering the peeling paint on the window frames. Winding Wood awoke after a long slumber, like a butterfly emerging from a chrysalis. It was not quite ready to shine in the sunshine again, but it soon would be able to fly.

The garden was yet to recover its former glories, and the beds which Violet had so loved were still devoid of flowers. Unable to employ a gardener, she and Thomas managed as much as they could.

Whilst she sewed with her mother one evening, she complained.

'Since Labour got in, no one wants to do that kind of work anymore.' Sophia fumed.

'They're nothing but bloody communists. If Attlee thinks he's going to steal any of my money to prop up Stalin, he's got another think coming.' In Sophia's long-held and vociferous support of Conservative politics, her working-class and cash-strapped roots were forgotten. She enjoyed the role of the grand matriarch of Winding Wood and was damned if those *'bloody socialists'* were going to affect her material position by *'stealing her money.'* In her frequent rants, she ignored the point that the wealth which propelled the Thomson family to middle-class status and their comfortable life at Winding Wood was inherited and not hers. Violet replied.

'They're going to be nationalising the air we breathe next!' The two women sighed and returned to their sewing. Clothing was only just off ration and still hard to come by, so even with money in the bank, things needed to be repaired again and again. Violet continued.

'I'm fed up with having to make do and mend.'

'I know, dear, it's trying. But not to chide you, we must remember that, like us, so many lost loved ones or their homes were destroyed.' Violet said.

'You're right, Mother; the only important thing is to remember Florence.' She returned to darning a white cotton blouse with a little rose motif stitched over the pocket. She continued.

'Then the awful news which came out of Europe, the terrible things the Nazis did. I'll never understand how ordinary people were taken in by their wicked spell.' Sophia replied.

'Pure evil,' and then Violet thought for a moment and, in a low grave tone, went on.

'We never heard anything else from the Hirsch family. I did try writing to the British authorities, but they could find no trace. I fear they perished in one of those terrible camps.' Sophia replied, her voice quavering.

'I'm very grateful you tried. When my aunt married a Jewish man, who could ever have thought it would lead to their whole family being under such an appalling threat.'

'I wish we could have helped, Mother.' Sophia gave Violet's hand a little squeeze and said.

'You did your best, Vi. How many other people would have opened their arms and home to a family fleeing from Germany? If only they'd managed to escape, they'd be living with us here now.'

'Did you ever find out what happened?'

'I heard from my other aunt that Eduard was arrested the night before they were due to make their escape across the border. Irma refused to leave the country without him, and a few weeks later, she and the children were also taken away.'

They both fell silent for a moment and then it was Sophia who moved on to a different subject, not wanting to dwell any more on the horrors of the Nazi camps.

'Violet, we've lost many over the years to illness and war, and those wounds will never heal. When I'm saddest, I think of Ekatarina Zagorski's words and remember our loved ones, safe and happy in the afterlife. That makes me feel just a little better. It also reassures me that when I go, I'll be with my family. I think I won't be here for much longer. Eighty years is a long time to carry this tired old body around. I'll be content if God chooses to take me soon. In fact, quite relieved.'

'Nonsense, Mother, I won't hear of it. There's nothing wrong with you, and I'm sure you'll be here for a good few years yet.'

'If that's what you think, dear,' said Sophia, sounding unconvinced. They stitched in silence for a while, then Violet said.

'I cannot imagine my life without you, Mother. You've been the bedrock of this family for so long. As you say, we've all suffered loss. You're the person who got me through that. Otherwise, I'd have been unable to continue. Thomas is a good man, but I've needed the strength only a woman and mother can provide.'

'You're far stronger than you think you are. I suspect you don't understand that I look to you for support, too. Let's not focus on tragedies but think of the things we have. Whoever would have thought Sophia and Violet Gosling from Plaistow would end up living in a house like this, with all the comforts we have? In many ways, the second part of our lives has been like a fairy tale. You're a good woman, Violet, and you deserve everything you've been lucky enough to be given.'

'Thank you, Mother. I must've inherited that goodness from you.'

The next morning, Violet went to wake her mother with her usual cup of tea. As soon as she opened the door, she saw something was not right. Her mother lay half in and half out of bed, slumped to the floor. Violet ran over, hoping to help, but when she touched her brow, it was cold. Sophia was stone dead.

Violet realised that she and Thomas would have to cope without the support of others. In her grief, she had a moment of clarity and strength thinking.

'I've come so far, I can manage, and now the younger generation will fill Winding Wood with love and laughter for years to come. I have been and remain a blessed woman.' And then she wept, realising that another of her family was gone, and she felt lonelier than she had ever done in her life.

Three days later, Violet had an intense dream about her mother. She saw Sophia in the place she yearned for all her life, back at the old family farm in the green Bavarian countryside, with a little duck pond in front. Her mother looked relaxed and many of the lines of the long years had dropped away from her face. She turned towards Violet and smiled, then her expression turned to sadness, and she said very clearly.

'Remember what you were told about Winding Wood, my darling. The dark heart of the house of secrets will be revealed.'

Then Violet awoke, the words still echoing through her mind. She was sweating and shaking, the clarity of her dream quite shocking. She loved to see her dear mother in her personal Heaven, but hearing Ethel Trout's foretelling, echoing down the years, brought a great sense of foreboding.

Chapter Three
Letters

Beachcombers
High Street
Salcombe
Devon

June 3, 1953

My dearest Violet,

I had to write to you because I am bursting with excitement after watching the coronation on television. What an extraordinary event!

The splendour of the ceremony and the sight of our young Queen completely entranced me. Watching it unfold, I was reminded of our nation's resilience, something we all need to hold onto, especially after the trying years we've endured. I believe a new variety of roses will be bred in honour of Queen Elizabeth. Wouldn't it be lovely to plant one in your walled garden?

I hope you were able to watch it as well, do you have a television yet?

Duncan is pleased with the toy shop's progress and thinks we will make a good profit this year. It is a blessing that, because of your inheritance, you do not have to worry about money. Times have been lean, but it does feel like things are starting to get just a little better.

In your last letter, you told me Bryony and James are trying to start a family. I hope Winding Wood reverberates with the sound of young voices again soon. You are a brave and resilient woman who deserves joy in your life.

Take care, dear Violet; I look forward to hearing from you soon.

Edith

Winding Wood
Crofton Lane
Forest Row
East Sussex

1st July 1953

My dearest Edith,
Thank you for your letter.
We, too, watched the Coronation. How wonderful it was to be able to see it as it happened. Who would have thought a few years ago, that we would have things like that in our own homes?

Thank you for your kind words about my resilience. It's been a hard journey; I cannot deny it. However, If I were to fall into the rancour of bitterness, it would serve no one well, not my family or myself. I visit the graves of my lost dear ones in my prayers each day, and by doing that, they always remain close to me.

Now, I have exciting news. Thomas tells me our investments are doing well, and we have decided to go to Spain for our holidays next year. We'll fly from Manston Airport in Kent and stay somewhere called the Costa Brava for two weeks. The hotel is in a village called Rosas and sounds charming. What a lucky woman I am!

Write again soon!
Much love

Violet

Chapter Four
Missing Edith
1959

For the first time since 1921, Violet nearly managed to meet up with Edith, but destiny decreed this would never happen.

The date had been arranged for months. Edith had to visit London for a legal matter concerning her aunt's will. She wrote that she would have an hour between her appointment with her solicitor and the train from Paddington. They would have tea together, and they were excited at the opportunity to see each other face to face after years of being pen friends.

Violet left Winding Wood in an upbeat mood on the morning of the meeting, her heart fluttering with anticipation. She hummed *'Bali Ha'i'* from her favourite musical, *'South Pacific,'* which she had seen that week in East Grinstead. A taxi collected her, and she was in such a jolly mood that she tipped the driver double what she usually did. She arrived at the station fifteen minutes early for her train, and she sat on the platform waiting in the morning sunshine. It was chilly for April, but Violet had worn her winter coat, so she was warm enough and enjoyed the fresh spring air on her face.

'So many years,' she thought, her mind racing with memories.

'I wonder if she's changed. I certainly have.' That day, Violet put on her best suit and, around her neck, a fur wrap. She wore elegant, cream kid gloves and carried her smartest crocodile skin handbag. On the lapel of her suit was an elegant diamond broach, a dragonfly, which Thomas had given her the previous Christmas. Violet recalled that when she first met Edith, she had been wearing a shabby homemade dress, which she had repaired over and over again.

Violet reflected on the other changes that had taken place in her life since her last meeting with her dear friend. Moving to Winding Wood was the most obvious, but then losing Florence during the war was so terrible that even fifteen years later, Violet felt as if her life was defined by it. She put on a brave face and kept everything together for the sake of her family, but inside, she had never fully recovered. The pain was a constant, dull ache in her heart, a wound that never truly healed.

On this bright April morning, something shifted inside her. Violet decided that, finally, things had to change. Her mourning had gone on long and deep. Surely, she had a right to enjoy her life? Being in a state of permanent grief would not help her or her family. She wanted to be a good mother to Bryony and her husband, James. She was over the moon when her first grandchild, Emily, had arrived the year before. Indeed, they should be her priority now. There were days when she would withdraw from the world, so deep in her grief, and when she went into dejected seclusion. How could she be a loving mother and grandmother? Something must change.

At that moment, Violet knew what it must be. She would stop visiting the place where Florence had died, the ruins of the Guards' Chapel. Every month, she took the train up to London as a pilgrimage and had a moment of quiet reflection. Latterly, she watched the new church rise like a phoenix from the rubble. She felt close to her daughter there. There had never been a body to bury. Thomas and Violet were told that many of the victims could not be identified, and their remains were interred in a mass grave. Was Florence there, buried with people she had never met?

'I need to stop going. Florence, please forgive me,' Violet said out loud, her voice trembling with emotion. Her monthly homage tied her to her past, a long chain of grief trailing across the years. Now was the time to release that and let her daughter finally be at rest. Tears welled up in her eyes, but at the same time, a huge wave of relief poured through her.

At that point, the train came steaming around the corner, and Violet was snapped out of her thoughts. She decided she felt lighter than she had for years. Florence would understand; she was sure of it.

Sitting on the train, watching the spring-green countryside pass by, she remembered she needed to check exactly where she would meet Edith. She opened her bag and reached in to find the piece of paper she had written the address on. After fumbling around for a few moments, she realised she did not have it.

'Damn, I must've left it at home,' she muttered, recalling last seeing it lying on her dressing table. Not too concerned, she thought she remembered the address. Edith would be outside her solicitor's office. It was on Floribunda Street, Violet was sure of that. But she could not quite recall the rest of the address. She thought for a few moments longer; then it came back to her - Finsbury Park. Relieved, she planned to catch the tube and ask for directions when she arrived at the station.

After changing at Oxted onto the London train, Violet sat next to a jocular woman she recognised from Forest Row but could not recall her name. The woman was going to London to buy a new hat. They chatted about the weather and their holiday plans. Throughout the journey, Violet managed to conceal the fact she could not remember her fellow passenger's name, even though the woman clearly knew who Violet was. At Victoria, the woman said a cheery farewell.

'Lovely to see you, Mrs Thomson,' and Violet waved back, none the wiser. She caught the Circle line to King's Cross, where she knew she had to change for Finsbury Park. Violet did not enjoy travelling on the underground, finding the musty smell and clouds of dust most unpleasant, so by the time she got to her destination, she was relieved to come up the escalator into the daylight. She went to the ticket office, not knowing who else to ask for directions.

'Excuse me, can you tell me how to get to Floribunda Street?' Violet asked the man behind the glass partition.

'Never heard of it, love. Have you asked that policeman?' he gestured behind Violet. She thanked the ticket clerk and headed for the uniformed man.

'Excuse me, officer, can you help me find Floribunda Street?' Violet inquired. The policeman shook his head.

'Are you sure you've got the right address?'

'Yes, I'm supposed to meet an old friend there. I haven't seen her in years, and I'd be most upset to miss her,' Violet explained. The policeman thought for a moment.

'Hang on, there's a Floribunda Street in the City just off Finsbury Pavement. Do you think you may have come to the wrong place?'

Realising her mistake, she looked at her watch. There was no way she would get there in time and miss the chance to see her old friend. She thanked the policeman and set off on her long journey home, feeling extremely dejected.

On the train back to Sussex, she scolded herself over and over, but then eventually decided the day had not been entirely wasted. After all, she had realised that clinging to her grief for Florence for almost fifteen years was not helping anyone. Tomorrow, she would write to Edith, apologise, and then focus all her attention on her family. The ghosts of the past could not be allowed to dictate the lives of living, breathing souls in the present. Then she thought wryly to herself.

'And the other good thing today was I had all notions of premonitions put out of my head. If there were such things, I would've been able to divine the address! Edith, you were always right!'

At East Grinstead, she looked up and saw the unnamed woman from that morning in the corridor. Not wanting to engage in conversation, she pulled up her Woman's Realm magazine to conceal her face, till she was sure the woman had sat down in the next compartment.

Chapter Five
Summer days at Winding Wood
1965

The mellowing effect of the decades cast its enchantment on Winding Wood, transforming it once again into a much-loved sanctuary for the family. The garden, which had languished as a shadow of its former self for so long, had been lovingly restored to its pre-war glory. Garden societies arranged visits for the first time in years and commented glowingly about how the Thomsons had meticulously revived Phyllis Fenn's original design. Vibrant blooms provided a breathtaking backdrop to the house, their colours a vivid tapestry that contrasted beautifully with the lush green, secretive woodland beyond. The air was filled with the sweet scent of flowers, mingling with the joyous laughter of children and the gentle clink of glasses as the Thomsons enjoyed their summer evening drinks parties.

For Violet, the comfort and security of this blissful time saw her nightmares and visions come less often, though they never quite left her entirely. Now and again, the icy dreams and terror would return to torment her. Nowadays, she was clear that her dreams were nothing more than mental disturbances caused by the profound pain of the personal loss she had endured.

On this lovely summer day, Violet stood on the terrace, sipping a glass of Pimm's, her heart swelling with pride as she watched her grandchildren, Emily and David, playing catch on the manicured lawn. Emily, a spirited six-year-old with golden curls, chased after her brother, David, who, at four, was a bundle of boyish energy. Their laughter echoed through the garden, a joyful reminder of how wonderful life was at the old family home. She thought,

'This is what I always wanted. Could anything be better than this!' And silently thanked the forces of fate who had propelled her and Thomas towards this blissful life.

Violet recalled the days when her children played in the garden. She felt a deep pang of sadness thinking about how much she missed Florence, but how could she be dejected on such a lovely day as this?

Thomas, ever the doting grandfather, sat on his favourite bench beneath the shade of a sprawling oak tree, watching the children with a smile on his face. He had always been a man of few words, but his love for the family was evident in his expression. Violet joined him; she had a folded newspaper under one arm.

'Thomas, have you read the latest about Harold Wilson?' she began, her voice tinged with disapproval.

'I can't believe the direction this country is heading.'

Thomas remained silent, his expression thoughtful. He was a secret Labour supporter in a household that leaned towards Conservative politics. His wife always voted Tory and held strong views on the subject, which she expressed in no uncertain terms. He had learned to keep his views to himself. It made for an easier life. Violet continued, her tone rising with indignation.

'I don't understand how people can support him. It's as if they've forgotten everything we've been through and what we've fought for. Now we're selling out to Russia!' Thomas nodded and replied.

'You know, Violet, the Profumo affair shook things up. It's a reminder that our politicians are not always what they should be.' Violet looked at him suspiciously; was he speaking out against the Conservatives? She was going to quiz him on the subject but decided not to. It was such a beautiful day.

Emily and David were playing a game of hide-and-seek, their shrieks ringing around the garden. As the afternoon sun cast long shadows, Bryony and James joined Violet and Thomas on the terrace. They chatted, discussing plans for the summer holidays and how the children were doing at school. Violet said.

'Thomas and I wanted to talk to you about something. It's about Winding Wood. We think it's important that the house stays in the family, so we've decided to gift it to you and James in a few years. We need to arrange a meeting with our solicitor, but if we do it correctly, you can avoid paying inheritance tax when we die.'

'You're going to live for a long time! 'protested Bryony. 'But that's wonderful, Mum. James, what do you think?' He replied.

'It's very kind of you, but I'm not sure we can afford to run the house, and I'm no gardener.' Violet knew James had a point; the cost of maintaining the old property grew every year. Yet, in her heart, Violet believed the house weaved an irresistible magic spell and, in time, would draw him and Bryony back. She smiled to herself, confident her plans would fall into place and did not feel it necessary to press the point further.

In the evening, Bryony and James were preparing to take the children home. They stood in the drive chatting to Violet and Thomas. Bryony, sounding exasperated, shouted.

'David! Emily! Where are you? Granny's tired, and we need to go!' A few moments later, the children arrived breathlessly on the drive. David managed to get his words out first, between big intakes of air.

'Granny, we picked you a present! Look!' And the boy gave a flower to his grandmother. Violet saw it was the most perfect pink rose. Bryony admonished him.

'You shouldn't be picking flowers from Granny's garden. Mummy, I'm so sorry.'

'Don't be silly, Bryony dear, it's a lovely gesture. Thank you, children, I'll put it in a vase by my bed. It's so pretty.' As she said it, she noticed she had tears pouring down her face. The salty stream came without warning and for no reason, so she took her hanky and blew her nose.

'Must be hay fever,' she thought. Then in a sudden moment of crystal-clear clarity understood why the roses filled her with so much sadness . She tried to push the thought away, but in vain. In spite of the beautiful sun-kissed day, spent with her loving family, Violet went to bed that night with her mind swirling with recollections and emotions she would have preferred to forget.

Chapter Six
Fear of Flying
1967

Violet happily spent her afternoon in the bedroom, packing for their summer holiday. The thought of two weeks of sun-filled relaxation put her in a jolly mood, and she hummed as she folded Thomas's clothes. She looked out the window at the grey, drizzling day, longing for the warmth of the Mediterranean climate. It has been a most disappointing summer so far. Violet loved to spend her time in the garden, but the cool, damp weather had her spending most of her days indoors.

Returning to the same place for their holidays each year brought comforting familiarity. Since their first visit to Spain, she and Thomas tried several resorts before finally settling on the little seaside village of Tamariu. For ten years, they had returned to the Hotel Playa each year, where Señora Rosales greeted them like old friends. They adored the little sandy cove right in front of the hotel and loved to swim in the crystal-clear turquoise-blue sea, often agreeing that this would be their holiday destination forever.

Violet meticulously checked each item off her packing list to ensure she did not forget anything. She also had to consider Thomas who was much more disorganised and would likely arrive in Spain without something important, like his sun hat or razor.

As she went through the list, her thoughts turned to the flight. She was not a good flyer and found the whole process stressful. Each time she walked up the steps to the plane, she was racked with anxiety that the aircraft would crash, and she would always be airsick. The previous year, when they were landing at Barcelona airport, they had been caught in a violent thunderstorm, and the lurching roller-coaster ride left Violet green, vomiting and petrified.

Suddenly, she was consumed by a most unpleasant sensation. The bedroom floor swayed beneath her as if she were on the deck of an ocean liner on a high sea. She felt nauseous, and a sharp pain throbbed in one temple. A thick black mist descended over her eyes, and then she felt like she was falling through the air. She had to sit down to avoid collapsing.

Slowly returning to normality, she rubbed her temple with her fingers, the pain fading but still present. Then, a single dreadful thought burst into her mind.

'Oh my God, is this a premonition about the flight!' She recalled a similar experience years before when she thought she had foreseen the R101 disaster. She quickly pulled herself back, remembering her old friend Edith's advice - this kind of superstition was dangerous nonsense.

After finishing the packing, Violet went to the kitchen to make herself a cup of tea. She sat down, pleased to rest her legs, but her mind kept turning.

'What if Edith's wrong, and I can foresee things? Can I be absolutely sure she's mistaken?' Violet tussled with her doubts for an hour, drinking several cups of tea.

'I wish I could talk to Edith; she'd reassure me,' Violet reflected. 'I'm just being a foolish old woman.' But she could not forget what she had felt upstairs in the bedroom. Finally, she made a decision.

'We can't go on that plane. If there's a tiny chance Edith's wrong, and I can foresee things, I'm not prepared to take the risk.' Violet was a determined woman, and once she made up her mind about something, there was no going back.

She decided to tell Thomas she was too unwell to travel, then undressed and went to bed, removing her makeup to ensure she looked pale. Not long afterwards, Thomas found her feigning food poisoning.

'I'm so sorry, dear,' she said. 'I know how important this holiday is to you, but I'm simply too unwell to travel.' Thomas was displeased but eventually accepted there was no option. He thought the insurance would pay out, and they might rebook for later that year.

The following evening, after their flight was due to arrive in Spain, Violet tuned into Radio 4, anxiously waiting for news of a disaster. By 10 pm, she went to bed, and the following day, the Daily Telegraph confirmed no such accident had occurred. Violet felt extremely foolish.

'Why did I not stick with what Edith said? Now, Thomas and I have lost our chance to spend some time together in the sun. What a fool I am.' But then she thought, 'There's the flight back from Spain too!'

The day came for the return flight, and Violet repeated the process, scrutinising the news for any report of an air crash. There were headlines about the latest American offensive in Vietnam but nothing about airline disasters. She again felt extremely foolish, finally accepting her 'premonition' was nothing more than a fainting fit.

Two days later, Violet and Thomas sat together watching TV, enjoying one of their favourite programs, *Doctor Finlay's Casebook.*' Suddenly, Violet heard a strange, unfamiliar sound and saw Thomas with an odd expression, making a gurgling, strangled noise. Panic surged through her as she rushed over to him, finding him cold and clammy, struggling to speak. With her heart pounding in her chest, she suspected a stroke and frantically called 999. The ambulance arrived quickly, and Thomas was hurried off to the hospital in Tunbridge Wells, with Violet anxiously holding his hand.

Thomas's stroke was relatively minor, and six months later, his speech had returned almost to normal, though his mouth still drooped a little at one corner.

Violet felt an overwhelming mix of relief and gratitude, realising how fortunate it was that they had not been on the plane or in Spain when he fell ill. The thought of navigating such a crisis in a foreign land was unbearable.

One afternoon, whilst enjoying a cup of tea, she pondered.

'Good grief, was I warned? I wonder…' Violet's mind spiralled with the possibility that she had indeed been forewarned. The notion filled her with a nauseating dread, and she couldn't shake the haunting image of the deadly Ice Woman from her old nightmares. Terror gripped her heart, and she shivered involuntarily, feeling as if a cold hand had brushed against her soul.

Chapter Seven
Violet's Diary

25th April 1975

I miss Edith's letters a great deal. It's sad; we corresponded with each other for half a century, and she supported me through my darkest times. Friendships like these are rare, and I was happy to have had Edith in my life for so long. I still find it hard to accept she stopped writing. My diary has become my only listener, and I should commit my thoughts to it more frequently.

And dear Thomas, his death five years ago left a big gap in my life; he was a good, loving husband. Much of my generation is gone. My only surviving brother, Wilf, is in Canada. Loss has accompanied me all my life, but now, as I approach eighty I have come to terms with it.

I must not complain because my wonderful daughter Bryony and her husband James are living with me. It took a lot of persuasion to get him to agree to move in, but I had no doubts that, in time, he would fall under Winding Wood's spell. My two grandchildren are very kind to me, even though they have their teenage troubles and tantrums. Mind you, the pop music they play is dreadful! James is always shouting at them to turn the stereo down.

Whilst I am blessed with my family, I miss having someone of my generation to share stories about times gone by with. The early part of this century is so far away now. To think, when I was a child, the first flimsy aircraft were taking off. Now, man goes to the moon, and we can fly across the Atlantic at supersonic speed on Concord

1ˢᵗ October 1977

    Recently, my terrifying nightmare of the Ice Woman returned more vivid than ever. I couldn't get the image out of my head for days. Edith was always very firm with me about my dreams, insistent that they meant nothing. I do hope she's right. I wish she were still my friend.

    My mood has been subdued. It is a shame that we have to be more careful with money. Thomas always dealt with our investments and after he died I discovered there was not a great deal left. To compound that, James's business has failed, so all in all we are in straightened times. There are urgent things needing doing to the house we cannot afford; I try not to notice its state. Best ignored!

    I am determined to keep as much of the garden going as possible. I am still winning awards for my roses, so I simply refuse to neglect them.

    It strikes me that Winding Wood is a very demanding mistress. She is like an avaricious old lady with a penchant for jewellery and beautiful things yet cannot afford them. She looks to others for their generosity.

    I wonder who will come to Winding Woods' rescue this time, for to consider her decaying into her final days is too much of a thought to bear. In my more positive moments, I don't believe that she will ever allow this to happen.

Chapter Eight
The Great Storm
1987

The mild, damp October night darkened, and the wind outside began to howl with an eerie intensity, restless spirits whispering secrets through the trees. Violet was in the sitting room at Winding Wood, her eyes fixed on the television. The familiar face of Michael Fish on the BBC weather forecast filled the screen, assuring viewers with complete confidence that there would be no hurricane. She pulled her cardigan tighter around her shoulders, then said good night to the rest of the family and went upstairs to bed.

The house creaked and groaned as the wind picked up, rattling the windows and sending shivers down Violet's spine. The gusts grew stronger, and Violet was certain the entire house was vibrating. Later, she lay in bed trying to sleep but found no respite from the raging storm. Huddled under the duvet, she tried to focus her mind on happy and calming things, and her thoughts turned to her family.

She lingered on how much she missed Thomas. It had now been seventeen years since he died; they had come so far together. Their early lives in the East End now a million miles away.

'Thank the Lord for Albert!' thought Violet. If Thomas's wealthy brother had not been killed, she would still be living in Westmoreland Street, eking out a cash-strapped retirement on the meagre state pension.

The year before the storm, loss struck at the heart of Winding Wood, when Bryony's husband, James, passed away unexpectedly. Bryony, who had always been the most positive of the family, seemed to cope with her widowhood with fortitude, although Violet sometimes wondered if this was a mask concealing a much deeper turmoil. There were times when she thought she detected hidden grief behind her daughter's optimism, but when asked about it, Bryony always said.

'I'm fine, Mummy. I just need to get on with my life now. And I've got my granddaughter to cheer me up.'

As the wind outside intensified, Violet rose from her bed and went to the window. She could see little in the dark but heard the trees bending and creaking under the strain, and the rain lashed against the panes. The storm was testing the fabric of Winding Wood to the point of destruction. She thought about the tall brick chimneys and feared one of them might come crashing down on the house. She returned to her bed, her thoughts lingering once again in the past.

Violet's grandchildren, Emily and David, had moved away to start their own families. Winding Wood, though still a place of happy memories, was quieter now that only Violet and Bryony lived in the large house. Then, Emily and her husband, Joe, chose to return and make it their home. The old house once again drawing its family back to it. To Violet, it possessed a magical ability to keep those who loved it close to its heart. The cycle was repeated, and the sound of children's laughter echoed through the rooms again.

As the storm raged on, Violet couldn't help but feel that the wind was an omen of things to come. Its fierce power was a terrifying reminder life was full of unpredictable bumps in the road. She had endured so many trials, and yet, through it all, Winding Wood stood strong, a beacon of resilience. The storm howled louder, and the house shuddered under its force. She closed her eyes, offering a silent prayer for the safety of her family and the preservation of her beloved home.

Bryony, too, lay in bed fearing the worst. At some point in the night, she heard the most horrendous creaking and then crashing sounds, and she feared many of the trees near the house would be lost. There was a knock at her bedroom door, and she pulled on her dressing gown. Joe stood in the doorway with the torch beam illuminating the room; the power had been cut off.

'Just checking you're OK, he said.' It's too dangerous to go out, but I reckon we'll lose a lot of the woodland. Let's hope nothing hits the house. Come downstairs, we're in the kitchen, and Emily's making hot drinks. We can sit it out together.'

As the family listened and talked, nervous about the damage the storm would cause, the winds eventually subsided, and about five in the morning, they found the peace of sleep.

Later, when they awoke, they were bleary-eyed from such a short night's rest. Emily was preparing breakfast, and Violet was keeping her company. So, Joe and Bryony put on wellington boots and gingerly went outside to explore.

A heart-wrenching sight greeted them: the majestic trunks of four enormous beech trees were lying across the lawn. They lay almost parallel with one another, neatly arranged as if by some unseen hand, resembling felled giants in their death throes. They had stood for two centuries, bearing dignified witness to the passage of time, the changing seasons, and the myriad events which unfolded beneath them. They were present when Winding Wood was built and, over the years, observed those who lived there going about their lives. They had seen families grow, children play, and generations pass. People came and went, but the trees were the constant. Now, their mighty forms lay prostrate, stripped of life by the brute force of nature.

Bryony felt saddened at the sight as she took in the scene of devastation. Beside her, Joe felt a lump rise in his throat, and he blinked back tears. They walked into the woods, their hearts heavy with apprehension, fearing the worst. Each step they took was accompanied by the crunch of twigs and vegetation underfoot, the remnants of nature's fury strewn across their path. The air was thick with the earthy scent of crushed leaves and sap, a reminder of the storm's intensity.

As they ventured deeper, their anxiety began to ease. To their immense relief, much of the woodland had been spared. Broken branches littered the pathway, adding to the scene of disarray. Here and there, they came upon a felled beech or oak, their massive trunks lying abreast the path like guardians. Their duty was complete, and it was time to rot and enrich the soil beneath so that new life would spurt forth in time.

Joe glanced around, his eyes lingering on the fallen trees and the scattered debris.

'It'll take a bit of clearing up,' he said, 'but we'll recover.'

Later on, when they watched the pictures on the news of the total devastation of some woodland areas, they understood theirs had a relatively lucky escape. Joe said.

'A friend of mine called this morning and drove up to Toys Hill, the National Trust place near Sevenoaks. He said it looks like an atom bomb's gone off. There's hardly a tree left standing. We're protected a little because the woods are in the lee of the slope.'

Violet was relieved Winding Wood had faced up to its challenge so well. In time, the sad, fallen trees would be cleared, and fresh young growth would force its way up to replace them. But the storm augured changes which were confronting her in her own life. The old and familiar would be blown away and presaged a grim new future.

Concerned that she was becoming increasingly forgetful, she visited the GP. After numerous appointments and tests, she had been diagnosed with early-stage dementia. Her life would begin to fade away, and Violet was terrified. The awful storm served as an overture to the dark times which lay ahead and eventually would mean she would not recognise her family any longer.

This would be her final ordeal.

Chapter Nine
1989
Roses

Violet grimaced as she glanced at the tray the disinterested carer placed in front of her. The overcooked, grey food in the home was grim, and its colour reflected the façade of the austere Victorian house which housed the residents. The plump middle-aged woman did not even utter a greeting. As far as she was concerned, the 'inmates', as she called them, were too 'batty' to care, so why bother with pleasantries? She had been doing the job for more years than she cared for and now only stayed out of habit and necessity.

Tonight's culinary delight was a leathery toad in the hole, swimming in grease, nestled against a limp pile of flaccid vegetables, followed by cold tinned rice pudding. The latter enjoyed the addition of a dollop of cheap strawberry jam. Its artificial red jelly made the whole look even cheaper and less appealing.

Violet toyed with the unappetising food for a while with a fork, but she found the chewy batter difficult to swallow and gave up. She cast her mind back to meals she used to cook for her family. Ever the dreamer, she turned her thoughts to something tasty she would enjoy eating. Perhaps her favourite treacle tart. It was those thoughts and daydreams which sustained her, now she was moving towards the end of her story.

Violet dreamed all her life. In her earlier days, she daydreamed about escaping from the malodorous city and having a beautiful house and a pretty garden, far distant in the lush green countryside, a world away from the black smoke. Then her dream came true.

But not all her dreams were good; as a horrible counterpoint to her fairy tale life came the recurring nightmare of the terrible Ice Woman. As she got older, it came less frequently but never entirely left her.

When her family decided it was time for her to be *'put away'* as she described it, her emotion was one of overwhelming relief. There was no doubt she had dementia, and she had come to terms with the fact she would fade away. But to ensure there would be no debate on the subject, she hammed it up to make her condition seem worse than it was.

Names and occasions often escaped her and she struggled to recall what dinner had been or what she had done the day before. However, she still maintained a sense of who she was and knew who her family was when they came to visit. Violet didn't encourage them, finding it stressful, and, in any case, she must keep up the pretence that she was more forgetful than she actually was.

Much of the time, Violet spent in a dark cloak of sadness. She retreated to it as her recall of more recent events faded. So many heartrending memories from a life defined by loss. Her father died young, her brother mown down on the Western Front, darling little Grace lost, her youngest Florence gone during the war, and then her mother, followed not many years later by dear Thomas. All gone.

Violet was not bothered about her daughter visiting. She had no interest in Bryony twittering about the WI or what her granddaughter was doing at school. Better a life, dreaming in her austere little room, dealt with by efficient but distant staff.

The living had to be lied to, and that caused a tight, uncomfortable sensation in her chest. Violet was content in her lonely and limited life, with memories starting to slip away from her because here she could be alone with her loss and secrets. She had made a deal with God that her deepest truths would never be told. Too many people would be hurt.

A little later, one of the carers came to collect Violet's tray. Joan was the only one who talked to her like a grown woman, instead of the patronising tone used by other staff. She noticed something in Joan's hand.

'Good evening, Mrs Thomson. How are you today? Did you have any visitors?' Violet shook her head. She could not be bothered to have a conversation.

Joan reached out her hand and said.

'I've picked a couple of lovely roses for your vase.'

Violet stiffened at the sight of the soft pink flowers, and as she caught a hint of their fragrance, a fat vein throbbed in her neck. She shouted.

'Take them away, you stupid girl, you should know by now I can't stand roses. Disgusting things!'

'I, I'm sorry Mrs Thomson, I thought you'd like them.' Violet spat at the girl.

'Just get the fucking things out of here.'

Shaken, Joan backed out of the room with tears pricking at her eyes. She just wanted to be kind. Then she pulled herself together.

'Poor dear, she doesn't understand what she's saying.' Instead, she decided to give the roses to Dora Miller in the next room, a much nicer person, she thought.

Left alone, Violet's fading mind twisted and turned, and a single desolate thought kept burrowing and probing over and over.

'It's always the roses, the bloody endless roses. Will I never get any peace? The damned roses.'

Prologue to Part Three

In the stillness of the night, I sometimes find myself propelled into a realm far darker than my cherished dreams. I strive to escape, to force myself awake, but I'm trapped, descending deeper and deeper like a swimmer ensnared by a relentless rip tide. Pulled into the abyss, I fear I may drown in the bottomless black pit.

I love to visit Winding Wood, returning to my beloved home filled with happiness and love. Yet, in this dreadful nightmare, the joyful, love-filled place is replaced by a landscape far more troubling. It tears at my heart, creating a visceral sense of dread in my stomach. Oh, how I yearn for my sweet, flower-filled garden, but for now, I must endure a journey into the desolate unknown.

Instead of lush lawns, vibrant borders, deep woods, and birdsong, I find myself on a narrow, dark path. No light illuminates the way, yet somehow, I navigate the twisting route ahead. On either side of me, I hear the cries of lost souls, but I'm helpless to offer aid. They suffer the same torment as me, and I feel a tight sense of empathy, but this is a closeness born of despair. A hand reaches out and touches mine for a fleeting moment before it vanishes, the owner wailing in grief for what they have lost as they are carried away into the void.

Ahead, a looming structure begins to take shape. It's a brooding edifice towering high above me, making me feel tiny and insignificant. Atop it sits a tall, imposing tower, and as I draw nearer, I spot long, church-like windows punctuating the grubby brick walls. Everything is dark, grey, and foreboding. From the building emanates an energy of the purest misery, and I feel it pass through me like a flood of foul water draining my very soul. It is as if the wretched building itself is a repository for every sad emotion, every lost soul, and every stolen day that ever existed, bleeding out to taint the unwary passerby.

I look up to one of the windows, and a sharp stab of fear penetrates my core. This is no church. Shocked, I see myself standing at the window, staring out across the scene of dark desolation. My face is drawn, and I've been crying. Then, in a heartbeat, my reflection spots me and waves frantically as if trying to warn of some unspeakable horror within.

Then I wake up. My senses struggle to adjust, and I am caught between a nightmare and reality. I grapple with confusion, uncertain of what is real. Am I the dreamer, or perhaps the dreamer is my mirror self at the window?

My tears begin to flow freely, a torrent of anguish. I cannot stop them, no matter how hard I try. Sobs rack my body, deep and uncontrollable, echoing through every corner of Winding Wood, each single salty tear, a mirror of the sorrow weighing on my heart.

The echoes of my grief permeate the house, intertwining with its walls and floors through every room and corner. The sadness seems to seep into the ground, mingling with the roots of the old trees that have forever observed my turmoil. The weight of my dream clings to me, a heavy, dark cloak I can't shrug off.

As I lay there, I feel the house mourning with me, its structure absorbing my cries of despair. The grief spreads, touching everything in its path. The pictures on the walls, the furniture, and even the flowers outside wilt and fade in empathy. Winding Wood has taken on my pain, reflecting my inner turmoil in its silence.

Part Three
Secrets

Chapter One
The pond
1989

Thud! came a dull noise, something heavy being dropped on the floor in the attic above Bryony's bedroom. In her furtive imagination, it sounded horribly like a dead body falling to the ground. Chilled, she turned over to try and go back to sleep again, pulling the duvet tight around her as if to ward off evil spirits. She was adamant that she would not investigate what was happening in the loft at 11 o'clock at night. She told herself the wind had blown something over, and until recently, she would have believed that. Now, that rational thought became seeded with doubt. In the weeks since her granddaughter Elsie announced she had seen the ghostly figure of a woman in the playroom, something had changed in the old house. A presence, a subtle shift in the energy of the place.

Winding Wood, so comforting and secure, home to generations of the family. As children, Bryony and her sister Florence played shrieking in its corridors or ran shouting at the top of their voices around the minstrels' gallery. The adults enjoyed sparkling parties and languorous summer lunches on the lawns. The story of Thomas and Violet Thomson's lives and their descendants wove its way through the long years. There were both joyful and sad times, but before now, nothing dark or unsettling ever disturbed the old walls.

It was the kind of house which gave you a warm, honeyed hug as you entered. No ghosts glided through the corridors here. Yet, something had changed. The strata of the earth seemed to have shifted beneath the old foundations, and in doing so, a crack formed, which allowed something unbearably sad, a grey mist of misery to come through. An unnamed presence, a whisper of what was to come, but not yet fully revealed.

Bryony's initial complete dismissal of Elsie's phantasm to the rest of the family was a strategy to reassure herself. She had not wished to admit the house may be haunted as, in doing so, that would make it more real. But sitting in the security of denial was something she now found hard to do. Her daughter Emily and son-in-law Joe avoided talking about the subject, and she suspected they, too, were struggling with the possibility of a ghostly presence.

A few days after the thud in the attic, Bryony was enjoying one of her regular walks around the garden. Firstly, she checked out the vegetables. She asked Joe to keep them watered as June had been hot and dry that year. Everything took on a brown, scorched appearance, and she longed for rain. Never quite trusting him, she wanted to check he had remembered to do the watering. On this occasion, her suspicions were proved wrong, and when she bent and touched the soil, it was moist. She mentally apologised to Joe for doubting him but then corrected herself.

'Most of the time, he's so useless. It's not surprising I think the worst of him.'

Her walk took her away from the cultivated garden, past the abandoned and overgrown tennis courts, then glanced at the moss-covered sundial and towards the pond which her mother had insisted on being dug half a century before. These days, the pond's surrounds were thick with nettles and tree saplings, as this was one of the many parts of the garden the family did not have the time or money to look after. Joe said he liked the 'wild' aspect, but Bryony thought it horrid and unkempt.

Bryony remembered from her childhood, how lovely it had been. The pond itself remained, but it now looked sad and neglected. Here, bog grass proliferated, and the water was covered in a thick layer of duckweed. She found the fallen log where she often liked to contemplate, brushed the surface with her handkerchief, then sat down. It was a place where she could be away from the bustle of the family—a quiet and overgrown corner of the garden where she would be unlikely to be disturbed.

In this moment of reflection, it was natural that her thoughts turned to the recent ethereal presence that had come to her home. The faint sound of a woman crying echoed throughout the house, day and night. Some days, no one heard it at all, others more often. It was always soft and distant but persistent. It became an earworm, impossible to overlook and hard to forget, as much as one may try.

But more than the crying, the chilling atmosphere penetrating Winding Wood held the deepest sense of foreboding. It could not be defined, but when the earth seemed to crack beneath the house and something unnamed drifted through, it brought with it a taint, a deep, sad chill.

'I wonder if we should get someone in to help us?' Bryony thought whilst still pondering the green-covered pond. Maybe a priest or someone who understands this type of thing,' for she had no idea about it. Snapped out of her thoughts, she jumped as a flock of crows flew overhead, cawing rudely as they went. She stood up, ready to return to the house and then took a few steps, where her foot collided with a fallen log covered in undergrowth. She started toppling over and flayed her arms around, but there was nothing to grasp onto, and she fell face down into the pond, taking a mouth full of muddy, rank water as she did. Three feet deep at this point, she had the most horrible sensation of slipping and sliding further in. Bryony thought she would drown alone in the pond that Mother had four men from the village dig years before.

In a panic, she reached out her arms, trying to grasp something. She had foul, muddy liquid in her eyes, mouth and ears; then, to her surprise and relief, a firm hand gripped her arm. The hand belonged to someone with great strength, and she felt herself being turned over. Now, her face was above water, and she propelled herself on her bottom towards the bank. In the shallowest part of the pond, Bryony managed to stand. She was covered in mud and slime and coughing from the odorous liquid she swallowed. She looked around her, expecting to see Joe or Emily, yet there was only the rustle of birds in the trees to be heard and the familiar sights of the overgrown garden around her.

Shaking with shock and cold, she made her way back to the house and bumped into Emily in the hall as she tried to sneak up to the bathroom without telling anyone about her ordeal.

'Mum, whatever happened! Good grief, are you OK?'

'Nothing to worry about, I slipped by the pond. Now be a poppet and make me a cup of tea. I'm going to have a shower and change. See you in a moment, dear.'

Chapter Two
The walled garden

Joe pondered in his studio, staring blankly at the canvas before him. His hand held a pencil, and it hovered over the surface. He struggled with the motivation to draw or paint. In the far corner, the portrait of Sir Harold sat untouched on its easel. Joe had no desire to finish it. Painting portraits was stultifying and pointless. He yearned to do something creative yet could not find the will to start, or indeed did not have any fresh ideas.

He blamed some of his lack of enthusiasm on Bryony, his mother-in-law. Each time she nagged him, a little more resistance to doing anything built up inside.

'Have you tried to look for any real work lately?' Bryony's voice echoed in his mind. She had the habit of breezing into his studio unannounced and always brimming with opinions.

'Art's fine, Joe, but you need to be practical. You've got a family to take care of. Emily works so hard. Don't you want to contribute more?'

He yearned to let his creativity flow, yet between the incessant nagging and the constant sense of loss he held close to his heart, it was stopped in its tracks. There was a blockage, a high emotional dam, stopping the current of life-giving river water, and any ideas shrivelled from the drought below.

He sighed and reached for his wallet. He wasn't sure why. Maybe it was the barrage of Bryony's disapproval or the empty feeling of loss which hung heavy on him today. He opened it, then fumbled past receipts and old business cards until his fingers found a small photo tucked inside.

He paused and trembled as his thumb brushed the edge of the picture. He didn't pull it out, but he knew the image by heart. Its corners were worn from years of being carried in his wallet. It was the only thing which kept him tethered to someone, but he rarely allowed himself to look at it for long.

As much as the loss dug deep, he was fortunate to have his family around him. Little Elsie was a joy, and Emily doted on him. His mother-in-law was a bit of a pain, but she provided a roof over their heads, and who would not be enchanted by the lovely place they lived in? The past must not be allowed to bleed through into the present and disrupt the harmony of life at Winding Wood.

He pressed the wallet shut and put it back in his jeans pocket; an uneasy feeling pervaded him. He would not dwell on it, not now, not with everything so fragile. Instead, he stood abruptly, the need to be in the fresh air.

The walk to the Rose Garden wasn't too long. It was his favourite part, one of the areas that remained cultivated. They managed to keep this walled treasure, the vegetable beds, and a broad herbaceous border well-tended. but much had to be turned back over to lawn. In other parts, the hungry tendrils of unwanted plants, persistent and intrusive, crept into every corner. The wicked fingers of these weeds destroyed all that had been elegant in their unstoppable path.

Joe looked forward to seeing how the Rose Garden would be today. June was when the vibrant show would be at its peak and even with the hot, dry weather this summer, he expected to be pleasantly shocked when he entered it. He wanted to enjoy the spectacle of the flowers in their full splendour.

Some of the plants were descendants of roses from Emily's grandparents' time. The family had continued with only growing traditional breeds. He expected a gorgeous display of pink, white and cream blooms, and their heady fragrance would softly fill his senses.

As he stepped through the brick archway into the walled garden, he stopped in his tracks. The roses, once lush and colourful, were all dead. Every bloom had withered and shrivelled into dry husks. The petals, usually soft and rich with colour, had turned brittle and brown. Not a single bloom remained. He remembered Bryony had been watering here, so what caused this?

He knelt beside one of the bushes, brushing his fingers over a dead flower. The petals crumbled and fell to the ground. It was as if life had been drained from all the plants overnight, leaving behind nothing but decay. He stared at the now barren walled garden, something deep and sad settled over him.

The garden had always been a sanctuary, a place to escape the noise of the world. But now, it looked more like a graveyard, a painful reminder of what he had lost. He reached into his pocket again, his fingers finding the familiar shape of his wallet. For a moment, he considered taking out the photo, looking at it, letting himself remember, but resisted again.

Joe walked away from the desolation, the smell of dry earth and dead roses clinging to the air. The atmosphere around him had become brittle. As he made his way back toward the house, he couldn't shake the sensation that something odd was happening at Winding Wood. The nightly sound of the woman crying and the sense of sadness prevailing in the desolate Rose Garden mirrored his feeling that the thing he used to have, so special to him, was slipping far away from his memories.

Chapter Three
Emily

The claggy humidity clung to every pore in her body, and it did nothing to lighten Emily's mood. The perpetual sound of the crying woman dragged down on her each day, and she struggled to keep upbeat. She had a heap of tedious tasks to complete but struggled to make a start. There was a lengthy list of the everyday things that needed to be done to run a home: banks, gas bills, and booking an appointment at the GP for her mother. She sighed; it was always her that took on these tasks.

Joe was useless in that sense. She loved him dearly, but he did not have a practical bone in his body. 'Perhaps artists never do,' she pondered. Her mother was vociferous on the subject, but Emily did not mind him being like that. The dreamy-eyed man she fell in love with when they met four years beforehand was no different from the man now. She was not in a position to complain. Her mother's refusal to take much of the load of running the house was more irritating. Bryony took the attitude she was head of the household; her daughter and son-in-law lived at Winding Wood thanks to her generosity, and if she wanted to dole out instructions, she would. And she frequently did.

She wished her brother were here; between them, they could stand up to their mother better; he had always been Bryony's favourite. His life in Dubai sounded exciting, and he often called to share the news. But she missed him.

Sitting at her desk in the book-lined study, Emily decided the bank and gas bill would wait and instead flicked through her wedding photos. As always, when she thumbed through the pictures, she felt a warm glow of happiness. What a joyful day it had been, marrying the man of her dreams.

Joe and Emily had a brief romance and engagement. They were brought together through their shared interest in art. He the artist, she the enthusiast, and their eyes met at a Pre Raphaelites exhibition at the National Gallery. In front of the painting of the Lady of Shallot, they struck up a conversation. She said to a friend afterwards.

'I couldn't take my eyes off him. He's that cliché, tall, dark and handsome and he has a wonderful mop of black hair. It was love at first sight.'

Both keen and blushing, they stumbled over their words in that awkward moment of two people meeting who instantly liked each other. Phone numbers were exchanged, and in a week, the couple were dating and, in a month, engaged. There was an air of urgency to Joe. When he proposed, he said.

'What's the point in waiting? Let's marry soon. We're in love, and we should waste no time because we have so much life to live together.' Before the wedding, Emily found out she was pregnant, to her mother's disapproval. Six months after they married, little Elsie presented herself to the world.

Emily loved Joe's lost-boy air, sometimes she glanced at him, and he seemed to be a hundred miles away. She would hold his hand and say.

'What are you thinking of, darling boy?' And he would reply vaguely.

'Not a great deal, working out how to start on my next painting.' And she was pleased knowing he was off into his realms of fantasy and creativity. With his air of mystery and romance and dark, handsome face, she sometimes thought he was perhaps the reincarnation of a medieval troubadour or a Roman actor.

Before they married, they planned to live in Joe's rented flat in Lewes and Emily would give up hers in Brixton. He liked the town, saying it attracted creative people, and she was happy to move out of South London. After being brought up in Sussex, she found the city intense and stressful. A few days before the wedding, Bryony spoke to Emily on the phone one evening.

'He's never going to earn much money, dear. Why don't you come and live at Winding Wood? The house is far too large for Granny and me, and we would love to have you here. I can't imagine you bringing up the baby in his one-bedroom flat. Look at what you would both have.' Emily thought it was a good idea but replied.

'Thank you, Mum, that's a lovely offer. I need to talk to Joe about it, though. I'm not so sure he'll be keen. He's more of a town boy.' It was not entirely true. Her real concern was what her fiancé would think about sharing a home with his mother-in-law.

As suspected, Joe expressed concern about the proposal.

'I'm not sure. The thought of living with your mother doesn't appeal to me. I don't think she approves!'

'She'll get to love you just like I do. Now, you've only ever been to Winding Wood at night when you dropped me off that time, so you never had the chance to see how beautiful it is.'

Not long after that, Joe and Emily went for lunch with Bryony. It was a sharp blue skyed spring day, the kind which made you feel fresh and alive after the dark toll of the winter months. They walked around the garden, carpeted with daffodils, and from the edge of the woodland, looked back at the graceful architecture of the house. He said.

'It's the most amazing place; we'd be fortunate to be able to live somewhere like this. Do you think your mother would warm to me in time?' Emily laughed.

'I have no doubt. Shall we tell her we've agreed to move in?'

Winding Wood had cast its spell on Joe, it had that effect on people. Drawing them in, seducing them and keeping all who came to it in a tight embrace.

Immediately after the wedding, the couple moved in with Bryony as planned. Joe's concerns were put aside. The thought of spending his days surrounded by nature and beauty intoxicated him with excitement.

Emily flicked through the photo album. What a happy day their marriage had been. What an awful hat Joe's Aunty Dot's wore! What a fun reception! Gosh, didn't Ida Coombs drink too much and make a fool of herself?

Emily reflected that she loved Joe very much, 'I've never had anyone in my life before who knows me so well. I feel safe when I'm with him.'

Then with a slight intake of breath, she remembered what she wanted to forget, the memory which she could not escape from.

'The thing he doesn't know. I wish I could tell him. But I'm scared of what he'll think.' This recollection brought a surge of guilt, which overpowered the warm, happy feeling she had whilst browsing through the album. As always, she had to push back on this. Otherwise, the guilt would be all-encompassing, and she would break under its weight in the end. She reassured herself.

'I did the right thing. I'm sure of that.' To distract herself further she went towards the shelves on the opposite side of the room. She wanted to find a book she remembered with details of woodland walks in Sussex.

Suddenly, she felt the most peculiar sensation. It was as if someone passed through her as she stood in front of the rows of books. A mist mingling with a mist, a feeling which was impossible, yet one which Emily had no doubt she was experiencing. She felt soft hair flow through hers. Then, the powdered smell of a woman's make-up followed. The merest brush of delicate skin touched Emily's face. There was another fragrance too, a sweet flower essence which she could not place.

The woman's emotions overlaid with Emily's, and she became consumed with an overwhelming sense of sadness. It wasn't the emotion of a momentary loss or a heated but brief row with a loved one; this was a deep-rooted sadness, an intrinsic part of the woman's soul. Emily began to cry, tears poured down her cheeks. There were the woman's memories, too, but they flashed through her mind too quickly for them to be grasped. It was like catching soap bubbles, as soon as you get close, they pop and leave no trace, and you forget they have ever been there.

'Who are you?' she sputtered, but it was too late. The warm, perfumed mist of the woman passing through her disappeared in an instant, and the room remained still and empty.

———————

Chapter Four
Letters in the attic

Joe thought having tea with his wife and mother-in-law was not his idea of fun, but he agreed when Bryony mentioned it in a tone which tended to indicate it was an instruction. He would rather be out in the garden immersed in nature. There was an embryo of a painting buzzing around his head, and the woodlands he so often walked in were fuel to his imagination.

He had the impression that Bryony wanted the family to discuss something, which was an uncomfortable prospect. It was easier to go through life day by day, only ever discussing the weather or what they were having for dinner tonight. Serious topics like emotions or what had happened in the past were best considered forbidden territory.

Later, after the family were sat together Bryony cut slices of Victoria sponge, then poured tea, and said.

'We need to talk about what's been happening. You know, the crying and the weird atmosphere.' Despite initially resisting the conversation, Joe decided his wife and her mother should be told what he had seen.

'I agree. It's getting a bit much,' he said. I'm starting to feel spooked.' He spoke of his sadness and bewilderment on finding the devastated, dead roses. Bryony had assumed her day dreaming son-in-law failed to look after the garden, not realising how quickly it had withered and died.

'I had a most peculiar experience too.' She said and then relayed how she slipped and fell in the pond and how the ethereal hand helped her to get a grip and save herself from drowning.

'That may have saved my life,' she concluded. 'There are not many people who can say they have been rescued by a ghost.' After telling her family what happened to her in the study, Emily said.

'Are we accepting the house is haunted?'
'I don't think we've any choice,' replied Bryony.

The family had put up with weeks of distant crying and waves of an intangible sadness which permeated the house, an insidious fog of tears. It came to feel as if Winding Wood itself was in deep mourning, its brick walls and foundations emanating a tragic funeral dirge. Initially, they tried to ignore it and pretend the sound of crying was the soft summer wind in the trees and the overwhelming emotion only their imagination. Over the days, they came to understand maintaining everything was all right was not an option.

'Whatever are we going to do?' asked Emily. 'This is starting to shred my nerves.'

'We could find an exorcist!' said Joe. Bryony's response came swiftly, and she did not sound in the slightest bit amused.

'Joe, I can assure you, as we might be haunted by one of my dead sisters, we'll not be doing that. I can't imagine for one moment why either of them would want to make us so troubled. If Grace or Florence were to come back from the other side, I would want to be able to talk to them. Oh, for goodness sake, listen to me; this is a load of nonsense, isn't it?'

'I'm not sure we can find an explanation other than ghosts,' Joe replied.' So no, I don't think it's ridiculous.'

Emily went on.

'Is there anything we can think of which would give us a clue to what the hell's going on here?' Bryony said.

'It's probably my overactive imagination, but one night, I heard the sound of the woman crying just as I had before. It went on for ages and kept me awake. Then, there was the most God-almighty thud from the attic. It sounded like a body falling over, I hid under the duvet and then forgot all about it. We should check it out and see if that gives us any clues! Maybe it was a body!'

The three of them made their way up to the first floor, and then to the door which led to the attic. Bryony walked up the narrow, uncarpeted, and creaking steps and felt a wave of nostalgia for her childhood. She was sad Florence never grew up to have children of her own, who would have enjoyed the secret dens which they had played in together under the steep, slanting roof.

Joe clicked on the switch at the top of the stairs, and a single bare bulb revealed the attic. Some light also came into the other end from a dirty skylight, but it was difficult to see anything. The cobweb-strewn roof space had never been converted to proper rooms. There was more than enough space in the house for the family, but like many attics, it served to store the family's accumulated detritus: childhood toys, tired old leather suitcases, with stickers telling tales of long-ago adventures.

The other thing which attics are good for are children's secret places. Discarded old furniture built into spaceships, pirate caves or fairy castles. Bryony and Florence loved to play up here as children, and then later Emily and David made the space their own. They played 'Doctor Who' and one of the old wardrobes stood in for the Tardis. David would run around shouting *'exterminate!'* until the two tired of the game and ran downstairs for supper.

In a few moments, their eyes adjusted to the dim light and they were able to make out the contents of the attic. Here an old doll, minus its head, there, a pile of 78 RPM records which had been the pride of Violet and Thomas's collection. In another corner, Joe made out a stand with a moth-eaten fur coat hanging from it. There was a wardrobe of suits which had belonged to Thomas, and no-one had the heart to throw out after he died. The throaty smell of mothballs assaulted Bryony's nostrils as she pushed her hand through the row of jackets. The attic was boarded and the floor creaked as they explored.

'It seems like your grandparents were hoarders,' said Joe to Emily.

'I remember Granny saying Grandpa would never throw anything away.' As if to confirm that point, Joe picked up a World War Two gas mask and showed it to his wife.

'Joe, Emily! Come over here, I've found something!' called Bryony.

'What is it, Mum?' and the two walked over to where she knelt on the floor. The floorboards protested as they went.

'Look, this box has fallen off the shelf, and it's right above my bedroom. It must be what made the thudding noise.'

'What's in it?' asked Emily. Her mother had opened the flap of the battered cardboard box and was exploring the contents.

'It's old papers.' Bryony flicked through the pile. Some of it was bank statements, school reports for her and Florence, green shield stamp books and even a £5.00 Premium Bond.

'Not very interesting unless the Premium Bond's still valid!' she exclaimed. Then she noticed a bundle of letters tied up with a green ribbon. She untied the ribbon and looked at the first one. It was from someone called Edith Bates, dated 3 May 1920. She thumbed through a few more. They were all from Edith. It appeared they maintained a regular correspondence.

She recalled her mother had mentioned her pen pal Edith but had no idea how often they wrote. There were letters from her friend, every two weeks or so. She was drawn to the last one at the bottom of the pile, wondering why they had stopped writing. Maybe Edith died. Bryony said.

'They wrote to each other for fifty years. This last one is dated 26th July 1970 just after Dad died.' She read out loud.

Violet,

I read your letter with shock and bemusement. The things which you have told me have shaken me to the core. I now know that your life at Winding Wood was built on a lie, and you have been prepared to sacrifice all human decency in order to perpetuate the deceit.

You once said your life was like a dream come true and you found your dream home with roses growing around the door. It's now apparent those roses withered and died a long time ago. I always thought you were a fine and kind woman, but this is not the case.

I believe the only route to salvation for you, is to tell your family the truth and maybe they will find forgiveness. Or perhaps only God will judge you.

What you have done is so egregious that I do not recognise the person you are and will not write again.

Yours with sadness

Edith Bates

———————————

Chapter Five
Edith Bates

Bryony spent the whole of the next day in a state of utter bemusement and shock. Whatever was Edith Bates referring to, and how dare she talk to her mother in this way? There were moments when the foundations beneath her seemed to have shifted as if riven by an earthquake, and others when she thought it was a storm in a teacup. Perhaps the two old friends had fallen out about something, and Edith had lashed out. And yet, the woman's harsh final words were in direct response to something Violet wrote. But what the hell was it? 'Probably a misunderstanding,' she tried to reassure herself.

Bryony considered going to visit her mother in the care home and question her on the subject but decided against it.

'Mother barely knows the time of day and probably won't remember Edith, so is there any point?' But the words in the letter cut deep, and she could not forget about it. She needed to discover more and thought she would try and contact Edith if she was still alive and find out the answer.

'And if she was just being unpleasant to Mother because they had a spat, I'll give her a piece of my mind.' Bryony decided the best plan would be to write Edith Bates a note and ask if she was able to throw any light on the matter.

Winding Wood
Crofton Lane
Forest Row
East Sussex

25th July 1989

Dear Mrs. Bates,
Please excuse me for troubling you, but I have discovered some old correspondence between you and my mother, Violet Thomson. Your letter to her dated 26th July 1970 would indicate you had some kind of falling out with each other. I can't discuss this with Mother as she suffers from dementia. Please call me on Forest Row 231448 so we can talk about this.
Yours sincerely,

Bryony Marshall

The days went by and became a week. Bryony began to think the woman was either dead or the letter failed to reach her. She would never find out what prompted her mother's friend to write such angry words. Then, two weeks later, she picked up the phone one afternoon, and a voice she did not recognise asked her:

'Is that Bryony Marshall? This is Edith Bates. I received your note.'

'Edith, thank you so much for calling me.'

'You're welcome. I can only apologise it's taken so long, but your letter went to my previous home. I lost my husband ten years ago and moved to a retirement flat in Dartmouth. The couple who bought our house still had my address, and they forwarded your letter.'

'That's wonderful. Thank you again for taking the time to call.' Bryony desperately wanted to find out what the letter to her mother was about, but it seemed rude to press the matter straight away, so the two women exchanged pleasantries, with Bryony finishing.

'Yes, I live at Winding Wood now. We moved back here after Dad died. I think it was in 1971. Such a lovely place.' She now felt ready to move the conversation onto the subject she was anxious to discuss.

'If I may ask, what lay behind the last thing you wrote to Mum? You were so angry. Did you fall out with her about something?'

'You don't know, do you? She never told you. Dear Lord, I thought she would've had the decency, but clearly not!' Bryony stiffened at Edith's tone.

'Know what? Edith, you're not making any sense. I have no idea what you're talking about! Please tell me what upset you so much that you stopped writing to Mother.'

'Bryony, I'm sorry but I'm not in the position to discuss things which Violet should've told you years ago. It's not my place to do so. You need to speak to your mother.'

'That's not possible. She has dementia and barely recognises me.'

'Then Violet's secrets must go with her to the grave.' Bryony began to be angry that the woman was becoming obstructive.

'You're being unreasonable Edith. I have a feeling that whatever my mother did, it may have a bearing on things which are happening at Winding Wood at the moment. We believe we're being haunted, and perhaps it has something to do with what my mother told you.' Edith did not respond for a moment, then said, in a grave tone.

'If that bloody place is haunted, it would not surprise me for one moment. It has too many dark secrets. But I'm sorry, I cannot be the one to tell you. There's been enough betrayal in your family, and even though your mother's acts were heinous, I'm not going to betray her now. I'm going to finish this call. Good day,' then the phone clicked off.

Chapter Six
Bryony's secret

Bryony's head spun with a mixture of conflicting emotions. She was loyal to her mother and did not like Edith Bates casting doubts on her character in such a vociferous manner. In Bryony's eyes, Violet was a decent and kind woman who raised her family well and dealt with considerable personal loss. But why was her old friend adamant her mother had done something so unspeakable? She could not believe this was possible. And if her mother had, why did she eventually spill the beans to Edith? Confusion filled Bryony's head, unable to fathom what the truth may be.

Bryony had always been a woman of habit and meticulous routine; she found this turn of events to be unsettling, and her smoking increased as a result. In the days that followed, she lit cigarette after cigarette, often stubbing them out, only half smoked, to only light another a few minutes later.

And yet, something niggled away at the back of Bryony's mind, a whisper of a memory from younger years. Something she could not put her finger on, an unspoken truth, a vague hint of a deeper layer to the Thomson's saga. She recalled she had wanted to confront her mother about it many years before, but she didn't, fearing she was being silly.

Now, whenever the thoughts returned, she tried to dismiss them as nonsense, for Florence and Bryony had enjoyed a charmed life after they moved to Winding Wood. There was a huge garden to play in; Mother was happy in her smart new clothes from the best shops in Oxford Street. Neighbours visited for tea or a summer lunch party.

Mother joined the WI and Father the golf club. It was a typical if unremarkable middle-class life, one a million miles from where they came from in smog-laden Docklands. But Bryony remembered that on occasion, she would glance at her mother and father, relishing all the good things they enjoyed, perhaps entertaining the Vicar over a sweet sherry or mother returning from the garden with perfect roses she had cut for the crystal vase in the hall. And in a moment of intuition, think,

'Something's not right.'

Still, the vague niggle pervaded, and each time she tried to think about it, she could not get it. She thought it was like trying to recall someone's name. You know you know it but cannot recall it at the moment. Lighting yet another cigarette and inhaling deeply, Bryony pondered.

'This house feels like it holds many secrets, so I suspect Edith's right and Mother's keeping something from us.' Then, she reflected wistfully.

'I know all about secrets because I hide one of my own.' The truth which had been festering away within her for three years, was that Bryony was an unhappy woman. She couldn't share this with her family. How could she? She kept them on the straight and narrow. How would they manage if they found out that inside, her happiness had shattered into a million broken pieces? Emily and Joe's lives were constantly hung by a financial thread. Someone had to guide them and provide them with stability. If they lost her shining light, how would they function? No, she must subjugate her needs below those of others.

Up to three years earlier, Bryony had been a different woman. That was until her beloved husband James died. It was sudden and brutal. There was never any hint of illness, he appeared healthy, and they looked forward to their retirement. Then, one afternoon, he left home with a wave to Bryony and shouted, 'I love you.' She never saw him alive again. He dropped dead in a single moment following a massive stroke on the 5th Hole of the golf club. There had never been anyone else for either of them; his loss created a gaping gap in Bryony's heart.

To the outside world, Bryony coped, and her friends commented how brave and strong she was, but inside, she shattered into a million grieving pieces and retreated into a quiet and dull existence, for nothing would ever be the same, no experience would be enjoyed in the way it had been when her beloved husband was alive. At first, people kept asking her if she was OK and how she was getting on. Faced with a brick wall of being told everything was fine, they stopped in time.

One by one, the bricks sealed her into a prison which she built for herself, and no one had the glimmer of an idea how much she continued to suffer. To survive and continue living some life, she retreated into a narrow path of normality, and in time, it made her misery worse. In her lowest moment, she decided it was her and not her dear sister Florence, who should have been killed during the war. She often thought.

'What use am I to anyone?' She had read the modern perceived wisdom that one must talk about one's loss and issues but dismissed this as "trendy" nonsense. She would grieve in the way that she wanted; to do anything else may allow the sadness to dissipate, and then she would have lost the sense of him forever. The moment had to be held to keep James's memory close by her side.

Bryony never told a soul quite how she felt. Once the condolences and platitudes of well-meaning friends ended, she smiled again, and everything seemed normal, but inside her dwelled a dark, empty place.

Chapter Seven
Wanting Florence

June's sparkling days, so full of burgeoning promise, faded into a blisteringly hot and angry July and then into the long, dejected month of August. The lawn at Winding Wood turned sad and brown, so when Elsie played on it, clouds of dust whorled into the air. Even the beech trees in the woods began to lose their leaves in protest. Joe found it upsetting that the beautiful woodland was distressed but hoped it would recover the following year.

Many oaks and beeches fell during the Great Storm, and he did not want the old wood to suffer any more damage. After inspecting the garden, he went back into the kitchen to make himself a cup of coffee, and just as he did, the phone rang.

'This is Edith Bates; who am I speaking to, please?'

'I'm Joe.' For a moment, he had no idea who the woman was, and then the penny dropped. Before he could add anything further, she said.

'You must be Bryony's son-in-law?'

'That's right, and I believe you and Violet corresponded for all those years! What an amazing thing to do. I'm not sure anyone would bother these days.' He regretted saying this, as it felt slightly disparaging; he had not meant to belittle her. She replied.

'Well, more's the pity. Now I've something important to discuss. Did Bryony tell you about our conversation?'

'She did; I understand you didn't want to talk about the last letter you wrote when you told Violet you wanted to cut off the friendship with her.'

'That's right, and I've not changed my mind. However, I think it's only decent that your family finds out the truth. I've thought long and hard about it. I cannot divulge Violet's secrets, but I want to help, and maybe we can encourage her to talk.'

'I think her dementia's too advanced for that.'

'That's possible, but I'm hoping if she sees me, it might jog her memory; it may work. We never met again after I left London in 1920. That's almost seventy years ago, but our friendship endured all those years via our letters. Violet was always such a good friend to me, and I thought she shared everything, but later, I understood what she told me was a pack of lies. That was so hurtful.' Joe did not know how to respond, so decided to turn the conversation back to Edith's plan.

'What are you suggesting?'

'I have to come up to London next week and visit the doctor. Old age means I spend more and more time there! I can easily catch the train to Sussex. We can meet Violet in the care home and see if we make any headway.'

The following week, Joe picked up Edith Bates from East Grinstead station. He spotted her straightaway: a diminutive woman in a tweed suit with pure white hair piled into a bun. Although almost ninety, she walked across the forecourt at a fair pace, pulling her tartan suitcase on wheels behind her.

During the drive to the care home, they chatted but avoided the subject of Violet's secrets; there would be enough time for that later. It was clear to Joe that this woman did not have the slightest hint of dementia. She spoke about how she and Violet met during the Spanish flu epidemic. Her memories were as clear as a bell. As they drove across the Ashdown Forest, taking in the sweeping view, she said.

'What a beautiful place. Violet and Thomas landed on their feet living out here. She did hate the East End so.' But Joe felt it was said with an undertone of disapproval rather than celebrating her friend's success in life.

Soon, they arrived at the care home, an expansive stone-clad Victorian house set amongst banks of overgrown rhododendrons. As arranged, Bryony and Emily were outside waiting for them. Bryony went to the door of the car and helped Edith out.

'It's so lovely to meet you, Edith. It seems quite strange Mother never met you in person again after you left London, yet here you are now. It's extraordinary!'

'It is indeed a wonderful thing, dear. I apologise for being abrupt when we spoke on the phone. All this is difficult territory for me. I'm clear I can't discuss Violet's secrets. They're far too profane for anyone else to divulge. It would be wrong, but it's time the people involved find their redemption. I fear that even that's not possible. God only knows, but Violet mustn't take this to the grave with her.'

Bryony did not want to press her at this point. When Joe told her about the plan to visit Violet to try and encourage her to talk, she was sceptical that it would work. Her mother most often retreated into silence; was she capable of saying much? When she did have moments of lucidity, the conversation was limited to inconsequential memories from forty years ago. But she would go through with it and see what happened.

After signing in at reception with an efficient but brusque nurse, they made their way through the long corridors towards Violet's room. The décor had seen better days, and the carpets were threadbare. Prints of old masters adorned the walls—here, the Hay Wain, and there, Van Gogh's Sunflowers. Their faded condition only highlighted the sad and dejected state of the old house.

Bryony knocked on the door of the room. There was no answer; there never was one when she visited. It seemed polite to knock, so she pushed it gently open, and the family entered. Violet sat in her high-backed chair with a crochet blanket on her knees. She did not acknowledge their presence and continued to stare straight ahead as if looking at something important in the far distance. An undrunk cup of tea sat coldly on the small table beside her chair. The long windows were open to the garden and sunlight poured in, but it made little difference to the dreary beige décor or Violet's washed-out pallor.

'Hello, Mummy,' said Bryony, and she bent over and kissed her mother on the cheek.

She went on. 'Now, today, I have a treat for you. Joe and Emily have come with me. We'll have tea together.' The nurse is bringing it in a moment. She promised to bring a plate of shortcake biscuits too; they're your favourite.' Violet said nothing, pulled her blanket a little higher, and continued to stare straight ahead. Joe and Emily pulled visitors' chairs to the bedside and kissed her. Still no reaction. Bryony thought.

'This is a waste of time; she's away with the bloody fairies.' But said.

'There's also somebody else who would love to see you—someone who you've not seen for many years. We thought we'd keep her as a surprise for you. She's come all the way from Devon.' At that point, Edith came into the room.

'Violet dear, do you remember me? It's Edith Bates. It's seventy years since we've seen each other.' There was a brief glimmer of a reaction from Violet, an altered expression that crossed her face like a shadow, and then nothing more. Bryony said.

'I think this is a waste of time. She doesn't recognise you.' Bryony looked at her mother and noticed Violet's mouth started to move slightly. She was trying to form words, but nothing came out. Then her face flushed, and without warning, she stood up with a jerk. The blanket fell to the floor, and she knocked the teacup off the table, and it smashed, the cold tea soaking into the crochet blanket. Standing over her family, she managed to snarl out some words. Spittle flew from her mouth as she did; her face flushed, and her hands jerked around like a marionette.

'Bitch,' she snarled at Edith.

'Fucking bitch!' Violet reached for the walking stick propped by her chair and threw it at Edith. Fortunately, it only struck her on the stomach and fell to the floor with a clatter.

'Bitch,' snarled Violet. Get her out of my sight, and the rest of you can fuck off too. Where's Florence? I want Florence. I don't like any of you.' At that, she sat down again, slumped into the chair as if she had run out of steam, and stared straight ahead once more. Her eyes reddened with anger, and spittle dribbled down her chin.

'Edith, I'm so sorry, she's not normally like this,' Bryony said as she bundled the family out of the room.

'Nothing to apologise for, dear. It was my idea. I didn't realise quite how difficult things were. I should never have come.'

———————————

Chapter Eight
Remembering Patrick

Joe walked slowly along the broad, sandy track through the Ashdown Forest, his footsteps crunching on the path leading to the part called The Airman's Grave. He loved the distant views towards the soft green line of the South Downs and relished the tranquillity of the place. All around was silent, save for the rustle of leaves in a far group of trees and the occasional calls of birds.

Sometimes, there would be a hum of a jet starting on its descent into Gatwick; otherwise, it would be just glorious peace and quiet. He thought the vapour trails they made, lining across the big Sussex skies, were things of beauty, on occasion crossing and creating intricate and delicate white patterns.

There was something sacred about The Airman's Grave, with its memorial to a crashed World War Two bomber standing a lonely guardian on the open heathland. As Joe approached the grave, he felt the familiar weight lift a little from his shoulders. The serene beauty of the Ashdown Forest contrasted with his inner turmoil. He reflected that Winding Wood was a place of secrets, including his own, and lately, they were beginning to unravel.

Joe's thoughts drifted to recent events, with Bryony discovering her mother's correspondence with Edith Bates. The letters appeared to be a signpost towards unravelling the past and finding out why the house had acquired a ghost, bringing only tears and sadness. But Joe also had a growing sense of dread. What if she ever stumbled upon something which revealed his hidden past? That was unlikely; he had been so careful to cover his tracks, but all the same, the emotion would not leave him.

He approached the stones, which marked the spot where the Wellington bomber met its fiery end in 1941, and the names of the six crew who died in the flames were remembered. Joe knelt by the grave, reading each name etched into the stone. He wondered if those airmen carried secrets of their own. Someone must remember them, as next to the memorial was a glass bottle with a single velvety red rose in it. It was still vibrant with colour, so it had only been placed there in the preceding days. Who still loved one of those lost boys?

As he stood up, he felt a shift within. There was something about the forest, its ancient strength, which gave him a moment of clarity. He realised the burden of his secret was too much to bear alone. The fear of losing everything was still present, but the need to be true to himself was far stronger.

He went and sat on the grass a short distance away. It was a warm September day, and the ground was dry to his touch. Just like the garden at Winding Wood, the forest had a parched and yellowed appearance from the long, hot summer. He thought back to the turbulent events of five years before, and as he did, tears ran down his cheeks. He was unsure if he cried for what he had lost or the tragedy of the dead airmen.

Patrick had been his first and most visceral love. They met at university, and for both of them, there was an instant, almost animal attraction; some would say love at first sight, but Patrick always said it was too corny.

'It was lust at first sight for you, mister.' There was never anyone else for the two of them. They both had their first sexual experience with each other, and from that moment, Joe fell deeper and deeper in love with the man. He loved his soft Cornish accent and gorgeous sea-blue eyes, but beyond that, he had a gentle and kind quality to his character, which made Joe sure they were soul mates and would be together always. He once said to Patrick.

'Perhaps we've met before, in another life, and that's why we're so comfortable with each other, why we feel so familiar.' Patrick replied, looking at him with his dreamy blue eyes.

'That may well be.' Then kissed him.

They talked often about their future, the things they would do, the adventures they would go on and the homes they would make together. They dreamed, planned, laughed, and cried, wove their lives and love ever deeper. There would be nothing which would stand in their way. The only barrier was Joe had not told his parents he was attracted to both men and women. He was too worried about their reaction, and his mother was a nervous woman. He thought it might give her a breakdown. He did not want to be responsible for that.

Once before, she had been doped up on Valium over some family problem or other, and it was a risk he did not want to take. He loved his mother, and the thought of upsetting her troubled him. For Patrick, things were more straightforward. His parents disowned him when he came out and threw him out of the house. He had no one to be accountable to.

The one wasp that spoiled the summer day of their love was that despite Patrick's frequent pleadings, Joe would not move in with him.

'What would I tell my parents,' he would say, or 'What would the neighbours think?' and once, when the subject turned into an argument, Patrick responded.

'Maybe this has to do with what you think about yourself. Have you considered that?'

Their happy, rainbow-tinted world began to see storm clouds approaching when news dribbled in from the USA about a mysterious disease which had started killing gay men. Joe tried to pretend it was an American issue and would not affect people in England, but then the first cases began to be reported in London, and he could no longer deny it. Along with the illness came the prejudices and the awful newspaper headlines about the 'Gay Plague.' This had Joe shrinking even deeper into himself and less able to be open to the world about his love and sexuality.

One evening, he met Patrick after work for a walk in St James' Park. When his boyfriend saw him, he could see he was distressed.

'What's the matter? Whatever's happened?'

'I can't do this anymore. I'm so sorry.'

'What do you mean?' stuttered Patrick through a wave of emotion fearing what may come.

'I mean us. I can't be gay anymore.'

'You don't have a choice; you are what you are. But why the hell are you saying this now? You've been happy in my arms for the last two years. What's changed?' Patrick's voice shook with emotion, feeling that what he treasured most was about to slip from his grasp.

'It was at the office today. One of the other guys who I work with spoke to the manager and told her he would not sit next to me because I'm gay.'

'Jesus, that's awful. What a fuckwit! But are you going to let him ruin what we have? I love you, Joe, and want to be with you forever!'

When Joe's work colleague uttered his ignorant words, they had the effect of creeping into an existing fault line of self-doubt which ran deep in him, like frost penetrating a rocky crevice, only to push it even wider open. Something snapped, and he knew he could not tolerate the looks, cruel comments, and downright rejection. He loathed himself for thinking it, and a raw pain stabbed at his heart at the thought of losing Patrick, but in the end, his doubt was bigger than his love.

Patrick begged and wept, but nothing changed Joe's mind. Sometime later, he walked off towards Green Park tube, his world having been shattered during one conversation. Joe never saw him again.

Joe left London and rented a flat in Lewes, where he grew up. It was far enough away from anyone he knew. No one would know about his previous life; he would become a straight man. A few weeks later, he met Emily at an art gallery. He had always been attracted to women as well as men, and with her gentle kindness, she helped heal his wounds. He loved her, but it was a different love from what he had with Patrick, which had been deep, animal, and spiritual.

Her kind and bubbly personality made him feel safe, and yet, something was missing, an intangible quality that could never be replaced. He once thought it was like looking at a black-and-white picture instead of a coloured one. Emily was equally lovely in black and white but somehow not quite real.

He missed Patrick and thought about him every day. He kept a little battered photo of him in his wallet. Each time he looked at it, he was riven with conflicting emotions: guilt, loss, confusion, and fear.

That day, In the clear air of the forest, he understood what he should do. Joe knew the alternative would be to walk away from Emily and Elsie forever. He could not manage the conflict created by his lies, alongside his love for them. The sun started to go down, then he turned, walked back up the hill to the car park, and drove home, his mind made up. Emily needed to know the truth, and he would share with her the part of himself he had kept hidden for so long. It was a grave risk but one he was willing to take. The path ahead was dim and uncertain, but he had to keep moving forward, one step at a time.

Chapter Nine
Thoughts on a train

Emily sat by the dirty window of the crowded commuter train, her gaze fixed on the countryside, which opened up after the long tunnel through the North Downs. The rhythmic clickety-clack of the wheels on the tracks was a soothing counterpoint to the anxious thoughts swirling in her mind.

Her meeting, pitching to a demanding new client in London, had been draining, and the irritating crowds swarming through ever-louche Victoria Station did nothing to calm her down. To her further annoyance, the man sitting next to her was large and spilled over the edge of his seat onto hers, squashing her into a narrow space. To compound the problem, he insisted on unfurling his Daily Telegraph so it kept brushing her face.

She wanted, above all else, to find out what the hell was going on at Winding Wood. The previous night, the woman's crying reached a new pitch, and she found it impossible to sleep until the awful wailing stopped at about 3 am. In the morning, she cursed her fatigue, knowing she must be at her best for the meeting. She didn't want to blow the opportunity.

By now, the family had no doubts that their home was being haunted, and they sensed that somehow, it could be related to what Violet had told Edith Bates. The constant sense of sadness that hung around the house had the three of them talking less and less as they each retreated into their own silent space. Only little Elsie remained unaffected, and she cheerfully played while the adults sank still further into their introverted mood.

Winding Wood became a place of quiet and reflection. Emily once told her mother that she thought the house felt like a living entity, an observer of the lives which unfolded within its old brick walls. The house had many stories to tell, whispered through the creaking floorboards and the cobwebs in the attic. Emily felt its presence more acutely since the day she moved back with Joe. As a child, it was a happy place, a wonderful playground, but now, sometimes, it felt as if the house watched her; it could probe the depths of her soul and everything which dwelled in her heart.

As the train sped through the countryside, Emily's thoughts drifted to the burden she carried, hidden beneath layers of composure. Friends often commented on what a good mother she was, how she cared for Joe, and how they admired her for juggling home life with a successful career. All those things were true, but that façade concealed something else.

She had once sought solace in the confessional of a Catholic church, hoping to unburden herself to a priest. She had never been in one before that day, but she had heard that you may find salvation there. It was an act of desperation, trying to come to terms with what she had done. The memory was vivid: the lofty, dim interior, the sun shining through the stained glass, the scent of incense hanging in the air, and the sharp edge of guilt cutting into her.

But when the moment came, she could not speak the words. She ran from the confessional booth, leaving the bemused priest to his prayers. The load of her secret was too heavy, the fear of judgment overwhelming. She left the church that day with her burden still intact, convinced her truth would never be told.

Her mind wandered back to the man she helped die five years before. The memory of his pain, his desperate pleas for release, haunted her like a spectre. AIDS ravaged him with innumerable awful conditions, and he could take no more. Will had been her best friend at university, and he took her to gay clubs where he introduced her to his friends. They all loved her, and she would dance the night away, comfortable and happy in their non-threatening company. So much better than the drunken, fumbling straight boys.

She acted out of compassion, but the guilt of what she did gnawed at her soul. She procured heroin to end his suffering, staging the scene to appear like a suicide. It was an act of mercy, done out of love, but the shadow of that night followed her, a constant reminder of the line she had crossed. Once, the previous year, she thought she would go to the police and confess, but almost at the police station, she stopped in her tracks.

'I'll go to prison. I'm not sure I would deal with that. How could I leave Joe and Elsie?'

Emily glanced around the carriage, briefly meeting those of the woman sitting opposite before she turned away. She wondered if anyone had ever glimpsed the agitation beneath her composed exterior. To the world, she was a loving wife, a devoted mother, and a talented designer. But inside, she was unravelling, trapped in her turmoil.

Her thoughts turned to Joe. She loved him and had no doubt he loved her in return. She adored how he looked at her with his soft brown eyes, asking for approval, but sometimes, they had a distance between them, an unspoken gap she couldn't bridge. She sensed he, too, hid something, a part of himself which he couldn't share.

As the train approached East Grinstead, Emily took a deep breath and retrieved her bags from the rack. She gave the large man with the Daily Telegraph a withering stare, and he went home to his wife, wondering what he had done.

The haunting of Winding Wood would continue to loom over her. Her secret was also like an ever-present ghost, as impossible to ignore as the crying woman. She wondered if she would ever find the courage to reveal her secret to her family.

Stepping off the train, Emily felt the cool evening air on her face, in stark contrast to the warmth of the carriage. She made her way to the car park, her mind still churning with worries. As she drove home through Forest Row and into Ashdown Forest, the familiar woodlands passing by, she spoke a silent vow to herself: one day, she would discover the strength to face her past, to confront the ghosts which haunted her. But not yet.

Chapter Ten
The diary

The soft glow of the evening sun cast shadows on the walls of the sitting room, which was filled with the gentle hum of the radio. Bryony's favourite programme, 'The Archers', could just be made out, but on this occasion, she was not concentrating on the everyday travails of Ambridge folk. She inhaled on her cigarette; the smoke curling around her felt comforting. Not focussed on the soap opera, her thoughts turned to her family.

She had always been the strong one, the pillar of the clan, and she embraced the role she considered her destiny. Cheerful, composed, and ever-proper, Bryony maintained a delicate balance. When she was younger, she was forever caught between her mother's perpetual mourning for her dead sister Grace and the sense that her sister Florence was a vulnerable creature who must be protected, like a piece of fragile and valuable porcelain.

After Florence died, the load of carrying her mother's grief only deepened. Bryony dealt with the family's needs with grace and mostly without resentment, but beneath the surface, she, too, was a woman haunted by the loss of her sisters. Grace and Florence's deaths cast a long shadow on the family, and it was to Bryony that they looked for her optimism and positivity.

When her father died and her mother was left alone in the house, Bryony once again came to the rescue. She said to her mother.

'We need to decide if it's time to let Winding Wood go. You could sell it and buy something smaller.' Violet replied.

'I don't think that's possible, dear. I have the feeling the house is not ready to let any of us go yet. I have a better idea. Why don't you move in with me? This is nicer than your house in Oxted, and the children will have a glorious time. It's such a lovely place to grow up in.' Before long, Bryony and James decided this would be a good plan, and in six months, they were ensconced with Violet in the old family home.

Her thoughts drifted to the diary she found in the box they discovered in the attic. Everything else had been sorted out, the letters from Edith Bates read, and anything of no use disposed of, but she chose this moment to read her mother's old memoir. It was a leather-bound exercise book, its pages yellowed with age. The cover was not dated, but flicking through the diary, she found sporadic entries that spanned much of the 1920s, and those Violet wrote after little Grace died were heart-rending.

Perhaps no one in the family wanted to listen. Was this her safety valve? She flicked through the book, her fingers trembling, as she turned the fragile pages.. Picking an entry at random, she saw her mother had written.

'*I went to the market in Canning Town today and bought some lovely apples.*'

Then, a page afterwards.

'*I wish the weather would improve; it never stops raining.*' It went on like this, pages recording the minutiae of everyday life, no revelations, nothing exciting. Then, an entry dated 5th October 1925 caught Bryony's attention.

'*Mother and I visited the famous medium, Ekatarina Zagorski at her house in Crystal Palace. She held a séance, and we received reassuring messages from Frederick and Grace. But then, one of the other mediums said something odd.*

'*Winding Wood's story will be told one day. The dark heart of the house of secrets will be revealed.*'

This can't have been meant for me. Miss Zagorski's house is called Winding Wood, so I believe the message was for her. Mind you, I did tell Mother that if I ever have a nice house, I will call it Winding Wood after that one. Such a lovely name.'

Bryony's heart pounded. What could it mean? This must have something to do with the tearful, ghostly presence which had become a resident of their home. It may also relate to whatever her mother wrote to Edith Bates, which caused her lifelong friend to cut off all contact with her. Reading the entry again, a chill ran down her spine.

She took another drag from her cigarette, the smoke mingling with the scent of the evening air coming through the open French windows. The radio played on, now light pop music, a soothing counterpoint to her swirling thoughts. Bryony decided that the effort of holding her family together was becoming too much to bear. She thought of her husband, James, and the deep void his death left in her life.

He had been her rock, her source of strength and comfort. Without him, she felt adrift, struggling to maintain the façade of composure everyone depended on. How could she reveal to Emily and Joe the depth of her pain when they all looked to her for strength?

Bryony closed the diary, then put it back on the coffee table, her mind racing. The words of the medium echoed in her ears. '*The dark heart of the house of secrets will be revealed.*' But which secrets was she referring to? Perhaps the lie she was a strong and happy woman would be unveiled, too, and what would happen then? Would the edifice she had maintained for so long, crumble and collapse? And what about the family? How would they cope if she could not?

She couldn't keep living behind the mask of composure forever. The secrets of Winding Wood were bound to come to light, and in time, so would hers.

Chapter Eleven
The signature

Joe spent the morning in the garden, the crisp autumn air heady with earthy scents of fallen leaves and late-blooming flowers. The trees, now dressed in hues of gold, amber, and crimson, swayed gently. Some of the leaves dropped to the ground in the breeze, indicating that summer's moment had its time. Something else, new and different, lay ahead.

In the darkness to come, nature would keep its secrets tight to itself, secure under the soil, only to arrive again with a rush of fresh joy in the spring. Then, all would be revealed once more.

He came to the devastated rose garden and knelt by the bushes, carefully pruning the withered blooms and stems. It was only now he found the heart to do this. Since he had discovered the brown and dying plants a few months before, he avoided the place, it hurt too much. His mind was leaden with his still unspoken truths. Joe had always found peace in the gentle rhythms of gardening, but today, the tranquillity eluded him. He thought the sad, dead roses murmured to him, urging him to confront the past.

As he worked, he thought of Violet and Edith. What was the story behind Edith's refusal to speak about the past, and why was Violet so angry when she saw her? Joe had decided that speaking his truth was the only way forward, and this must be the same for the family, too. Lies had festered long enough, and only by confronting them could they find peace.

With a determined sigh, he decided what he would do. He wiped the dirt from his hands on his trousers, then made his way inside the house to the desk in the corner of the study. He took out a sheet of writing paper and began to write a letter to Edith but in Violet's name. His hand trembled as he wrote the words, each one a further step towards the truth.

Dear Edith,

It is time for the facts to come to light. You have my permission to reveal the family secrets. It is the only way we can move forward and heal.

With all my love

Joe folded the letter and placed it in an envelope. This was only the first step—the easy part. The challenge lay ahead in convincing Violet to sign the letter and embrace the path to truth.

Later that afternoon, he kissed Emily on the cheek and said goodbye. She asked.

'Where are you off to?' He did not want to set an expectation he could resolve things, so he quickly thought of a lie.

'I need a part for the mower from the guy in Forest Row. It's making a terrible noise every time I use it.'

Joe drove to the care home, his heart pounding in anticipation. He signed in with the same brusque nurse who had dealt with them on their last visit. For a moment, he thought there was a question in her eyes.

'Why're you here again, and why did you come by yourself?' He then decided his imagination was in overdrive and ignored her.

He found Violet in her drab room, filled with the mellow light of the autumn sun, casting a warm glow on faded photographs on the chest of drawers. There was one of Violet's mother and father, their expressions fixed in solemn grimace forever, the Victorian photographer having had them stand still for what felt like an eternity. Then, a little girl with long ringleted hair, who he knew to be Emily's aunt Grace who died as a child. Lastly, a wedding photo of Violet and Thomas, she, pretty and demure in a cloche hat.

As before, he noted there was no picture of Florence which he thought most odd. Emily had said she thought it was because her grandmother found it too upsetting. In front of the pictures were a group of cheap-looking china trinkets, an ornament of a shepherd girl and a little box with a rose motif on the lid.

This time, Violet sat by the window, her eyes following the swirl of falling leaves outside. To his surprise, the faintest of smiles appeared on her face when she turned and saw him. Then he remembered Emily had told him how fond her grandmother was of him. He had made a wise choice to come alone on his mission.

'Hello, Violet,' Joe said softly, taking a seat beside her. He took her frail hand in his.

'I need to talk to you about Edith.' Violet's eyes widened, and she gave a faint nod. Her hand, though weak, squeezed his in a gesture of encouragement. Perhaps coming alone rather than confronting Violet with the whole family would see her agreeing to his proposal. At least she was not angry like she was when Edith Bates visited.

'I wrote this letter for you to sign,' he continued, holding up the envelope. 'It's time for the truth to come out. You need to let Edith tell us what she knows. Violet, I think deep inside that is what you want too?'

Violet's hand tightened a little around his, but she pulled back. Joe felt her hesitation, the years of silence pressing down heavily on her.

'Violet, I understand this is difficult,' he said gently. 'But I've come to understand something important. I have my own secrets, things I've kept hidden for too long. And I've learned that salvation can only come through sharing them. We can't find peace if we keep living in the shadows.'

He paused, letting his words sink in. Violet's eyes searched his, and he saw the conflict churning within her. She reached out and took his hand again, her grip firmer this time. She was breathing heavily as if the inner turmoil was taking a physical toll on her.

'Please, Violet,' he urged. 'Let's do this together. For the family.'

Violet's hand trembled, but she nodded, a tear slipping down her cheek. Joe placed the pen in her hand and guided it to the paper. She squeezed his hand again, indicating her agreement. With a shaky hand, she signed the letter. As she did so, a sense of relief washed over him. The first step had been taken, and the path ahead now had a glimmer of light illuminating it.

Later that day, Joe went to his studio. He wanted to paint. For a while, his creativity had been stymied, almost in hibernation, but now, ideas and images had come into his mind. He also felt a sense of satisfaction he was not used to. It was he who had visited Violet, which may help to solve the puzzle. Perhaps Bryony would approve of him more now? He sat at his easel and then began to sketch the draft for his new art-work.

He completed the familiar outline of Winding Wood; which he had painted on many occasions. This painting would be different, as recently Joe had heard a persistent voice within, urging him to paint roses. He would include the walled rose garden and paint it in full summer splendour, with glorious pink roses glimpsed through the archway in the brick wall which led within.

As he drew he thought.

'I can't get rose's out of my head, since I saw the sad, dead ones in the walled garden they've constantly been in my dreams. I can almost smell them, It's as if someone's trying to get my attention. Could it be Winding Wood's tearful ghost ?

Chapter Twelve
The journey to truth

The journey from Devon to Winding Wood was long and tiring. It did not help that the train broke down outside Exeter, and when it limped into the station, Edith and several hundred fractious passengers decamped onto the damp platform for an hour. The following train was packed, and it was only out of the kindness of a young man that she got a seat.

The journey dragged on, but Edith had a sense of purpose driving her forward. The secrets she carried had weighed on her for years, and now, she was ready to share them. Violet's letter gave her the permission she needed, and the day she received it, she called Joe to arrange to travel to Sussex. There was a sense of urgency to the matter. Being realistic about her age, she did not know how long she would be around for. Should she die before telling the family her story, they would never be released from the lies of the past. Even so, there were moments during the journey when she wondered if she would go through with it.

As the train sped towards the capital, she thought about Violet's family, and the impact her revelations would have on their lives. At Reading, she sent Joe a message telling him about the train from Victoria, which she hoped to catch. She liked the boy; he was so gentle and kind, yet she noticed a dreamy, distant quality to him. As if he thought about something beautiful that no one else could see.

Upon arriving at Winding Wood, Emily, Joe, and Bryony greeted Edith. The tension was palpable, but there was also a sense of hope in the air.

'I'm too tired to talk to you this evening,' Edith said to Bryony. 'Would you forgive me if I had an early night? Then I'll be ready tomorrow.' Whilst impatient, Bryony saw the exhaustion written on Edith's face, and she led her to the guest room, which nestled over the porch.

'Can I make you anything to eat, Edith? I don't feel I'm being a good host.'

'No, don't worry dear, I brought sandwiches which I ate on the train. That's quite enough for me, I've such a small appetite these days. May I trouble you for a Camomile tea? It will help me sleep. I've brought my own tea bag if you don't have any?'

Later on, the first mournful wail echoed through the oak-panelled hall, upwards to the minstrels' gallery above and onwards into the bedrooms. The sound of crying curled around each one, only avoiding the little room where Elsie slept, blissfully unaware of the turmoil her adult family were confronting. Then the sound wound back down like drifting smoke through the ground floor. There was nowhere to escape from it. Bryony wondered if she ran far away, even to another country, would it follow her; she would never be rid of it.

Emily spent several hours cuddling up with her daughter on the narrow single bed. She feared the wailing could be heard there, too, and wanted to hold Elsie tight to her. In fact, her bedroom was an oasis of tranquillity, and the child slept untroubled, dreaming of unicorns and fairies.

In the morning, the family ate breakfast together. Each of them was on edge, waiting for what would happen next, but felt it only polite for Edith to take the lead. After she finished her toast and a second cup of tea, she said.

'I'm refreshed and ready, but this is not the place for our conversation. I want to talk to you in Florence's old room. I remember Violet telling me she left it just as it had been the last time Florence used it. Is that still so now?' Bryony replied.

'It's never been used since; Mother forbade it, and the room sat empty all these years.'

'C'mon, let's go up there,' Edith pushed herself up from the seat with the help of her walking stick and led the way upstairs. She said.

'From what Violet told me, it's that room,' and she waved her stick in the direction of a closed door. 'I remember she said it was opposite the top of the stairs.'

'Yes, that's right,' said Emily. We were never allowed to go in there as children. It's such a shame, because it's a lovely room and with such a pretty view.'

'I believe overlooking the rose garden,' replied Edith.

Joe opened the door, and they entered the room. They saw it had long windows allowing light to pour in and a white fireplace still complete with china trinkets on one wall. It was furnished with a double bed covered in a faded pink bedspread. The room had not been decorated in over forty years; the floral wallpaper was of a style from long ago, and everything was shabby and, in places, peeling.

There was a musty but not unpleasant smell. Edith remembered Violet told her she kept the windows open in the summer to keep it aired. She cleaned it herself, not allowing her daily help to enter, so it was only after Violet went into the care home the previous year that the dust started to accumulate, and cobwebs hung from every crevice. On the bed sat a large and rather battered old teddy bear.

Along one wall was a walnut wardrobe and on opening it, Joe saw a rail of clothes. He ran his hand along the top of them, and a cloud of dust flew up. He said.

'Someone would have liked to have these clothes, or maybe the room could've been used as a spare bedroom.' Bryony replied.

'Well, at first, Mother forbade anyone to use it or touch Florence's things, but later, I think, we forgot the room was here. It was so strange, of course, if you asked me about it, I would have told you, but walking past it every day, it almost seemed like it didn't exist.'

By now, Edith had settled into a Lloyd loom chair, and Bryony perched on the end of the bed. She said.

'Joe, could you get a couple of extra seats, please? There's one in my room and one in the guest room.' Soon, the family was seated in a circle, ready to hear whatever Edith was going to tell them. Bryony lit a cigarette, and, on this occasion, Emily felt she could protest.

'Mum, do you have to?!' and Bryony, who had lit up without thinking, stubbed it out in an ashtray she found on the bedside table. Edith took a deep breath, preparing herself to speak.

'What I'm going to tell you will bring you some resolution, but it'll also change your lives forever,' Edith began, her voice steady but filled with emotion.

'The secrets of Winding Wood are tied to Violet and her family, and they are darker than you can ever imagine.' She paused, allowing what she said to sink in. The room held its breath, the air thick with anticipation. The family fell silent as the gravity of Edith's words settled over them.

From Edith's solemn tone, Emily, Bryony, and Joe knew how serious her revelations would be, but they also understood they had no choice. The ghostly cries must be silenced, and Violet's secrets revealed, and the only way to do that was to face the darkness of the past and bring the sunlight of truth to shine on it.

Part Four

Lies

"He who permits himself to tell a lie once finds it much easier to do it a second and third time, 'til at length it becomes habitual; he tells lies without attending to it and truths without the world's believing him. This falsehood of tongue leads to that of the heart, and in time depraves all its good dispositions."

Thomas Jefferson

Chapter One
A pair of dropped Gloves
Plaistow London
1913

At seventeen, Violet Gosling understood little about how her body worked, but she was not ignorant. In the end, it did not require much education to put two and two together. At first, she felt mystified at the changes within her. When she figured it out, nausea consumed her, and she grasped onto a nearby chair to steady herself.

Three months earlier, she met Thomas Goldsmith on the Underground. It is one of those tiny moments where lives, destiny, and family stories are changed forever. After visiting an aunt in Whitechapel, Violet dropped her gloves on the train. Before she could pick them up, a tall man standing beside her stooped to retrieve them. He stood up smiling, then passed the gloves to her, and she thought she had never seen someone so handsome in her life and flushed.

He oozed masculine charm, yet his soft blue eyes promised sensitivity and decency. Violet knew little about men and sex but responded to being attracted to a good-looking man and blushed. She stuttered out a thank-you and thought nothing more of it. After alighting at Plaistow, she found herself walking next to the stranger. Whilst embarrassed; it seemed rude not to strike up a further conversation.

'Thank you so much again; I only bought those gloves last month; I would've been most upset to lose them.'

'It's my pleasure. Do you live in Plaistow?'

'Yes, close to the station, on Crimea Road. I'm being impolite; I should introduce myself. I'm Thomas Goldsmith.'

'And I'm Violet Gosling. I'm going the other way, so I'll say farewell.'

She waved goodbye and walked off, then heard footsteps behind her. The dark winter night brooded, cold and gloomy, and for a moment, a prick of fear touched her, then she recognised the man from the train beaming at her again. Out of breath, he asked.

'Forgive me for being forward, Miss Gosling, but I wonder if you'd walk out with me. Could we meet in the park one afternoon? You're pretty as a peach and rather caught my eye.'

Violet was flattered; in her opinion, the handsome man was far out of her league. Mother would be furious, and she feared the harsh back of her hand but did not receive compliments from men like this every day. Feeling like a child about to dip its hand into a bag of forbidden, delicious sticky sherbet, Violet replied.

'Yes, let's meet at the bandstand tomorrow afternoon, how would that be?'

'That'd be delightful, Miss Gosling.' Violet bounced home, determined no one would learn of her secret assignment; her mother would most definitely disallow it. The idea of her daughter meeting a man at least five years older than her, or indeed any man at all, was not something to be entertained in Sophia Gosling's extensive and rigorous rule book.

Full of youthful pride and womanly joy, Violet fantasised about the date to come and wrote in her diary.

'Thomas is so handsome. I wonder if he will want to kiss me. He is just the kind of man I would like to marry.'

The following day, Violet met Thomas by the bandstand in the park at the end of her street. She put on her best blue frock and hat and walked with a flutter in her heart. She feared he may not turn up, but there he was, as arranged.

Soon, they chatted away; it felt so natural in this man's company. He talked little of himself, asking all about her. She told him how her dear papa had died two years earlier. As the oldest in the house, she had to leave school and work in a factory. She told him this with no tone of bitterness but rather an air of resignation.

Before long, Thomas's reassuring, masculine hand reached over and touched Violet's. Not sensing any resistance, he left it resting on hers. A further date was arranged, and Violet hurried back home, ensuring her story of returning a borrowed book to a friend was watertight. In her diary that night, she wrote.

'Thomas is such a gentleman; he made me feel special today.'

The following weekend, Violet and Thomas met by the bandstand again. After chatting for a while, he suggested a walk, and soon, they strolled through a quiet part of the park, her arm linked to his. It was much colder than the previous week, which kept many locals from their afternoon stroll. Brooding, dark-leaved rhododendron bushes encroached on the pathway.

Thomas's hand moved to Violet's waist, and he tugged her towards him a little; she enjoyed the sensation. He stopped, turned to face her, and pulled her tighter against him and pressed his lips on hers. Slight panic rose in Violet; she had only kissed a couple of boys before, and this was so soon, but his presence and raw manliness made her resistance collapse.

She returned his kiss, tongues exploring and probing, the tobacco-tinged man-taste of him was good. He pulled away and encouraged Violet towards a small, wooded area. Here, the path petered out, and soon, they were concealed behind a broad tree.

He started to kiss her again and put his hands on her breasts. With a further wave of panic, she understood there was something men and women did when they got married, but other than that, there was little detail. Her mother had bludgeoned into her the fact she must be a 'good girl', and men always wanted to do something to women, which got them into trouble. Men were animals to be guarded against unless you married one. Then, however they treated you, it would be fine. Her instincts told her she should not be doing this.

His hand probed between her legs through the thin fabric of her skirt. Her arousal was now an uncontrollable wave which removed all sense of knowing how a 'respectable' woman should behave. At that moment she wanted him more than anything else she had ever known before, even though she did not understand what it may entail.

Violet's grasp of the facts of life was negligible, but when Thomas unbuttoned her skirt and started to tug at the underwear, she knew, intuitively, what was happening. She felt the hardness of his arousal pressing into her, in turn making her more and more frantic to explore this forbidden territory. As he penetrated her, she gasped with pain, her virginity gone in a moment, pushed up against a tree in the park.

Soon, a deep longing and pleasure replaced the pain, yet so briefly enjoyed as he grunted, and she felt a warmth inside her and something dribbling down her thighs. Embarrassed, she rearranged her clothes, and they walked home; he said little, Violet filled with a mixture of emotions, feeling like a grown-up and desirable woman, but tinged with warm guilt.

The following week, the assignation was repeated. Violet, enthralled by the sensation of Thomas's lips and body, wanted more because she knew she was in love with him. She hung off every word he said, and her diaries were filled page after page, with entries about how wonderful and handsome he was and how she intended to be his wife. Thank goodness, there was a hidden place behind the chest in her room where the diary secrets may be concealed from her mother's prying eyes.

After the second date and a further brief encounter against the same tree in the park, Violet pushed a card into his hand as they said farewell, declaring her undying love in a few words of adolescent poetry. The following week, when she went to their normal meeting place, he did not turn up. Joy turned to pain in a brutal, cutting instance, and she found it hard to conceal her tears from her mother when she returned home later. Instead, she said,

'I think I'm coming down with a fever. I'm going to bed.'

In the following days. Violet's heart twisted into a thousand pieces and shattered; the man she wanted with a burning need had cast her aside. Other times, she fantasised he had been killed in an accident. This naïve dream dashed when concealed in a hiding place behind bushes, she watched his house and saw him return from work.

One day, she wanted to die; the next, she hated him, or she prayed he would come back and love her again. Retching into the bowl of the outside toilet, it never crossed her mind what the malaise meant. When her monthly cycle failed to come, in her innocence, she did not understand what it predicted. Only three months later, when she detected an internal change, a feeling of difference and a slight distention of her stomach, the penny dropped with clanging horror.

Chapter Two
Fearing Mrs Hindley

'You filthy harlot, you're no child of mine,' spat the enraged Sophia. She drew her hand back to strike her daughter, but long used to her mother's rage, Violet nimbly dodged away. Although a diminutive woman, Sophia was strong and hit her children hard when she wanted to.

'Mother, please! I didn't mean to; I couldn't help myself.' Violet wailed. 'I thought he loved me!'

'What nonsense! Any respectable girl wouldn't go out unchaperoned with a man. It's of no interest to me if he loves you or not. To allow yourself to be taken like this, when you're unmarried. In a park! Like a farmyard animal! You're a slut, nothing less! Do you know what people call such children? Bastards! How can you think this is a decent way to bring a child into the world? Did you not consider for one moment what the result of your actions would be?'

'I didn't know Mother, you never told me anything about men.' Violet was crying and shaking, terrified by her mother's rage, and desperately scared about her fate.

'That's because you're supposed to wait until you're married, and then your husband will teach you everything. When I wed dear John, I had no knowledge of this. I was horrified when he first touched me on our wedding night and thought it disgusting. In time, I came to understand that looking after my husband's needs was part of my duty as a good wife.'

'I don't understand. Are we not meant to enjoy it?'

'Don't be crude, Violet. This horrid act is for the creation of children and the satisfaction of men. Us women have no say in the matter.'

'But what will I do when the baby is born?'

'Don't be ridiculous, Violet Gosling. Are you an imbecile? You're not bearing a baby. The shame this would bring on us is too much to bear. This family worked long and hard to be respectable, and I'm not having you ruining our reputation for a few moments of lust up against a tree like a dog. No, we'll have to do something about it.'

'What do you mean, I don't understand?'

'There's a way we can prevent the baby growing inside you. For God's sake, if you weren't so stupid, we wouldn't have to think of such wicked things. I never for one moment thought a daughter of mine would be so crass and wilful. Did your father and I not bring you up with decent Christian values?' Violet could say nothing more and sobbed, her head buried in her hands on the table. Sophia continued with barely suppressed anger.

'I've been told of a Mrs Hindley in East Ham. She can deal with this and will get the brat out of your body before it grows. It's going to cost us a lot of money, which we don't have. We must pawn something to pay her fee. I have a gold sovereign Papa gave me when I was a little girl. Perhaps that would raise what we need.'

Violet had enough and found the thought of being sent off to a stranger to interfere with her body horrifying.

'If only he'd marry me, mother,' she wailed. 'I can't go through anymore.'

'If only he would. But you won't tell me who the dirty scoundrel is. How can I do anything for you if you won't tell me?' Violet had dug her heels in and refused to name her lover, fearing her mother's raging anger. But worn down and fearing Mrs Hindley's ministrations, she relented.

'It was Thomas Goldsmith.'

'You mean Betsy Goldsmith's boy! The animal! He's at least five years older than you. To corrupt a young girl is below contempt. The filthy scum. Where does he live?' Violet gave her the address, and Sophia prepared to do battle.

The next day, Sophia banged hard on Thomas Goldsmith's front door. All five-feet of her, a woman on a mission who would not be given no for an answer. Thomas answered the door, and once the stony faced, furious woman introduced herself, asked her in. It would not do for the neighbours to hear her allegations. During the ensuing discussion, he point-blank refused to marry Violet.

'I don't love her, Mrs Gosling, and I have plans which don't include a wife and child.' Her eyes narrowed. Sophia brought her face closer to his and said.

'Mr Goldsmith. I'd like to offer you a choice; either you do the decent thing and marry my daughter, or I'll be giving my four sons your address. They're fit boys, two of them are boxers. I'm wondering if in the future you might like to be a father, because I'll ask them to make sure you'll never be in a position to be one. Do I make myself quite clear?'

The deal agreed with Sophia left a grim Thomas brooding in the parlour. As she walked down the hall, he followed her and, at the door, said, in a menacing tone.

'Although I don't love Violet, I'll marry her. But I don't do so because I want to. I've taken your threats seriously and appreciate I've no choice in the matter, but one day, trust me, I'll pay you back.'

Chapter Three
The First Lie

Violet checked her appearance for the tenth time in the mirror. Unhappy with the curl of her dark hair, she unpinned one side and combed it, then fixed the locks up again. Unable to afford a new wedding dress, she hired one for the day and hoped it would make her look pretty. To her chagrin, her mother insisted the dress was two sizes too big to disguise the giveaway curve of her stomach.

She wanted to look her best for her fiancé. One day he would love her properly; she would make sure of it. She had no idea about the exact nature of the conversation between Thomas and her mother but suspected the feisty woman had strong-armed him into the arrangement. She was well aware of how terrifying her mother could be when she disapproved of something or wanted to have her own way.

Violet would woo her man by keeping a tidy home and cooking for him, looking after his bodily needs, and showering him with all the affection a woman could muster. Then, one day, he would love her. She finished applying her make-up, took a deep breath and went downstairs to show off her dress to the rest of the family. Her mother and brother Frederick were waiting outside the bedroom, and he smiled.

'You're pretty as a picture, Vi. He's bound to fall for you.' Violet and her brother had always been close, and she was pleased to have his support. Her mother remained cold and angry since discovering she was pregnant, and Violet appreciated Frederick soothed and did not scold her. Sophia scowled in the background. She insisted the wedding must be in church; a registry office would never do, but it should be as small as possible. The thought of busybodies spotting her daughter's pregnancy was too much to bear. Only Violet, Thomas, Sophia and Frederick would be present.

There was nothing Sophia could do to stop local women from counting the months on their fingers later in the year. They relished a bit of juicy gossip over the backyard fences. It would not be long before the chatter turned nasty and the dreaded B word uttered between mean and disapproving tuts. She decided to move the family to a different address a few streets away, just far enough so there would be fewer people to do the counting. It might work.

Decent properties to rent were in short supply, so when Sophia found reasonable rooms with Mrs Ida Haddock, she immediately decided to take them. Three rooms, no bathroom, W.C. in the garden and Mrs Haddock, a stout, formidable woman with a penchant for lily of the valley perfume and mothballs. Their cloying miasma blended and wafted around her as she showed Sophia the dingy accommodation. The lodgings had been a little better in their day, but now everything fell into shabby and worn old age.

Sophia thought Mrs Haddock had the air of someone who believed her premises were grand and that she was not the class of person she usually had as a tenant. For Mrs Haddock's part, she detected a hint of an accent in her prospective tenant and thought.

'Hopefully not Jewish.'

Despite Mrs Haddock's reservations about the background of the woman she was showing around her rooms, she needed the money and was delighted to have a new tenant, so she pushed any concerns from her mind.

Violet waited nervously by the altar, fiddling with her long imitation pearl beads. She had read stories of women being jilted by their fiancées at the last moment and feared Thomas would summon up the guts to refuse to marry her and defy her mother's ire. She was wrong, she didn't know of her mother's ominous threat to have his genitals removed. To her relief, when she turned and saw him walk up the aisle, she believed he had started to fall in love with her. Throughout the marriage ceremony, she looked at Thomas with adoring eyes, the man of her dreams who would one day love her passionately. He stood at her side expressionless, knowing he could not escape his grim fate.

The following week, Violet and Thomas, Sophia and Frederick moved to Mrs Haddock's. It would be a tight squeeze. Frederick slept in the main room, which also served as a sitting room and kitchen.

Each of the occupants of Mrs Haddock's rooms lived in their own bubble of emotions. Sophia wore a smug sense of satisfaction. She had made sure Thomas Goldsmith made Violet a decent woman. The child would have two parents and never suffer the stain of bastardy. Sometimes, she fretted they had not moved far enough away from their previous lodgings but stopped herself. No one knew them in the new street, and it would be easy to be vague about the actual wedding date.

Violet, meanwhile, spent her days in a warm, blissful haze. The baby growing inside her made her feel like a proper woman, and she had married the man she adored. She no longer had to work in the horrid factory, which hurt her back, and Thomas brought in just enough money to support them. What could be better?

As for Thomas, not only did he have to marry a woman he did not love but he also had to endure living with her fire-breathing dragon of a mother. Once, when Frederick and Violet were out of the room, Sophia hissed.

'And don't think I haven't got my eye on you, Thomas Goldsmith. I've met your type before, and if I see your eyes wandering to another woman, there'll be hell to pay.' In a vitriolic tone, he spat back.

'Don't forget what I said to you, Sophia Gosling. One day, I'll get you back for this.'

After supper one evening, Sophia said.

'Thomas, have you got your marriage certificate?'

'Yes, it's in an envelope in the bedroom.'

'Please find it for me.' Knowing better than to disobey her, he retrieved the document, and Sophia flattened out the creased paper on the table.

'Get me a fountain pen. There's one in my room.'

'Whatever are you doing, Mother?' asked a bemused Violet.

'We're making sure your baby never gets called a bastard by anyone who reads this certificate. I'm going to alter the date of your marriage from July to January then, when the child is born in October, it'll be legitimate.' Violet was not convinced this would make the slightest difference but decided not to say anything. Her mother ruled the roost and should not be tangled with; it was easier to agree.

———————————

Chapter Four
1920
More lies

The steaming summer day hung rancidly over Plaistow. Malodorous smoke belching out of factory chimneys lay leaden in the street. In the Royal Docks, ship funnels spewed more detritus, further adding to the choking haze. Violet thought the air would suffocate her and desperately needed to get out for the day. Being Sunday, Thomas was not working, so Violet suggested an outing. He would have preferred to go to the dogs with his mates but couldn't face an argument.

'How would it be if we took the bus to Epping Forest? Grace needs fresh air, and both Mother and I want to stretch our legs. It gets so stuffy in our rooms.'

The family caught the bus and, an hour later, were strolling through Epping Forest's leafy glades. Even though he had been dragged along, Thomas found the clean air pleasant and decided to make the best of it.

'Daddy Daddy! Can I ride on your shoulders, please?' Grace begged in her most wheedling tone of voice. Almost seven years old, her red hair bunched into long ringlets made her look striking. A sturdy child, despite her difficult birth which saw Violet in labour for sixteen hours, she barely suffered a day's illness since. Thomas smiled and said.

'Yes, sweetheart, c'mon, jump up!' Violet asked.

'Thomas darling, there's something I want to talk about please don't be cross. Things in the shops are getting more and more expensive since the war, and I'm having trouble making ends meet. Would it be possible for you to give me a slight increase with the housekeeping?'

'Violet, I've told you a thousand times, my job doesn't pay much. It'll be better in the future when Westborough promotes me. You must be more careful with the money I give you.' She said nothing and decided not to press the matter further for the time being, not wanting an argument.

Although he would not admit it, Thomas enjoyed the outing, so the family returned to Mrs Haddock's in a sunnier than usual mood. After supper, Violet and Thomas changed into their night clothes and went to bed. The normal routine would be for the two to say a distant good night to each other, then roll over to sleep. Tonight, with her mood elevated by the walk in the sunshine, Violet wanted to talk. She turned to face her husband's handsome profile. She reached over, stroked his shoulder and said.

'Thomas darling, I'm sorry I nagged you about money. I know you're doing your best. I'm going to work harder to stretch out what we have. But there's something else on my mind.' She stopped, preparing herself to deliver her request.

'I'd love to have more children. We've had such a nice time today. I was wondering…'

'Violet, there's nothing I'd like better, but our circumstances don't allow it. I'm not earning enough money. These rooms wouldn't accommodate another child. We're so blessed with our beautiful little daughter. One will be fine for us.'

'I supposed so, dear. You're so sensible, and here I am dreaming away. You're right, of course.' And she kissed Thomas on the cheek.

He turned over and pondered on the thing which his wife must never find out. Each week, part of his pay was spent on procuring young girls in Whitechapel to sate his appetites. It was an itch he had to scratch, and he had no guilt whatsoever that this deprived his family of some of the little luxuries in life. Maybe a new hat for Violet or a doll for Grace, and the chance for Violet to have more children. In his mind, it was part of the promised revenge against 'the dragon-in-law' as he called Sophia behind her back. How appropriate that the woman who desired respectability above all else had a son-in-law who was using whores in back streets. He often laughed to himself, picturing Sophia's horror if she knew. But, of course, he did not want her to find out.

Thomas's thoughts were interrupted by the sound of his daughter crying.

'Mummy, Mummy, I don't feel well!'

Violet rushed to the side of Grace's bed on the other side of the room.

'What is it, dear?'

'I feel sick, Mummy!' Violet knelt and pressed her palm to Grace's brow. It was sticky and burning with fever.

Two weeks later, Thomas and Violet buried Grace. Scarlet fever took her; it was fast and brutal. At their little girl's graveside, Violet collapsed into her mother's arms. It sounded as if the depth of her sobbing and grief would reach the ears of the angels in Heaven.

Chapter Five
Thomas
1926

Thomas perched precariously on the ladder, glancing down at the glistening cobbles below. He did not like heights and felt queasy. It was drizzling, but Violet had nagged him to inspect the blocked gutter on his day off. Every time it rained, a torrent of water poured down the wall. The house they rented in Westmoreland Street always needed something done to it, and his wife and 'dragon-in-law' would make sure he did it. As he pulled out chunks of moss and leaves, his mind meandered, thinking about his life.

After his forced marriage to Violet, their early years were marked by the war and their separation while he was away in the army. Those years were a great relief for him, and he made sure to have his share of fun with local girls in Yorkshire.

On his return, he took a long time, grudgingly coming to terms with the fact he married out of practicality, not love. He continued his 'revenge' against Sophia with his weekly trips to Whitechapel, preferring young and compliant girls, who fulfilled his appetites up against a wall in dark alleyways reeking of urine.

This intoxicating thrill came crashing down when Violet's mother nearly uncovered his illicit escapades. A neighbour spotted him scurrying along a back street in Whitechapel and mentioned it to Sophia. She interrogated him, and he managed to produce an excuse on the spur of the moment, but she knew he was lying, and he knew she knew. Fearing she would discover more about his activities and turn her brutal sons on him, he suspended his nocturnal trips; it was too much of a risk.

When his firstborn, Grace, died, the absence of her bright laughter left a void which echoed through their home, a haunting reminder of what might have been. He and Violet entered a state of shared grief, be it that they dealt with it in different ways. Violet's grieving was clear to all. Frequent bouts of crying, and then days where she wanted to just lay in bed, were in time replaced by a distance from others, lost in the longing for her child.

She needed to talk about Grace, yet no one was prepared to listen. Her mother flustered around, keeping busy and issuing commands, insisting everything was fine. Thomas never spoke of his daughter again. Once, Violet told him she had visited a medium and received a message from Grace in the afterlife. He dismissed it in a moment.

'What a load of nonsense. These people are charlatans and are making money out of the vulnerable.' Violet looked as if she had been struck and said nothing more on the subject.

He did not love Violet, but he would not leave. It was not that he thought his life was fulfilling; more, he could not summon up the courage to do anything about it. Through a combination of inertia and fear of being assaulted, he became complicit in further sealing any escape route from the trap he lived in. His youthful dreams of exotic travel to far-flung parts of the Empire, accompanied by nubile young native girls, were replaced by the mundanity and drear of Plaistow life. He often thought about how Sophia had ruined his choices and resented her fiercely.

Violet and Thomas argued a lot about where they lived. He found contentment in the grimy terraces of the East End; this was familiar territory, and he had no desire to be anywhere else. On the other hand, Violet loathed the place and hankered after fresh country air. When she raised the subject, he would say.

'We must accept the deck we've been dealt. There's no point in us getting ideas above our station.'

After Thomas stopped squandering money on street girls, there was a little more for the family. In time, he agreed with Violet that they could have children. He never admitted it because he would not talk about it, but he missed Grace, and having a young life around would help to fill a gaping void. As a result, Violet and Thomas had two more children: Bryony, born in 1924, and Florence, two years later.

The two girls could not be more different. As soon as Bryony walked and talked, she was a bundle of joy and energy. She held the approach to life that she would make everyone and everything around her happy. If her grandmother grimaced in pain with arthritis, she would give her a hug. If her mother looked sad, as she so often did, with the loss of Grace still draining her soul, she would cut a little bunch of flowers from the garden to cheer her. Florence was an entirely different kettle of fish, sensitive and emotional. The slightest blow would have her crying and running to Violet or Bryony for reassurance. Thomas loved them both and they were the only thing which bound him to his family.

The drizzle stopped, and a little sunlight shone through the overcast. Having finished his tasks, Thomas put the ladder away in the lean-to and went back into the house, thinking,

'Perhaps one day I'll get a stroke of luck; I might win big on the dogs! Then I'll be able to have some fun again, and I'll make damn sure it's somewhere Sophia will never find out about!' He sniggered to himself at the thought and shouted.

'Violet, is my tea ready? I'm starving!'

Chapter Six
Arnold Bastable
1932

Thomas arranged to meet Arnold Bastable, his boxing club friend, in the Queen's Head, a seedy, run-down pub just around the corner from Westmoreland Street. Arnold had mentioned he had something important to discuss, and Thomas was pleased to have an excuse to get out of the house for a while. Sophia had been particularly difficult recently. The pain of her arthritis made her even more bad-tempered than usual, but knowing of her discomfort, Thomas could not find any sympathy.

'Difficult old cow,' he muttered under his breath when he had been on the receiving end of her latest salvo.

He met Arnold in the dingy, smoke-filled lounge bar. Every surface was covered with a layer of grime, and the ceiling was stained sticky-brown from decades of nicotine. The man had scant strands of greasy hair scraped back across his scalp and smelled of body odour mixed with the pungent scent of hair preparation. The few other customers were all men, and if a woman walked in, heads would turn. Here, deals were done, threats issued, and bets placed. They sat at a table in the corner where no one would overhear them.

Arnold bought two pints of stout at the bar, and they drank them, then two more each, making small talk about the boxing club. Thomas scrutinised him, suspecting he was timing what he had to say for the moment when they were both lubricated by alcohol.

'What did you want to discuss with me?' Thomas asked.

'It's a delicate matter. I must know I can trust you,' Arnold replied.

'Depends on what it is,' Thomas said, sounding cautious.

'It's a way for you to make a lot of money,' his friend replied, leaning closer.

'And I take it from the secrecy this isn't something legal?'

'Bang on, mate! So, do you want to learn more, or should I shut up now?' Arnold replied, his eyes gleaming with mischief.

Much as Thomas grudgingly settled into the humdrum of his life, a part of him was intrigued. For a moment, thoughts of India or Shanghai and voluptuous young lovers came back to him. It would not do any harm to hear what the proposal was. He said.

'Tell me more, Arnold!'

'We need someone inside Westborough's, and being an engraver, you're our man. We want you to copy banknote plates from the originals.'

'Whatever for?'

'Isn't it obvious! We're going to print a load of fakes!'

'That must be risky?' Thomas replied as thoughts of being incarcerated flashed through his mind's eye.

Arnold laughed rudely, which turned into a snort.

'Of course, mate, everything has risks. But this is pretty foolproof. You make the plates and pass them over to one of the company's maintenance men on our team. He'll get them out of the Westborough building for us. We've got a printer with his own press, and then Bob's your uncle. They'll be sent off by boat to Argentina. It's some dodgy deal out there involving different parts of the government. We don't need to know any more.'

'It all sounds too easy!' replied Thomas.

'The boss has got it worked out; it can't go wrong.'

'We've all heard that one before. You're going to have to twist my arm. How much do I get for my part in it?'

'Twenty thousand pounds.'

'Jesus fucking Christ!'

'You heard me. Twenty thousand. So, we have a deal?'

'I'm not sure. I need to think about it. It's a hell of a risk.'

'Well, don't think too long. You may miss the opportunity of your lifetime!'

On the way home, Thomas pondered about the proposal. On one hand, he had settled into a humdrum life, on the other he felt a rush of hot excitement at the illicit plan. Torn, he had no idea what he would decide to do. It all sounded so risky.

'Perhaps I should tell Arnold I'm not up for it,' he reflected. Then a thought came to him: he would ask Violet to help him decide. After all, she would be involved. He would be taking a huge gamble; if he went to prison, she would have to cope alone.

Violet was alone in the kitchen washing up. Sophia and the children were in bed so he could discuss the plan with her without the scathing judgment of his mother-in-law or alarming the children. In some ways he wanted her to be angry and tell him putting his family at risk was the last thing he should do. That would be easy, and he would go back to Arnold and say his wife forbade him from getting involved.

He told Violet about the plan whilst she had her arms up to the elbows in soap suds, washing the last few plates. She stiffened, shocked at what he told her. Although part of him wanted her to explode in anger and put the matter to rest, he also feared the lash of her tongue, which in recent times had become as barbed as her mother's. She turned around, drying her hands on a tea towel.

'It sounds like we have a chance to escape, Thomas. My life so far has been tough. Many are in the same position, so I don't complain, but it's hard. When I was a little girl, I used to daydream I'd marry a lord and live in a beautiful house in the country. I married you because I was pregnant but thought I would win over your affections.

How naïve I was. I strongly suspect you're unfaithful to me, and the sad thing is I don't give a damn. I've dealt with the fact that you don't love me and never have.

You'll never understand how that hurt me once my innocence faded away. Look at me! Thirty-six years old, and I'm worn out. My hands are chapped and bleeding from housework; I have a constant cough from the smoke in the air. I can't afford to buy nice clothes, everything I wear I've stitched myself. I've lost so many people: my father, my brother, little Grace.' At that point, Violet's voice wavered with emotion; she breathed to steady herself and leant on the draining board.

'The hell with it. Yes, do it! This may be the one opportunity we ever have for a better life!'

'But I'm not leaving Plaistow,' insisted Thomas. We'll buy a house near here. Then, I can have the best of both worlds. Money in the bank, but still see my mates at the boxing club.'

Violet said nothing. 'One thing at a time,' she thought. 'I'll get him out of here if it's the last thing I do.'

Chapter Seven
The long road from Southend

Thomas began his covert endeavour with the greatest possible care. As a trusted foreman, he could work long hours, hunched over his desk unsupervised. This part of the heist would be easy. All he needed to do was copy one of the plates he had engraved the previous year.

During overtime shifts, he began to create the fake plates, which he concealed in a drawer. Each time he worked, he etched a little more of the intricate design and adrenaline coursed through his body. The fear of being caught palpable, yet exciting. Twenty-thousand pounds was an amount of money Thomas found difficult to comprehend. He earned ninety pounds each year, and the figure from the counterfeit plot promised a fortune. His fantasies of voluptuous girls were now supplemented by a car or a flight on one of the latest aeroplanes from Croydon to Paris. Luxuries beyond his imagination.

Every few days, Arnold arranged a further meeting at the Queen's Head to check how Thomas was getting on.

'I should think about another week or so,' assured Thomas. 'I have to pick my time carefully and not work too long. It would arouse suspicion.' But driven hard by fantasies, he finished the plates sooner than expected. The two men met to plan the next phase of the plot. Arnold instructed Thomas.

'Pass the plates to Fred Wilson, and he'll get them out of the works. As the maintenance man, no one checks what he's taking in and out, as he normally has no access to any of the plates or notes. They think their security's so tight, but it's like a leaky sieve. Stupid fucking bastards, they deserve to be stuffed.'

'That's good. So, when am I going to have my money?'

'The notes will be printed in three days; that's when you come in again.'

'What the fuck? I've done what you asked! I'm not risking anything else!'

'We need you to drive the consignment to the Essex coast, where we'll meet a contact. We give them our Argentine Pesos in return for proper pound notes.'

'I didn't offer to drive, and I don't want to be involved any further. Some other mug can do this for you!'

'Our normal driver came to the filths' attention, so we dare not use him. It could get the whole set-up banged up.'

'I don't want to risk it. I've done enough.'

'Thought you might say no. The boss said to mention to you; you wouldn't want your charming mother-in-law to find out you've been pleasuring yourself with street-girls in Whitechapel, would you?'

'How the fuck do you know that?'

'Walls have ears mate.'

'I stopped that years ago.'

'Sure, but I still don't think Sophia Gosling and her sons would take too kindly to that news, however long ago it was. Is it a deal?'

Two weeks later, Thomas drove cautiously along the mean arterial road back from Southend. He did not want to speed and attract the attention of the police. The miles dragged, the drive passing endless ribbon developments, which of recent times flowed out of the towns in an unstoppable tide of brick and tile. Here and there, a wayside café, but the men didn't stop; they wanted to get their job done. The excitement had Thomas hot and flushed, and a vein pulsed in his temple.

'What's the plan, Arnold? When will we ditch the rest of the cash and take our slice? I want to be shot of it!'

'We're going to meet the boss on Wanstead Flats. Then we split the money; twenty grand for each of us! I reckon I might piss off out of here and give it a shot in Monte Carlo and win more! What are you going to do with your share?' Thomas, concentrating on a dark, narrow section of the road, said nothing, then a few miles later spoke again.

'If it weren't for my girls, I'd be out of here and leave Violet and her fucking mother behind. But I can't leave Bryony and Florence. Maybe I'll buy a house.'

Soon, the van meandered through the London suburbs. Arnold was silent and in deep thought as if a kernel of an idea had come to him. A tiny worm burrowing through his consciousness. Not formed and so impossible, so daring. He rejected it, but a few minutes later, it percolated up again, now fully shaped and ready to give voice.

'The money's going to be divided five ways. That's generous of us, don't you think, Thomas? Have you thought for a moment we could split it two ways? Fifty-fifty, you and me. Then you can leave Westborough's and never work again, and I can piss off to Monte Carlo!'

'What the fuck! You devious bastard. We can't do that; the boss would have us both killed!'

'True, but he can't if he and the rest of the gang are banged up!'

'That's grassing!'

'I call it business.' Thomas struggled to catch up with Arnold's idea. He thought he was loyal to the gang, and this was a daring prospect which would put the pair of them on the wrong side of some very hard men. However, once Thomas thought further about his friend's idea, the lure of bigger cash proved difficult to resist. He began to work out quite how rich he would be.

'OK, Arnold, let's do it. But how the hell will we pull it off?'

'For fuck's sake! I thought you're so bloody clever; it's easy. Instead of going to Wanstead, we split the money, go our separate ways, and hide the cash. Then you phone the filth, give them the names, and say where they printed the notes. They'll be delighted to have an easy arrest. It saves them having to think.'

'But how am I going to cover my tracks? They'll find out it was an inside job at Westborough, and I'll come under suspicion!'

'Then we'll have to find a scapegoat. Can you think of anyone we can get to take the blame?' Thomas thought for a moment.

'There's a noxious little git who works on my team, Harold Jackson. He's a bit simple, good at his job but can hardly string two words together. Before the shift starts tomorrow, I'll plant one of the plates in his locker. They'll never suspect me. I'm the foreman. He's so dumb, he won't be able to argue his way out of it.'

'Sounds like a grand plan, Thomas, but if the boss goes down for twenty years, one day when he comes out, he'll track you down, and when he does, I wouldn't want to be in your shoes. I'm getting out of the country. What'll you do?'

'Got that worked out too. I'll change my name. It'll be like I never existed.'

On a side road in Leytonstone, they stopped and began counting out the cash. Thomas flipped between elation and fear, hot flushes and nausea. The bile rose up his throat, he jumped out of the van and vomited over a garden hedge.

'Not such a hard nut?' sneered Arnold. Thomas wiped his mouth with the back of his hand and snarled back.

'Right, this is it. You know the plan, I'm going home now, and I never want to hear from you again. As far as you're concerned, I don't exist, and in a month or so, there'll be no trace of me. Thomas walked off into the night, the cash in a bag, and headed for Plaistow.

Chapter Eight
The birth of Violet Thomson
1934

Thomas browsed through the Daily Mirror whilst enjoying the morning sun from his favourite garden bench. He read about how bad unemployment was and smiled smugly to himself, knowing he would never have to worry about money again. The warmth of the sun's rays and the gentle rustling of leaves lulled him into a sense of peace.

Life was good, even if Violet drove him to distraction, and her fire-breathing mother was worse. The only escape from that was his monthly visits to Streatham, where he procured the 'high-class' services of Mrs Anthea Hall-Morris. He was smug that he could afford her, several rungs up the ladder from the girls he previously used in Whitechapel.

He sometimes pondered what it would have been like to have other men in the house. Surrounded by four women, he did not have much to say. He thought.

'They do all the bloody talking.'

The family's move from Plaistow to Sussex two years before propelled them at dizzying speed to the comfortable life of the middle classes. Whilst Thomas would have preferred to stay in the East End, Violet and Sophia insisted on a country home. Besides, it got Thomas further away from the gangsters he feared. Violet quickly adapted, and her new life found her the well-dressed, country woman, socialising at ease with the neighbours at Winding Wood. Thomas found the difference between the East End and rural Sussex more troublesome and spent much of his time brooding, finding the people Violet chose to associate with to be 'up their bleeding arses.'

But in time, he, too, adjusted. After grumbling for many months about their new home, he began to appreciate the tranquillity of the place. However, on this lovely morning, his peace was shattered when a headline on page two caught his attention:

'Brutal East End Gangland Killing
Mr Joseph Rogers was found shot and injured in Poplar High Street at 3 am on Tuesday. He died in hospital from his wounds. It is alleged Mr Rogers was the victim of a gangland feud and the "Poplar Boys," a gang which ran the underworld in the area for many years, was responsible.'

Thomas's head spun, and his scrotum tightened around his balls; this was too close to home. He knew the Poplar Boys from his Plaistow days, and they had connections to the gang he double-crossed. He long figured that living in Sussex would keep him out of reach and planned to do something about changing the family name. In his money-cushioned apathy, he never quite got around to it. Now, jerked into the fear that when Reggie Hartnell, the gang leader he betrayed, eventually got out of Wandsworth, he might be able to find him. He had to do something and decided to talk to Violet later that day; he had no other option; they must change their surname.

He pondered for a while on what should replace Goldsmith before deciding on Thomson, his mother's maiden name. That evening, Thomas and Violet went to the chintzy lounge after dinner. He found the patterned curtain fabric and sofas overbearing, but his wife had selected them, and he didn't have the chance to contribute to interior décor choices. He insisted he had something important to talk about. Bryony and Florence were in bed. Violet had taken to the habit of drinking sweet sherry in the evening and poured them both a glass.

'So, what do you want to discuss, Thomas?' Violet asked, her curiosity piqued.

'I think it'd be a good idea to change our name by deed poll. I told you about Reggie Hartnell; he'd kill me if he found out where I live. I heard a while ago he made a bargain with the police and got a shorter sentence in return. He'll be out in three years; we need to have disappeared before then. I've been meaning to do something about it since we left Plaistow.' Violet replied.

'We must think about the girls' safety. But what name will we use?'

'Thomson. It was my mother's maiden name.'

'Why can't we use mine, Gosling?' Violet suggested. For Thomas, the thought of bearing the same name as the dragon-in-law was not palatable.

'When people hear your mother's name and ours, they'll think of us as unmarried, and that'd never do. No, Thomson it must be.'

Thomas explained to Violet he would contact their solicitor. She said.

'That's all very well; I understand the legal process, but what will we tell the neighbours? The postman will soon see we have a different surname. I can promise you it'll have tongues wagging.' Thomas replied.

'We'll make up a story. How about you tell them you wrote to a hotel to make a booking for a holiday. They replied and said they don't accept Jews.'

'But we're not Jewish!' protested Violet.

'Goldsmith can often be taken as a Jewish name, so I think it'll convince people. The Goldsmiths no longer exist, and we'll become the Thomson family. Then there's no chance Reggie Hartnell or one of his minions will ever find us.'

Violet decided this was all a thoroughly good idea. After thinking about it for a while, she decided she liked the name Thomson and that it sounded classier than Goldsmith. The decision was made, and she had a sense of relief, knowing they were taking the necessary steps to protect their family.

Violet Goldsmith's metamorphosis was nearing completion. Initially, her accent underwent a meticulous transformation during the elocution lessons with Ivy Wakerell. The echoes of her Cockney background were expunged, replaced by the cultivated, middle-class tones of the home counties. Confident in her newfound speech, she no longer fretted over dropping her Hs or feared detection.

Alongside her polished accent came an entirely new wardrobe. Once a woman who sewed her own garments, often struggling to afford fabric for new dresses, Violet now frequented smart stores in Tunbridge Wells and London. She created a sophisticated look that had people commenting on her impeccable style. Although in her forties, she was determined to stay abreast of the latest fashions, diligently perusing style magazines to ensure her attire reflected her elevated station in life.

The house and garden became the ultimate expressions of the Thomson's newfound affluence: the house tastefully furnished, the garden resurrected to its pre-Great War splendour, through the efforts of a dedicated team of gardeners.

The woman known as Violet Goldsmith, had been left behind, replaced by a new persona basking in the sunlight. Like a colourful butterfly emerging from its chrysalis, Violet Thomson had been born. Her past, moulded by years of hard labour and losses, had given way to a confident, well-dressed woman presiding over her beautiful country home and garden.

As Violet tended to the herbaceous border the following day, she reflected on the journey that had brought her to this point. 'Violet Thomson,' she kept repeating, savouring the sound of her new name and delighting in how it rolled off her tongue. She felt six inches taller.

Her transformation was complete, and Violet felt a profound sense of pride. Every step she had taken led her to this moment of rebirth, and she relished the new life she had meticulously crafted for herself and her family.

Chapter Nine
A letter
1936

Winding Wood
Crofton Lane
Forest Row
Sussex

25th February 1936
My dearest Edith,

Thank you for your letter. I am pleased to hear you got over your nasty bout of flu. My mother had it, too, and was quite poorly for a couple of weeks.

We received a letter from my sister-in-law the other day. My brother Bill is unable to read or write; he's been a bit simple since birth. His wife wrote that he could no longer manage working as a carpenter because his sight was failing. She asked if Thomas or I could do anything to help. She also suggested that they would love to visit us. When we left Plaistow we did not tell any of our family how wealthy we are and the type of life we enjoy. However, I think Bill's wife sniffed money! Not wishing to be uncharitable, I sent her a ten-shilling note. As for visiting! I think my dishevelled East End family would be a bit of a shock for the neighbours. Best to discourage them from ever coming here.

I often look around me and still can't quite believe how my life has been transformed. I am so blessed; after years of gruelling work, loss and misery, I have come home. These are my rewards. I have sworn a solemn oath that nobody will ever stand in my way and steal this happiness from me. The thought of returning to somewhere like Plaistow terrifies me, and I will do anything to ensure it never happens.

With much love as ever

Violet

Chapter Ten
Tea with Mrs Hatcher
1937

There was barely a cloud in the sky, and the June day was hot and clammy. Violet asked Thomas to put up the parasol on the terrace. Otherwise, her guest would find the heat too overbearing. She checked everything was ready on the table, adorned with a pretty embroidered tablecloth, her best Royal Doulton china, an assortment of freshly baked fruit scones and a selection of finger sandwiches. She heard a car crunch up the gravel and went to welcome her visitor.

Mrs Gladys Hatcher was a formidable-looking woman who wore black dresses nearly to her ankle, a style from generations before. Mounted on her head today was an expansive hat, resplendent with a peacock feather. Mrs Hatcher was at the beating epicentre of local gossip. Recently starved of juicy titbits, Violet decided it would be entertaining to invite her to tea and glean the more salacious details of Forest Row folks' indiscretions.

At one time, she feared their vipers' tongues, dreading they would detect her impecunious East End roots. Now, confident and secure in her new life, she wanted to be part of the Chinese whispers about other village residents.

Violet passed Mrs Hatcher the plate of sandwiches, and the woman snatched four in a rapid manoeuvre, which Violet thought was greedy. She said.

'It's shocking to hear Reverend Davies has been having an affair with a married woman in the village. Disgraceful!' Her friend replied.

'I heard it on very good authority; I cannot, of course, reveal my sources, but I fear the Davies' marriage will not last much longer. Mrs Davies is bound to hear about it. Gossip travels so quickly round here!' To Violet's wry amusement, the woman tutted as if to disapprove. Mrs Hatcher said.

'And then there's the dreadful business of the Hamilton girl. Only seventeen and with child!' Violet replied.

'Shocking! I presume the bastard will be taken away from the mother and sent to a children's home. We cannot be seen encouraging other wastrels to engage in such sordid behaviour!' After saying this, Violet recalled her own child, born six months into marriage, then decided, for no good reason, that the two pregnancies could not be compared. She justified herself by thinking,

'I was in love with Thomas; this harlot slept with a man for no other reason than lust.' Mrs Hatcher had completed her diatribe about Joan Hamilton and asked.

'May I have another sandwich?' and she reached over and helped herself. Violet noticed a crumb on the woman's chin. The combination of eating and talking meant some food had not reached its destination. Having consumed another two egg and cress sandwiches, Gladys Hatcher looked serious and said.

'There's something which I wanted to discuss with you, Mrs Thomson. Horace and I thought you may be interested in joining the organisation we belong to.'

'And what would that be?' replied Violet, thinking Mrs Hatcher was about to mention another gardening club.

'We've joined the local branch of Mr Mosely's organisation. It's called the British Union of Fascists.' Violet had heard a little of the movement, although she did not involve herself in politics. The garden was her priority, and issues that affected other people were not her concern. She replied.

'What does that involve? I'm not sure I know much about it.' Mrs Hatcher sat up in the chair, looking emboldened and flushed.

'We went for cocktails at Lord Harrington's last month and we met a group of people there who are very involved with the movement. They explained how they could improve things in this country. Look at the sorry mess our politicians have got us into!'

'I can't disagree with that,' Violet replied.

'The most important issue is that Mr Mosely tells us we must deal with the Jewish question. Do you know they run the banks? They defraud money from all of us; they interfere with every aspect of a decent society and are intent on taking over! Their homes are filthy and children repugnant. They revolt me, and the sooner we deal with them, the better!'

Violet was taken back at the ferocity of Mrs Hatcher's response but made no reaction. She did not want to get on the wrong side of this woman by disagreeing with her. She had expended a lot of effort in building up her reputation in the village, and making her an enemy would be an extremely dangerous move. She feared that one day, someone would discover where the Thomsons came from, and Mrs Hatcher would be the first to distribute the gossip around the village. Instead, Violet said.

'Oh dear, how ghastly.' Mrs Hatcher, invigorated by her anger, continued.

'If you are to join, we need to ensure there aren't any Jewish connections to your family. You told me once you changed your family name for fear of being thought Jewish.' She stopped momentarily, looking embarrassed and composed herself to deliver the killer blow.

'It's just that your mother mentioned to Mrs Milton at Greenacres that her Aunt married a Jew, and her cousin and family are seeking to leave Germany and settle here. I do hope that's not true? We don't want any more Jews in Forest Row.'
Violet fumed inwardly about her mother's indiscretion.

Sophia's aunt Henrietta had indeed married a Jewish man. Their son Eduard Hirsch had written to Sophia expressing his grave concerns about Adolf Hitler and saying that he was trying to get his family out of Germany and to safety. Sophia told Violet that perhaps they should invite them to stay at Winding Wood. She thought it might encourage the Home Office to allow the family into the country.

Violet formulated her response as quickly as she could. She did not want Mrs Hatcher to think she was prevaricating. On one hand, the Hirsch's were her family, and why should she deny who they were and what blood ran in their veins? But then anxiety crept in, and her stomach churned, fearing the disapproval of this all-powerful woman. News that the Thomsons had Jewish relatives would run around Forest Row at the speed of light, and in an instant, their hard-earned reputation would evaporate. She could not bear the thought. Reaching a decision, she replied.

'I'm so sorry Mother's given you the wrong impression. We're worried that she's becoming senile and often talks nonsense. Clearly, she's made this up and troubled you for no good reason. I don't have a cousin Eduard, and I can absolutely assure you that if I did, he would most definitely not be a Jew. We have no such taint in my family. Imagine!'

Violet decided she would speak to her mother about the matter later. Sophia must be made to understand she needed to be more discreet. The letter from cousin Eduard should be ignored. He must not be encouraged to come to England with the family. That would never do. In any case, she thought the business with Adolf Hitler had been exaggerated by 'the bloody Jews' and would blow over soon; most likely, Eduard was being overdramatic.

Mrs Hatcher looked reassured; she would report back that her fears were misplaced and said.

'May I have another scone, please?'

Chapter Eleven
George
1944

Violet and Thomas listened with mounting excitement, to the news crackling out from the radio. After five terrible, long years of war, they finally had something to be hopeful about. The much-anticipated invasion of France had commenced, and Violet dared to think the fighting would soon be over.

'How long will it go on?' she asked Thomas, who replied.

'Difficult to say, but it sounds like the allies are making great advances in Normandy. They must be in great peril, though. It's a blessing for Florence that George isn't fighting.'

George and Florence had been seeing each other for almost three months after a chance meeting at a friend's birthday party. Florence's shyness and anxiety evaporated in his company, and she felt taller and more confident. In truth, George was not as confident as he made out; he was simply good at putting on a front, and she, too, made him feel so much stronger when they were together.

Both were gentle people who benefited from the support of the other. This was love in its nascent stages, one of those meetings where two souls' lives held the potential to begin a lifelong journey as a couple and meld into the most blessed of unions.

Florence had already decided this was what true love must be like. She wanted to write romantic poems and sing songs one day; the next, she would be in floods of tears, fearing her new boyfriend didn't care for her. She had never experienced the emotion before, but she was sure the flushed, giggly feeling which overtook her whenever she was near George must be it. She thought he was so handsome, accomplished and kind!

When Florence first took George home, there were disapproving looks, followed by tutting and harsh words muttered under her grandmother's breath.

'What's he doing here when our boys are being killed fighting!'

But she softened and cooed fawningly all over George when Florence told her his father was Sir Arthur Warren, owner of the car manufacturers in Tonbridge, now building Spitfires. As the head designer, George would not be called up. Violet also assessed the young man's credentials with mounting joy. Not only had Florence found a suitable potential husband who was likely to inherit a fortune, but George's family were titled. The icing on the cake.

One disappointing grey June afternoon, Florence rushed into the kitchen at Winding Wood. She had returned from lunch with George's family and panted, breathless with excitement. Violet was at the sink peeling potatoes, needing to pad out the meagre amount of meat left over from the family's rations.

'Hello dear. Did you have a nice lunch at the Warrens?' she asked. Florence gushed.

'They have a house near Maresfield; it's Georgian and huge! George told me it has forty rooms! It's more like a stately home. They have about one hundred acres. Before the war, they ran a stud, but it's all turned over to crops now.' Violet smiled, thinking as she often did, quite how far the family had come since Plaistow days. Florence continued.

'They're lovely people. Sir Arthur was kind to me and told me how lovely it was to see his son with such a charming girl. I blushed when he said that. His mother was ever so nice, too. She ran a milliners in Mayfair before she married Sir Arthur. They spoiled me, but I never quite understood what George saw in me. He's so handsome and I'm very unconfident. I stuttered when he introduced me to his mother and father. They must think me silly.'

'Florence dear, a little shyness isn't a bad thing. I'm sure they'll love you just as we do.'

'Maybe. Anyway, I have some exciting news!'

'Tell me, dear, has he proposed?'

'I'm not sure he would ever want to marry someone like me. No, it's that we've had a lovely invitation to church in London next Sunday. George's friend Bill is in the Household Cavalry, and they hold a weekly service at the Guards' Chapel in Birdcage Walk. Bill invited us to join him. It sounds so glamorous.'

At that point, Violet's legs almost gave way under her, she swayed, and her vision fogged over, completely black. She heard a terrible roaring noise and then collapsed to the floor. She was only unconscious for a few moments, then started to come to, feeling sick and with an unpleasant metallic taste in her mouth.

'Mummy, Mummy, wake up.' Florence shook her mother, and after a minute or so, Violet opened her eyes. She thought she would awaken to find the debris of her bombed house around her but was shocked to see the kitchen in its usual neat and ordered self and that she was lying on the floor with her daughter looking down at her with a most concerned expression on her face.

'Don't worry yourself, Florence, I'm fine,' Violet protested and, after a cup of sweet tea, was soon sitting up and chatting with her daughter. Florence asked.

'What brought that on, Mummy? I was worried about you. I thought for an awful moment you'd had a stroke. Do you think I should call the Doctor?'

'Please don't fuss, dear. It's just my time of life.'

Violet was terrified. She had experienced similar feelings when waking up from her horrible dreams. She knew little of such things and never understood if her nightmares were telling her anything. However, sitting and talking to Florence, and returning to normality, she was convinced the darkness and violent noises were a foreshadowing, and there was no way on earth she would let her youngest go to the service. She had to find a way of stopping her.

Chapter Twelve
The Guards' Chapel

Violet called Florence into the sitting room. She had been on the phone to George and was still flushed and excited as she came into the room. She asked.

'What did you want to talk to me about Mummy?' Violet replied.

'Sit down dear, I have something important to discuss. Your father and I have been talking, and we're worried you're getting too close to George for a girl of your age; we don't want you to go to London with him to the church service.'

Violet could see her daughter's face dropping with dismay. She steeled herself and went on, 'You're spending too much time with him, and a whole day out together is too much. We're concerned that he may expect certain things of you, and we have your decency to consider.'

Still shaken, Violet was determined her daughter would not go to the service. She did not have any idea what the terrible sense of darkness she sensed augured, but it must mean something. After all, wasn't there talk about Hitler's secret weapons being aimed at London?

'How could you be so mean?' shrieked Florence. 'I'm going to the service with George, and you can't stop me!'

'I'm also worried about bombing, Florence.'

'Oh, that's nonsense, Mummy. They'll have air-raid shelters, and I'll be perfectly safe. You can't tell me what to do!'

'Let me remind you, young lady, until you're twenty-one, I will tell you exactly what I want you to do. You aren't going to London, and that's the end of the matter.' Florence shouted.

'You're being cruel, why do you always want to ruin everything? I think you're jealous! You've spent so much of your life in misery, mourning for Grace, I don't think you can bear the thought of anyone else being happy!'

Violet, boiling with anger at the criticism and shocked by her typically compliant daughter's defiance, hardened her resolve and snarled angrily.

'If you're going to take that attitude, young lady, then I think it's time your relationship with George is brought to an end, and I'll hear no more about it.' Florence burst into tears and stormed out of the room.

Still furious about Florence's behaviour, Violet tussled with the decision to call Sir Arthur Warren and tell him the relationship would be ended. She liked George but was not prepared to allow Florence to be wilful and rude. How cruel her daughter had been to mention Grace and then be accused of being in permanent mourning for the child. She hardened and decided Florence must be taught to be more obedient. She told Thomas what she had decided and expected him to support her on the matter.

When Violet called Sir Arthur, he was polite but bemused. He liked Florence and thought her gentle nature would be a perfect match for his shy son, but he did not think he could object to Violet and Thomas's decision; after all, they were the girl's parents. He put down the phone, left with the distinct impression Mrs Thomson had not been telling him the whole truth.

In the days that followed, Florence, point blank, refused to speak to her parents. Always such a kind and well-mannered girl, she now glared at her mother when she passed her in the hall. Her job as a shorthand typist took her to Croydon every day, and she was pleased to escape from Winding Wood and her mother's anger.

What had always been a joyful family home for her, a place where the gentle soul felt protected against the stresses of life, now loomed ominously like a prison. Its red brick walls might have well been granite bastions. She thought her heart may break and confided to a friend in the office she was not sure she could go on living without George.

Violet thought she would come around in time. She was only young, and there would be plenty more Georges. Her friend Muriel had a decent-looking son, and an introduction could be arranged.

The Sunday of the service at the Guards' Chapel came. Florence sulked and cried all day in her room, refusing to come down for food, shouting only once at her mother as she tried to coax her downstairs.

'You've ruined my life!'

Just after seven pm, the phone rang, and Violet answered it. It was Sir Arthur Warren. When he started to speak, Violet's stomach churned. He spoke in the tone of voice of someone who was about to deliver bad news.

'Mrs Thomson, I'm going to have to ask you to brace yourself for the most awful news,' he began, his voice heavy with dread. 'One of my contacts at the Air Ministry just called me. I'm so sorry to tell you that the Guards' Chapel was hit by a flying bomb during the morning service. It seems that most of the congregation were killed. We've heard nothing from George and fear the worst.'

Her hand trembled as she clutched the phone, the gravity of the news sinking in. The world around her slowed, the edges of her vision blurring as if shrouded in a dark, suffocating fog. Her strength drained, and she dropped the phone. Sir Arthur's voice could still be heard coming out of the earpiece.

Breaking the news to Florence was awful; Violet was torn between guilt and emotion. She climbed the stairs, dreading how she would deliver the appalling blow. Violet sat on Florence's bed and reached out her hand to her daughter. Florence pulled hers away, refusing to engage with her mother and turned to the wall.

'Florence darling. You're going to have to be very strong. Sir Arthur just phoned. Something awful happened today at the Guards' Chapel, a bomb. He believes George may have been killed.' Florence turned round her face, white as chalk and said nothing. No tears came, and she refused to speak when her mother tried to comfort her. In time, Violet left her alone in her room, not knowing what else she could say.

Chapter Thirteen
Listening at the bottom of the stair

In the days which followed, Florence did not say a word to either of her parents. Bryony was away in the Land Army, and her grandmother had been rushed into hospital to have her appendix removed. She had no one to talk to, and her isolation deepened her grief still further. She cried and sometimes howled, the loss tearing at her heart, the man she loved was gone. During stiller moments, in between her tears, she fumed, her anger festering, deep and acidic.

One morning, Violet looked up from her breakfast, sensing Florence's presence. Thomas engrossed himself in his newspaper. He couldn't stomach another argument. Florence stood in the dining room doorway, silent and stony-faced. Violet said.

'Florence dear, are you a little better?' Thomas glanced up from his toast. Florence spoke in a flat and emotionless tone.

'Why did you stop me going to the Guards' Chapel? Please tell me the truth!' Violet decided honesty was the best policy and replied.

'You know I have strange dreams and feelings about things which might happen. Do you remember I told you I had a premonition about the R101 crashing in France? Florence, still silent, glanced at her mother with tearless, traumatised eyes. They looked as if they were asking a question for which Violet would never have an answer. Her mother continued.

'Well dear, I had a premonition about the Guards' Chapel, that's why I stopped you going. I hope you understand I was trying to protect you. Florence's eyes opened still wider. Violet saw the girl was trembling, it seemed with emotion, but when she started to speak it was from an outpouring of anger.

'You cruel bitch! You had a premonition, and you let George go! Do you not have one shred of decency in your rancorous heart?! What have you turned into? Violet stood up and hit her daughter hard across the face. Florence put her hand to her cheek; it was throbbing badly. Her mother's blow had loosened one of her teeth. A little trickle of blood ran down one side of her mouth, which she dabbed with her hanky. Stunned at her mother's violence, she took a few moments to compose herself and speak.

'I don't think you'll ever understand what you've done. You're heartless and without morals.' Violet had never heard her youngest talk like this before. She was used to her words being full of love and kindness or about her anxieties, but this was different. Her tone cold and emotionless, she continued.

'You've stolen my one opportunity to be happy. I'll never forgive you for this.' Violet interrupted.

'But darling, we were trying to help.' Florence spat back.

'You have a strange way of helping me, making sure the man I love was killed.'

'I didn't know; I didn't think…' Florence cut her off and turned to her father, who, up to that point, had been trying to keep out of the argument. Her face was flushed red with anger and she was now glaring at Thomas.

'I know what you did!'

'Whatever are you talking about?' replied Thomas, sounding confused. Florence shouted back.

'I know all about Westborough's.' The words struck Thomas like a blow, and he recoiled back in his chair.

'How the hell…!' Florence cut him off.

'You thought I was the anxious one. "Poor little Florence" you called me. You thought I was just made like that; I remember hearing you saying once, "she was born with a temperament so much more sensitive than Bryony's." But I wasn't born that way. It was all your doing.'

'Whatever are you talking about?' asked Violet. 'All we ever did was to try and look after you.' Florence glared directly at her father again.

'You never suspected for one moment what made me nervous, but it was your fault. When I was a little girl, I got into the habit of creeping down the stairs at night and listening to your conversations. I thought it would make me grown up hearing what the adults were talking about. You never had any idea. I was so careful; you caught me on one occasion, and I told you I had a bad dream. If only you knew.'

'One night, just before we left Plaistow, I heard you both talking about what you did at Westborough's. Not only are you a forger but also a grass! And you put the blame on an innocent man! Harold Jackson did nothing and ended up in prison for what you did. Imagine how this made me feel. I doted on you Daddy, you were my hero, and then I found out what you were capable of. I was six years old! My entire world, my child's innocence, was murdered in a moment!' Thomas said.

'You wouldn't have been old enough to understand what we were talking about.'

'You're right, I didn't understand all of it, but from that moment, I knew damn well you were a criminal and not a hero. I never forgot what you two were discussing. As I got older and listened to more of your conversations, I understood everything. Little by little, I worked every bit out, and as I did, it chipped away any remaining respect I had for you.' Thomas tried to regain control of the situation.

'None of this is your business and you're not able to protest. Look at the lovely life you have here!' Florence glanced at her father with an expression of derision.

'This lovely life was built on crime and the misery of others. I was at school with two of Harold Jackson's children. They had to go to the poorhouse because you got their father blamed for your acts. How can you live with yourself?'

'Needs must, dear. I had to protect you all,' replied Thomas coldly.

'You're both as bad as each other,' continued Florence.' I think it's time for recompense. Mrs Jackson will find some comfort when justice is done at last.'

'What do you mean?' replied Violet, alarmed at the direction the conversation had taken.

'I'm going to the Police, and I'll tell them everything. Once they are on the trail, I wonder how long it'll be before the other men in the gang find out about it. I wonder if some of them are out of prison now. I expect they'd be pleased to discover where you live.'

Violet intervened. She thought trying to appeal to Florence's better nature may work.

'Florence darling, I do understand how upset you are, but would you want to see Daddy go to prison? We'd have to sell Winding Wood. You're such a kind girl, you must appreciate we'd lose everything. I may have to go back and work in a factory again. Please, for my sake, drop this.' Florence turned to leave the room and shouted back.

'Frankly, I hope you both rot in hell. You deserve it.'

Chapter Fourteen
The Dark heart of the house of secrets

Violet and Thomas talked long into the afternoon, desperately trying to think how to stop Florence from going to the police. Thomas shut the door to the hall as he did not want the daily help listening to their conversation, which, if relayed to the neighbours, would have the local gossip mongers' tongues wagging. They had their reputation to think about. Thomas said.

'We could send her to stay with your friend Edith in Devon until she calms down?'

'Don't be so wet, Thomas; we need to do something a little more drastic than that. In any case, I don't think she'd go. She's determined to ruin our lives. We've come so far, the thought of losing everything scares me.'

'Then I've no idea what else to suggest. Let's hope the Police think she's made it all up or has gone insane. I have a good reputation in Forest Row. People think we're upright pillars of the community. We've worked hard to earn their respect. I'm hoping to be chairman of the Golf club next year. No one will believe a word that comes out of her mouth.' Violet sneered back.

'You've always been so fucking weak. For God's sake, you never would have agreed to the Westborough's job if it wasn't for me. We'd still be poor. We must come up with a plan, it's too risky. Something's going to have to be done.' A seed of an idea began to form in Violet's mind. She said.

'A woman in the village told me they sent their daughter to an asylum. The girl was promiscuous, and they decided it'd be the best way of controlling her bad habits. What if we had Florence committed? We can tell them she's hysterical because of George being killed. That much is true. Who'll believe her if she tries to tell them about Westborough's? She'll calm down after she's been there for a month or so, and maybe then she'll see reason.'

'Would you really do that to Florence?' Thomas asked, aghast that his wife could think up such a drastic plan. 'I thought she was your favourite. You're always telling me so.'

'If it means saving you from prison and keeping Winding Wood, then we have to consider it,' replied Violet, looking around at her beloved home.

The following morning, Florence heard her father on the phone in the hall. She planned to creep onto the landing so she could catch precisely what he was saying. Turning the door handle, she realised she was locked in. She could make out her father saying.

'It's a terrible business, Doctor Holford. She's hysterical, and we're worried she may harm herself; we cannot calm her; she's been like this for days now.' There was silence as Thomas listened to the reply, then continued.

'So, you can take her tomorrow at ten if we decide to proceed? I'll call you later and let you know. Thank you so much for everything you're doing for her.'

Florence did not like the sound of this but could do nothing. She tried the door again, but the lock was firm and the wood solid. She would have to wait the next morning to discover what her father meant. She lay on the bed all day, holding her old teddy close to her, frequent tears mixed with a creeping sense of foreboding.

Later, Thomas cornered Violet in the kitchen.

'I've spoken to Doctor Holford, and everything's arranged. An ambulance will take her to the asylum in the morning if we tell him to go ahead. I do have my doubts, though. Is this the only way?'

'We're doing the right thing' insisted Violet. She had tussled long into the night with the decision. Sleep evaded her, and her mind whorled with conflicting emotions. She would miss Florence's loving presence around the house, yet each time she weakened and thought they should face her daughter down, the thought of the loss of reputation and poverty loomed. By the morning, she had steeled her resolve and convinced herself they had no choice in the matter. She continued.

'The Police may well believe her story, and you'd be arrested. Then what would become of me? We can't take the risk. We'd lose everything and the scandal Thomas. Do you want that? She needs dealing with.' Thomas replied.

'I suppose you're right; they'll treat her hysteria, and she'll be calmer and more rational. Perhaps this will make her a happier person. I have grave reservations, but you seem determined to do this.' Violet said nothing but stared at Thomas, her cold eyes betraying her commitment to the plan. He continued.

'Doctor Holford has arranged for her to be sectioned so she does not have the option of coming home without our agreement.' Violet replied.

'That sounds sensible; we don't want her back here making a fuss, and what's the treatment?'

'Apparently, they've been experimenting with something called a frontal lobotomy. I understand they're getting excellent results when treating women with hysteria. So, shall we go ahead?'

Violet knew nothing of the procedure, but if it silenced Florence and saved them from penury and disgrace, she decided it was not such a bad thing. In any case, she had always been a delicate child, and Violet feared she would end up a neurotic and highly strung adult. She thought.

'Maybe this will help. Surely life in the asylum would be better for her, protected from everyday life?'

Violet cast her eyes around her, taking in the beautiful dining room and its long windows overlooking the garden. The doors were open, and the sweet fragrance of honeysuckle floated in. The July morning was alive with the sound of birdsong, and the day promised gentle, warm sunshine, the fresh Sussex air such a contrast to the leaden smoke-spoiled sky of the East End.

The thought of losing Winding Wood, the horrors of poverty. No, that was too much to bear. She pushed any concerns aside, assuring herself that an experienced doctor would only do the right things. She said.

'We have no choice. Do it.'

Winding Wood recoiled and shuddered, an unwilling witness to Violet and Thomas's wicked act. The dark heart of the house of secrets finally manifested. Its echo would ripple down the decades, tainting the lives and choices of generations of the family to come.

Prologue To Part Five

The pursuit of truth and light is the beating heartbeat of our salvation. Within the clarity of truth lies the pathway to wisdom, illuminating the darkness which lies in the deepest abysses of our minds. Secrets, however, are dark shadows which cloud our judgment and corrode our souls. They create barriers that hinder our journey to enlightenment, trapping us in a web of deceit and ignorance.

Embracing the light of truth frees us from these bonds and, in the process, reveals the hidden mysteries. It is through this light that we transcend our material form and find tranquillity and ecstasy in the celestial realm.

Ekatarina Zagorski

Golden Pathways to Wisdom

Second Edition 1932

Part Five

Golden Pathways to Wisdom

Chapter One
The reckoning

The Rose's Promise (anon)
'A single rose blooming in the snow, A promise of love that will forever glow. Despite winter's chill and icy embrace, This fragile bloom holds steadfast grace.'

Edith's revelations created brutal surges of emotion in Bryony, Joe and Emily. They reeled, in a state of shock and anger, having found the story of their family, which they had been told all their lives, was nothing but a pack of lies. There was a long silent pause, punctuated only by bird song from the garden and the distant ticking of the Grandfather Clock on the landing.

Reminders of Florence filled the room: the china trinkets on the fireplace, the open wardrobe door showing off her rail of clothes, and the battered old teddy bear on the bed. The bedroom closed in around them, and their minds struggled to comprehend the unspeakable things they had been told. Bryony clutched Florence's teddy, her fingers stroking the worn fabric as if seeking comfort from a more innocent time. Her voice quivered as she spoke, and from her questions, she was clearly having trouble processing what she heard.

'You're telling me Florence wasn't killed by the Flying bomb. That it was all a lie?' Edith's gaze remained steady, her face sympathetic.

'Your sister's fate was far more tragic than you were led to believe. Your parents had her committed to an asylum and lobotomised to keep her from revealing the truth.'

Joe's hands clenched into fists, his knuckles white with barely contained fury.

'They did this to their own daughter, just to protect themselves?'

Edith spoke gently; what she had told them must be excruciating to hear and hard to comprehend.

'Florence knew too much. She threatened to go to the police, and your parents did what they thought they had to do to hide their secret.'

Emily's voice shook, her eyes brimming with tears.

'How could they do that to her? How could they live with themselves?' Edith sighed.

'Fear and desperation can drive people to do unimaginable things. Violet and Thomas were terrified of losing everything, and they made a terrible, unforgivable choice.' Joe then asked.

'Did you ever suspect, before then, that Violet could be capable of something as heinous as this?'

'Who would?' replied Edith sadly. 'But if I'm truthful with myself, I started having doubts many years ago. I chose to ignore them. After Violet moved to Winding Wood, she changed and was not always the gentle, kind woman I first met. A rather vain and brittle person replaced her. I remember a letter she wrote sometime in the thirties. In it, she swore no one would ever take her new life away from her. It seemed overzealous, and I didn't know what to say and never replied. Perhaps, over the years, I enabled her by not challenging her. Some of the blame must fall on me.' Bryony said.

'No, that's not true, this was Violet and Thomas's doing and no one else's. Why do you think she confessed to you in the end?'

'I believe she wanted someone to vindicate what she did. Not long after I wrote that last letter, she replied to me. I can't recall exactly what she wrote; I tore it up, but she was full of self-pity and asked me to try to understand her actions. I think she thought of this as her confessional, and she expected me, her over-loyal and always supportive friend, to understand and give my blessing. I did not reply.' Joe looked thoughtful and said.

'We seem to be placing all of the blame on Violet, surely Thomas was equally guilty?' Edith replied.

'He played his part too, but I do think out of the pair of them, she was far worse. He wouldn't have been part of the banknote fraud if she hadn't encouraged him, and it was her idea to have Florence committed. Thomas was a weak individual, and Violet was always the driving force, so yes, I do blame her more.' Bryony continued; she was having trouble speaking between racking sobs.

'My life, and my children's lives, have been built on lies. When I was young, I sensed there was something indefinable and unspoken, but this! I thought my parents were kind and loving people. We were raised to believe we came from a good family. But now, I find my father was a thief, a grass, and he allowed someone innocent to go to prison to cover his tracks and as for what they did to Florence…' At that point, Bryony could speak no more, and she collapsed into Emily's arms, who did her best to comfort her mother.

The room fell into silence again. Now, the only sound was Bryony's occasional sob. They sat in stunned disbelief, their minds reeling as they tried to grasp the enormity of what they had learned. The foundations of their lives, built on the illusion of a respectable family, shattered, exposing the darkness that lurked beneath the surface.

Vivid memories of Florence flooded Bryony's mind. She remembered her sister's infectious laughter, the way her eyes sparkled with mischief and kindness. She recalled the quiet moments they shared, the stories Florence told of her dreams and aspirations, fairy castles and handsome princes forever silenced by their parents' cruelty. Bryony could not begin to imagine or want to think about what she went through during her incarceration.

Joe's voice broke the silence.

'We need to find out everything. No matter how painful it might be. What hospital was she in, and how long did she live? We can find out where she's buried or where her ashes are and visit.' Bryony nodded in agreement.

'We have to make sure Florence's memory is honoured. She deserves that much. I can never forgive my parents for this. Mother's dead to me.'

Emily wiped her tears away, her expression resolute.

'Elsie must never be told about any of this. Ever. Let her think she comes from a kind and loving family. The story stops with us; it doesn't need to be handed down through the generations.'

The family stayed in Florence's bedroom for a while longer in silence. It was time to face the dark truth and to honour the memory of the woman they had lost to the family's terrible secrets. They felt Florence's presence in the room with them, urging them to find justice for the life which had been stolen so cruelly from her. Armed with the truth, they would find a way to put her ghost to rest.

As if to acknowledge to the family that the awful truth had finally been recognised, Winding Wood fell into holy silence that night. No sound could be heard except the pipes creaking and occasionally snoring from Bryony's bedroom. The house's ghosts would find their way to resolution and peace, the living would make atonement for the ill deeds of others in the past, and the spirits would, at last, be at peace.

Chapter Two
The list

Edith Bates' words hung over the residents of Winding Wood. As if to emphasise the gloom, the autumn, which had shown so much promise a few weeks before, had deteriorated into a dank, foggy grey. The world Bryony, Emily, and Joe once believed in had been turned upside down, leaving them grasping at the frayed edges of their reality.

Bryony's mind swirled with a thousand questions, each more troubling than the last. Yet, amidst the chaos, a glimmer of positivity emerged: she, Emily, and Joe began to talk more openly, breaking the cloister-like silence that had shrouded Winding Wood for months. Their shared sorrow forged a newfound unity.

Still, Florence's weeping ghost had not been laid to rest. The family hoped unveiling the truth would bring peace and her haunting cries would cease. But every night, the unrelenting, mournful wails persisted. In desperation, Emily and Joe took to sleeping with the radio on in a vain attempt to drown out the heart-wrenching sounds.

Bryony insisted that as Florence's sister, it was her duty to see this through to the end. Emily and Joe stepped back, pledging their love and support. Bryony decided that a crucial part of honouring Florence's memory would be to uncover where she had been in the hospital and, if possible, locate her grave. She would lay flowers each year on her birthday. That was the very least she could do; she felt helpless, unable to heal the wounds inflicted by the grievous sins of others.

With her work complete, Edith returned to Devon. The family expressed their heartfelt gratitude and urged her to stay in touch. She agreed, though she harboured doubts. Despite the kindness Emily, Joe, and Bryony showed her, a perpetual gloom lingered over Winding Wood. The house unsettled her, and she vowed never to return. She promised to keep in contact by phone, answer their questions, and offer reassurances, knowing full well she would never see them again.

One bone-chilling November afternoon, Bryony called Edith. After the customary pleasantries about the weather, Bryony broached the subject she was anxious to discuss.

'We're trying to find out more about what happened to Florence. When Mother wrote to you, did she mention which hospital she was sent to?' Edith sighed.

'I destroyed the letter many years ago. Handling it made me feel dirty, as if the words themselves were cursed. It's been so long, but I'm certain Violet didn't name the hospital. However, I remember she mentioned it was in Surrey, which was odd since they lived in Sussex. I can only assume Violet and Thomas arranged it to lessen the chances anyone would discover Florence was still alive.'

'Thank you, Edith. That's most helpful,' Bryony said and went on.

'We must arrange for you to come and visit again soon.'

'That would be charming, dear,' Edith replied smoothly, the lie so elegantly delivered that Bryony believed she meant it.

Bryony had no idea how many asylums there were in Surrey, but her friend Louise had just retired from years as a GP in the county. Surely, she would know. Bryony called her, and although Louise couldn't recall all the psychiatric hospitals offhand, she assured her.

'I can find out for you. Shall I write with the names and addresses?'

True to her word, a few days later, a letter arrived. Bryony's heart pounded as she opened it, revealing a neat, typed list of hospitals:

Netherne: Hooley
Cane Hill: Coulsdon
Brookwood: Woking
Warlingham Park: Chelsham
West Park: Epsom
Horton: Epsom
Long Grove: Epsom
Manor: Epsom

Louise also wrote.

'You'll find some of these hospitals have already closed, so I fear if Florence was in one of those, there might be trouble finding her records.'

Bryony typed the same brief letter to each hospital, unwilling to engage in unnecessary dialogue with the wrong institution.

Winding Wood
Crofton Lane
Forest Row
East Sussex

15th October 1989

Dear Sir/Madam,
I am trying to find out any information you might have about my sister, Florence Thomson, who may have been admitted to your hospital in July 1944. If you have any records of her time with you, it would be most helpful if you would write to me with the details.
Yours faithfully,

Bryony Marshall

Two weeks slipped by, and then another. Bryony tried to curb her impatience, understanding the slow-moving nature of the NHS, especially when inquiring about a patient admitted over forty years ago. Were such ancient records even kept, and how easy was it to access them? One morning, a letter arrived from Warlingham Park Hospital, apologising they could find no admission record for anyone by that name. A few days later, a similar letter came from Cane Hill. Bryony's spirits plummeted, fearing her mission to be in vain. Emily offered words of reassurance.

'You're doing your best, Mum. If it comes to nothing, at least you've tried.'

On a grim winter morning, Bryony returned from shopping in Forest Row. As she opened the front door, an official-looking letter lay on the doormat. Suspecting it was from another hospital and dreading a further dead end, she headed to the kitchen, fumbled for her reading glasses, and tore open the envelope.

Nightingale Ward
Brookwood Hospital
Woking
Surrey
GU21 2FE

4th December 1989

Dear Mrs Marshall,

Thank you for your recent letter. I apologise for the delay in contacting you. We are short-staffed as the hospital is being prepared for closure. I can indeed confirm your sister, Florence Thomson, was admitted on the 10th of July 1944. If you wish to discuss this matter further, please call me at the number on the letterhead.

Yours sincerely,
Doctor Helen Buxton

Bryony felt a whirlwind of emotions. Until now, there had been nothing tangible to anchor Edith's story. She believed her, but the doctor's confirmation made everything more real, brittle, and immediate. She smoked two cigarettes, drank a cup of black coffee, and picked up the phone to make the call. The call connected to Doctor Buxton's secretary, who then put her through.

'Good morning, Mrs Marshall. I'm pleased you called because I'd like to help you with Florence. Our records list the next of kin as Violet Thomson. I believe that's her mother?'

'That's right. Violet's our mother, and she's still alive, although she suffers from dementia, so I can't ask her much about this.' Doctor Buxton continued in a tone that made Bryony think she was carefully selecting her words.

'We never knew that Florence had a sister. Only her mother visited, and that stopped in 1959.' Bryony thought.

'Mother did have some limited sense of conscience.' Then she had a change of heart and reflected 'Those visits would have tortured Florence. She must have begged her to take her home. It was cruel to visit and give her hope. I can only think Mother wanted to find her own salvation.' She said aloud.

'It's important for us to find out as much as possible about Florence. We've only just learned she'd been sent to an asylum. We were told she died during the war.'

'How deeply upsetting for you, I'm so sorry. We hear many sad stories, and sometimes relatives are ashamed to admit a family member had been a patient at the hospital and want to cover it up. What you tell me is not unusual.'

'More like guilt than shame in Mother's case,' thought Bryony. She continued.

'One of the things we want to know is when she died. How many years was she a patient at Brookwood?'

'I'm sorry, I don't quite understand,' replied Doctor Buxton, confused. Bryony clarified.

'If we know when she died, we can find out where she's buried or where her ashes are.'

'Mrs Marshall, I had no idea you didn't know. Please forgive me for my insensitivity. Your sister isn't dead; she's been here for forty-five years as a resident of Nightingale Ward.'

Chapter Three
Brookwood

Later that afternoon, Bryony asked Emily and Joe to join her in the sitting room to relay her news. From her shocked expression and grave tone, they feared there would be more awful information about the family to take in. Joe lit a log fire, and the flames crackled and roared, struggling to keep the room warm even then. It was crisp and cold outside, and the drafty old house was never easy to heat.

William, the family's bruiser of a black cat, lay stretched out on the hearth to absorb maximum warmth, blissfully unaware of the turmoil going on around him. Bryony rather envied William for his peace. With anxiety in her voice, Emily asked.

'What is it, Mum, you look awful? Have you found out something else? I can't think what other dark deeds my grandparents committed to add to their list of crimes. Bryony paused and took a deep breath, visibly seeking to compose herself.

'I called Brookwood Hospital today. They confirmed Florence was admitted in July 1944.' Emily said, her voice giving away her anger.

'Oh my God, so there's no doubt it's true. I suppose I hung onto the slightest possibility that Edith fed us a pack of lies.' Bryony went on.

'There's more, and this will be hard for me to tell you.' Joe and Emily looked at each other, their faces ashen, fearing what was to come next.

'Florence isn't dead. She's alive and has lived in that fucking place for forty-five years.' Bryony did not often swear, and her profanity only emphasised how deeply she felt about the subject. Emily stood up and started pacing around the room.

'It's horrendous. I'd naively hoped Auntie Florence died peacefully years ago and had been released from her torment. Perhaps that was wishful thinking on my part. But to discover she's been confined for forty-five years! It's terrible. What Florence has endured is pure and simple evil! I won't be visiting Granny again. As far as I'm concerned, she's dead.' With that, she sat down and buried her head in her hands. Joe, his voice choking with emotion, said.

'What I'm struggling to understand is how any mother could do something so monstrous to her own child. What kind of person was Violet?' Bryony replied.

'It's unthinkable. A mother's instinct should be to nurture and protect. I can only imagine Mother had a fatal flaw, a weakness of character, which surfaced when faced with a stark choice: either lose everything or lose her daughter. To her eternal shame, she chose the latter. She had a difficult early life; her transformation to her charmed existence at Winding Wood is not something that would have happened to many. But as a result, she became a monster. Doctor Buxton also told me Florence lives in a private room at Brookwood. At least she has that small dignity. And guess who was paying for it all these years?'

'Violet?' Joe suggested.

'Absolutely right,' Bryony confirmed. Emily continued.

'So, she knew Florence was still alive. All that time, she was paying the fees. It must've been out of what was left of Grandpa's illicit earnings. Do you remember the fuss she made maintaining she couldn't manage the cost of the care home fees. We thought we were going to have to sell Winding Wood at one point to cover them. It was only when we found those investments she'd forgotten about we worked out she could afford it.'

'What a bitch,' Emily spat. 'We could have helped Florence if we'd known. I would have visited her. This is too much. Today, I've found my aunt's still alive, but the person who I thought was my grandmother is gone; she never existed. I thought her to be a kind and gentle woman, but that was a façade. I'm mourning for the fact I don't have the grandmother I loved anymore.'

'Hang on,' interrupted Joe. 'Aren't we missing something here? We thought we'd been haunted by Florence's ghost for months; we'd hardly had a night when we hadn't had to listen to the awful crying, and now, we're told she's still alive. Who the hell's haunting Winding Wood, it can't be Florence?'

'You're right, Joe, it doesn't add up, does it?' replied Bryony. In trying to work out why we have a ghost, we've uncovered a terrible secret, but it's not the one that will help us solve the mystery of the crying woman.' Emily said.

'We may have to accept the ghost's someone who has nothing to do with the family at all.' Joe went on.

'I don't think we can live here anymore. I can't cope with the crying, and the sense something sad pours out of every brick is unbearable. Bryony, you have happy memories of your childhood here and you too, Emily. But is this a place to bring up Elsie? God knows what effect it may have on her. As hard as it might be to consider, Winding Wood's no longer a good place. Bad things have gone on here. I think sadness, the memories of the angst and pain has been absorbed into the fabric. It could be that Winding Wood itself is crying. Have any of you thought of that?' Bryony replied in a grave tone.

'I've not always seen eye to eye with you, Joe, but you're right on this occasion. I'll speak to the estate agents tomorrow and get the wheels in motion. The bloody house is getting far too expensive to maintain.'

She glanced around at the room which she had known most of her life, comforted by the familiarity of it, but also having the feeling she wanted to run away and seek to forget the awful things which her parents had done. Then, with a thud, she understood that would never be possible. How could she forget her sister? The pain would stay with her for the rest of her life. Violet and Thomas's wicked acts threatened not only to poison the family home for all time but ripple down through generation after generation, causing pain and havoc as they went.

Chapter Four
Andy

Bryony was adamant she would visit Florence in Brookwood by herself.

'Being confronted by so many people will be too much for her,' she declared when Emily tried to convince her otherwise. As a compromise, they agreed Joe and Emily would go with Bryony in the car, leaving little Elsie with the childminder.

'You can't face this alone, Mum,' Emily stated firmly. 'We're coming with you and will wait outside. No argument.'

The drive around the M25 was interminable; a breakdown had caused a serpentine traffic jam. Bryony sat in stony silence in the front, cursing their slow progress, while Joe reassured her they had left ample time to reach the hospital at the time arranged. Their mood was sombre, each of them acutely aware of the emotional burden which lay ahead. The lashing rain and leaden skies did nothing to help, only adding to the sense of foreboding.

Eventually, they arrived at the gates of the hospital. Joe turned to Bryony and asked.

'Are you ready to face this? We're still ready to join you if you would prefer.'

'You're very sweet, Joe. Thank you,' Bryony replied. Her critical and vocal views on her son-in-law had softened since the devastating revelations about her sister. Throughout her life, she took on the role of the strong one, first looking after Florence as a child and shielding the sensitive girl from life's turbulent currents. Later, Violet needed her support, and as the matriarch of Winding Wood, she provided a bedrock of support for Emily and Joe. Now, she felt vulnerable, looking to her younger family for strength. Where Bryony had once dismissed Joe as a dreamer and a waste of space, she now recognised his gentle qualities of love and kindness. She continued.

'I feel as if I failed Florence. I always took care of her, and in that awful moment when she most needed me, I was absent.' Emily reassured her.

'None of this is your doing, Mum, you didn't fail her.'

'Maybe. This is why it's important for me to meet Florence by myself. I have things to say I don't want to share in front of others. This is my atonement for the ills of our family.' Emily nodded in empathy with her mother.

'Understood, but we'll be outside if you need us.'

They made their way up the long drive, fringed on either side with ominous dark laurels, which in parts overhung the way, seeking to oppress the visitor. Soon, the asylum loomed into view. The sprawling, Gothic style buildings with dark masses of brick, slate and lead, whispering much about the multitude of lost souls incarcerated within its walls. Their lives and secrets subsumed to the overbearing structure.

They passed a tall building capped with a metal water tower, then pulled up in front of the arched main entrance. The hospital soared above them, a high square tower with a church-like spire, long Gothic windows, and a foreboding slate roof. Joe remarked.

'When they built these places, they wanted to demonstrate their power and make the patients feel insignificant. It's dreadful.' Emily responded.

'It gives me the creeps. Mind you, I'm not sure how much longer it'll be here. Look at that building.' Turning their heads, Joe and Bryony saw the oppressive ward block on the other side of the courtyard had windows boarded up with corrugated iron.

Joe parked the car. Bryony got out and pulled her coat tight around her to shield from the cold rain. Emily said.

'I love you, Mum.' Bryony remained silent but offered a faint smile in response. She spotted a sign pointing to Nightingale Ward and left her family behind. She had never been lonelier.

Her route first led her through an enormous, empty room. Its vaulted ceiling soared above her, and her footsteps echoed on the stone floor in the silence. She wondered what the room had once been used for, and then she saw an old black and white photo mounted on the wall of staff and patients seated at long tables, so maybe it had been some kind of dining hall. Whatever its purpose, it now brooded with an atmosphere of decrepitude. The dark smell of damp permeated the air, and the only furniture remaining was a few folding wooden chairs stacked against one wall.

At the other end of the room, another door creaked open, revealing a courtyard. The paving stones had heaved up in places, allowing fingers of weeds and grass to proliferate. On the opposite side, Bryony saw a further door labelled 'Nightingale Ward'. She turned the handle, but the door was locked. Confused, she noticed a bell push and pressed it, hearing a distant tinkling. Before long, the sound of footsteps came, and with a clunk, the door swung open.

'Good morning,' she said. 'I've come to visit Florence Thomson.' The young male nurse replied.

'You must be Mrs Marshall. I'm Andy Whitmore, one of the nurses who takes care of Florence. I've been expecting you. Follow me.'

'Thank you. Can you tell me why this door's locked? It seems most odd in a hospital.'

'This is a locked ward, Mrs Marshall. The patients are not free to come and go.'

The knot in Bryony's stomach tightened further. Was this a hospital or a prison? Andy Whitmore led Bryony up a flight of narrow stairs. At the top, he unlocked another door with a set of keys jangling from a chain clipped to his belt. Ahead, a long, wide corridor stretched away into the distance. It was sparsely furnished, with the odd chair and table dotted along its side.

'Come into the office, Mrs Marshall. Would you like a coffee?'

'Thank you. It's been a long drive, so it'd be appreciated.' Now seated and more relaxed, she took in the nurse for the first time. She thought he was in his late twenties, a small man with reassuring brown eyes and fashionably bushy sideboards. She decided she liked him and continued.

'I expect Doctor Buxton explained to you that until recently, I had no idea Florence was alive.'

'She has, and may I first say, how sorry I am. On our part we didn't know Florence had anyone other than her mother, and she hasn't visited for many years. This is such a sad situation.'

'So, can you tell me a little about Florence and what I can expect when I meet her?'

'Yes, of course. I've been working here for seven years. I've grown very fond of Florence. She's a lovely lady, but you have to brace yourself; her condition has deteriorated, and now she's completely blind.'

'What's caused this? Can you explain, please?'

'When I first met her, she could still communicate. She had severe difficulty with her speech, and her conversations were, may I put it this way, a little childlike. She would stumble over words and then forget what she was talking about. This was the result of the operation they performed on her. But she was so full of love. Her language was limited, but all she ever spoke about was joyful and warm with loving words.'

'Sometimes, she would cut little bunches of flowers from the hospital garden and give them to me. When a new patient was admitted, she tried to help them become accustomed to the place; she took them under her wing. Such a kind lady. You would think she would have been bitter, but all she ever expressed was love. I remember her talking about you and how much you cared for her.'

'And what's changed?'

'Within the last year, Florence started to fade away and then lost her sight. Instead of our conversations, be it that they'd been a little limited, she fell silent. Then, in the last few months, there were long periods where she cried for hours on end. It broke my heart to hear it. I would sit with her and hold her hand, then eventually she calmed down.' Bryony stiffened, crying and tears had tormented them at Winding Wood for so long. Andy went on.

'Now there's something else I have to tell you. I don't know how open you are to considering the possibility there are things we don't understand in this world, powers and forces beyond our comprehension?'

'With what's happened recently, I'm open to anything!'

'When I first started to care for Florence, she told me about her beautiful family home in Sussex, and when she explained it was called Winding Wood, I couldn't at first quite believe it!' Bryony replied.

'Why, what's so special about the name?'

'My Grandmother was a famous medium and psychic called Ekatarina Zagorski, she lived in a house called Winding Wood in Crystal Palace.' Bryony's eyes opened wide with amazement, remembering the story which her mother had often told her. Andy said.

'Bryony, I think I was brought here for a reason, so I could take care of Florence. I don't know how the two houses of the same name are connected; can you explain it to me?'

Chapter Five
Golden Pathways to Wisdom

Bryony finished recounting the tale of her mother attending the séance at Ekatarina Zagorski's house all those years ago. Andy, with his eyes gleaming with excitement, responded.

'As I said, I was brought here for a reason. I'm so happy to have learned of this connection. It's put the last piece into a jigsaw I've been puzzling out for years. Let me explain: I believe I've inherited some of my grandmother's psychic abilities, and I always sensed I was connected to Florence. When I visited Grandma at her Winding Wood I used to love a beautiful scale model of the Crystal Palace she had made for her. It was such a beautiful thing.' Intrigued, Bryony said.

'When I was a little girl, my father drove us up to the North Downs, and we watched the Crystal Palace on fire. I've never forgotten that sight, horrendous and glorious at the same moment. Then I remember Mother telling us about the model in Ekatarina Zagorski's house. Andy smiled and opened the desk drawer. He withdrew a sheet of paper and said.

'Look at this. It seems Florence never forgot that sight either.' She saw a line drawing of the Palace, coloured in with crayon. At the bottom, Florence had signed the picture. Andy continued.

'Your sister used to draw every day; her pictures were often of the Palace. There was no doubt, I was linked to her and had a duty to look after her. I made absolutely sure I did everything possible to make her comfortable and feel loved.'

'Bless you, Andy. It's comforting that you genuinely care for my sister. She's endured much and I'm grateful for what you have done for her. But what made you come to Brookwood? You said you were drawn here to care for Florence, but how did you know?' Andy replied.

'I can't tell you exactly how, but when I applied for the job here, I sensed that all the barriers were being removed one by one. I saw the job advert in a magazine I did not normally read. I got the job even though my qualifications were not up to their requirements. On the day of the interview, my car broke down, and I only got there in time because a total stranger stopped and gave me a lift; he drove ten miles out of the way. Destiny is a powerful force and looking back I'm convinced that a higher power was pointing me to Brookwood and Florence.' Bryony fell silent for a moment then asked.

'Can I see her now, please?'

'Yes, but please prepare yourself, she may not remember you.' With that, he led Bryony out of the office and down the long, echoing corridor, speaking softly as they walked. A few female patients shuffled around aimlessly or sat slumped in chairs along the way, adding to the desolate atmosphere. Andy said.

'I came to work here, full of hope and determination to change the world for the better. But I've realised this place is a repository for those society wants to forget. See that woman? That's Doris. She came in twenty years ago after a panic attack. They coshed her with drugs, fried her brain with electric shocks, and look at her now. She won't ever be going home.' The woman in question was small, hunched, and flinched like a whipped animal as they passed. Andy went on, his voice even lower.

'That nurse,' and he gestured at a stout woman with a bulldog's neck; 'she has a penchant for roughing up the patients if they do something she doesn't like. Crimes like not eating their supper.'

'Dear God,' said Bryony.' It must be tough for you working here and having to see that. I hope Florence...' she tailed off, her voice quavering. Andy reassured her.

'I can assure you, for all the years I've been here, no one laid a finger on her. She's been loved and protected, but I can't look after all the others, the system is too broken. See that room,' and he gestured to an open door. 'That's the strip-down room. When the patients are admitted, they're kept there for days. No windows, no TV. Nothing other than a mattress, and they're only allowed their underwear. It's like a prison cell, to break them down as they enter the system.'

At the end of the corridor, he gestured.

'This is Florence's room. Shall I come in with you?'

'No, thank you, this is something I must face alone.'

She smiled and touched his arm in thanks for his kindness, then opened the door.

Florence sat on a chair in the middle of the sparse little room. This was barely the pretty, vibrant young woman Bryony remembered. Her hair was pure white and cut short to her head in a helmet, little attempt at any style. Her face had a grey pallor from too little sunshine and bland, repetitive hospital food; it was, however, remarkably unlined for a woman of sixty-three years.

She wore a shapeless plain cream skirt and brown jumper, which was covered with a plastic bib and apron. Florence's eyes were both hidden behind a white caul. Either a gift to protect her from seeing the misery around her, or was it to conceal the sacred secrets of her soul from prying eyes? Bryony was unsure which. Florence stared straight ahead, unseeing, captured in a perpetual shadow world.

The room smelt stale, the meaty odour of lunch still lingering. It was furnished with little more than a metal-framed single hospital bed and two chairs. The floor was covered in green lino, and the one small window was draped with a thin curtain. The only other furniture was a small wardrobe and a bedside cabinet on which rested a photo frame. Bryony picked it up, and tears ran down her cheeks as she saw a picture of her and Florence as children. Next to it was a battered old book. It was *'The Snow Queen.'* Bryony recalled her parents gave it to Florence one Christmas when they were children. She carefully turned over the fragile cover, inside was a pressed flower, a rose, and from its condition, looked very old. Holding it to her nose, she detected just the merest hint of fragrance.

She pulled over the visitor's chair next to where Florence sat and, for a few moments, prepared for what she would say. A voice in her head kept saying she could not cope with the situation, and she wanted to run outside to smoke a cigarette. Still, she reminded herself she had always taken care of her sister and would start again now, picking up where she left off so many years ago.

'Florence darling, it's Bryony. I've come to visit at last. Please forgive me it's been so long.' There was no response from her sister. She went on.

'I had no idea you were here in this hospital. They told me you were killed at the Guards' Chapel. I cannot begin to tell you how sorry I am that I've not been here all these years to love and care for you.' Still no response from the silent, sightless woman.

Over the next hour, Bryony talked and talked, remembering so much of what they shared together, and reminiscing about all those little memories which make up a life. The games in the garden at Winding Wood, the dolls they played with, the holidays with mother and father. At some point, Bryony took Florence's hand in hers, squeezing it every now and then for reassurance. All the time she talked to Florence, she thought, 'I can make this better; I'll do everything I can to help.' Her love for her sister was as alive and vibrant as it had been in 1944, the years of absence and loss did nothing to dim its flame.

'And do you remember that Christmas when we played sardines, and no one could find you, as you had hidden in the coal shed! It took Mother hours to clean you up again!' Still, there was no reaction from her sister.

In time, Bryony felt exhausted and decided she would conclude her visit for the day. She said.

'I love you so much, Florence. I'll come and see you again next week and gently pulled her hand away. As she did, Florence stretched her hand back, placed it over Bryony's and squeezed it. At that point, the emotional strain became too much for Bryony, and her long-overdue tears flowed, but she knew Florence had heard her words. She left the room, not wanting Florence to hear her sobbing.

Shortly, Bryony was sitting with Andy in the office, having another coffee. He said in a caring tone.

'That must've been incredibly painful.'

'It was, but in a way, I feel better now. At least she recognised me, and I hope she understands she's not been abandoned by her family. That's some comfort.' Bryony drank her coffee. Andy said it would be fine if she smoked. She said.

'The strange thing is that for the last few months, we've been haunted at Winding Wood by a woman who cries and cries. It's heartrending, and we were sure it must be Florence. But she's alive, it must be someone else and there's another mystery to unravel. To be honest, it's become so draining we're going to sell the house. Another family can deal with the problem!'

'Maybe,' said Andy, 'but let me tell you this. I learned much from my grandmother; she was a remarkable woman. She explained to me there are many things we don't understand, and we should always have an open mind to the mysteries. When I started working, she gave me one of her books. Look, I have it here; I keep it on my desk. I believe this is another reason we were destined to meet, so I could help you solve Winding Wood's riddle.' He passed her the old, leather-bound book, which was called

'Golden pathways to wisdom'

'There are a couple of passages which I think are relevant. I'd like you to read them later; I'll mark the places. I believe you'll find them comforting.'

Bryony bade her farewell, thanking him profusely for his kindness, and arranged to visit Florence again the following week.

Emily and Joe were still waiting for Bryony in the car. Bryony indicated that she could not speak much about the visit; she was too drained. They drove home in silence, the emotional overload having sapped every last bit of her energy. Bryony assured them that she would share everything the next day.

Later on, Emily ran her a bath and poured her a double gin. After relaxing in the hot water for half an hour, she got out and dried, put on her dressing gown and went back to her room, where she sat on the edge of her bed. She opened the book at the first place Andy had marked:

'There are those whose minds and memories are not what they once were, and some of them are very sick and troubled people. They hover in a twilight void between life and death, where the boundaries of what we understand to be life become blurred. Who is to say they cannot travel beyond the confines of their mortal bodies, slipping the chains which bind them to this earthly existence, and visit places that held special meaning for them? Perhaps, in the stillness of the night, they are drawn back to the homes they cherished, their ethereal forms seeking the solace of familiar surroundings. Their tears echo through the corridors of time, a lingering reminder of the love and memories they hold dear.

These spectral wanderers, caught between worlds, may find themselves retracing the steps of their past, returning to the comfort of places they once loved. It is said the heart's longing can transcend the limitations of the physical body, reaching out across the vast expanse of the unknown to touch what was once beloved. In these moments, they might find a semblance of peace, a fleeting respite from the torment of their fractured minds. The places they loved, now shrouded in the mists of memory, become sanctuaries for their restless spirits, offering a brief reprieve from the shadowy limbo they inhabit.'

Chapter Six
The Snow Queen

The young carer entered Violet's room to bring her medication and collect the untouched dinner. She couldn't blame her for not eating it; the food served to the residents was far from appetising. Tonight's offering of dry, curled-up ham and greasy chips would not have tempted anyone. She glanced around the room, searching for dirty plates and cups to take to the kitchen. Christmas was four days away, and the staff had made a half-hearted attempt at festive cheer, draping a piece of gold tinsel in each room. The carer thought to herself.

'Not sure why we bother with this tack. They have no idea what day of the week it is, let alone Christmas.' She moved to the window to make sure it was tightly shut. The weather forecast predicted a freezing frosty night, the coldest for years, and the rambling old house was difficult to heat. She fumbled with the catch, and it seemed to slide home.

'Goodnight, Violet,' she said as she left the room. There was no response.

That night, Violet slept deeply and dreamed more vividly than she had for years. To accompany her slumber, a fierce wind whistled and howled through chimneys and crevices. The window rattled in its frame, fearing it may come open and allow in the bitter cold, Violet decided to check it was securely latched. She gingerly swung her legs out of bed and found her slippers where the nurse left them for her. But then she decided she was asleep and still dreamed.

Then, a sound, a rhythmic knocking loud enough to be heard over the wind and the rattle of the window. Fear gripped her insides. What was making the noise? She tried to reassure herself it was just the wind. Something must have come loose and was being blown about. She moved closer to the window. Then, with a sick thud she remembered her awful nightmare which had repeated over and over, the ice cold woman, determined to kill her. A dream nested within a dream, was it she who had finally caught up with her?

Knock! Knock! Knock! Knock!

Louder and louder, it reverberated around the room. Her fear surged again, bile rising in her throat. She wanted to get back into the protection of the bed and hide away, but first, she had to find out what was making the noise.

Knock! Knock! Knock! Knock!

She decided the knocking sounded as if it was being made by a mortal hand, not the random banging of something caught in the wind, but how could that be? Her room was on the second floor. She pulled back the curtain and pressed her face close to the window but could see nothing through the dirty panes. For a moment, she thought she had awoken, then decided that without any doubt, this must be a dream. No one could be making the strange noise.

Knock Knock! Knock Knock!

Violet shook with fear, terrified of what may be outside. Her mind thought of a thousand possibilities, but none were rational. She struggled with the sticky catch, then found the strength to force it open. Driven by the wind, the window swung violently into the room, almost striking her. The freezing blast of air dug like knives into her face, but she had to know what the knocking was.

Violet's mind twisted over and over with confusion: asleep or dreaming? Whichever it was, terror dug deep into her soul. She tentatively extended her trembling hand through the open aperture to explore the unseen. The incessant banging on the frame reverberated through the night, a haunting rhythm that sent shivers down her spine. In that dreadful moment, as if time itself had stilled, an icy hand clasped hers in a vice-like grip, sending waves of chilling dread through her veins. It was the same icy hand that had brushed against her face in that old, recurring dream.

As her eyes adjusted to the dim night light outside the window, a shadowy outline materialised before her, and it was the face of the Snow Queen, Violet remembered from an illustration in the book she had given to Florence. She wanted to shout out but found no sound would come from her throat other than a strangled moan. An old memory came up from the deepest part of her fading mind, and she heard a quote from the book echoing through the wind.

'The Snow Queen's beautiful palace was built on the tears of a thousand broken hearts.'

Then, the face dissolved and reformed, and she saw the woman from her nightmares. Now aged and etched with deep lines, the visage exuded an aura of malevolence that froze her to her very core. To her visceral horror, she recognised who the face belonged to. The awful realisation of finally knowing who the woman was after a lifetime of dreams the most gut-wrenching terror of all. Her heart pounded like a drum in her chest as she stood paralysed, ensnared in a nightmare made manifest.

Violet howled like a wounded animal, hoping someone would come to save her, then begged a God she didn't believe in. But with the night staff occupied watching videos on the floor below, there would be no salvation.

In the morning, a different nurse came in to bring Violet her breakfast. Upon opening the door, she was instantly assaulted by the icy cold and saw, to her horror, the window flapping and banging in the wind. Violet was lying prone on the floor, her thin nightdress no protection against the frosty blast. There was no doubt she was dead, her eyes wide open in questioning horror, her face blue, and her lips covered in a white frosting of ice.

Chapter Seven
The Graveyard

Joe meandered through the walled Rose Garden, captivated by the glorious blooms and savouring their soft, perfect fragrance. The radiant display was in stark contrast to the yellow-brown desolation of the previous year.

'This is a happy place now,' he thought, and he realised he wasn't only speaking about the garden but Winding Wood itself. Purged of its secrets, the old house exhaled a long-held breath, transforming into a haven of light and joy. The mournful cries and atmosphere ceased, replaced by an air of warmth and contentment.

Once a repository of the Thomson family's hidden truths, the house now became a sanctuary where shadows no longer dwelled. The spell was broken, the truth about Florence revealed, and after she died peacefully in her sleep the previous month, she was, at last, liberated from her suffering. The weeping stopped, and immediately, the veil of misery lifted away.

The family noticed a new presence in the house, and now, the ethereal visitor only brought happiness and love. Bryony would feel a gentle hand on her shoulder if she felt distressed. Emily said if she was lonely, she would sense a comforting aura. Joe noticed the rose garden blooming more abundantly than it had for years. The plans to sell the much-loved home were quietly forgotten. Winding Wood would keep its family close to its heart and nurture them in return.

Before then, it had been the shrine of intrigue, and in the fertile soil of hidden truths, all secrets flourished. Now, the story of Winding Wood had been told, the purging sunlight of honesty purified the place and allowed all to be revealed.

Joe found divulging his past to Emily a monumental challenge. The weight of his words pressed heavily upon his heart, for he feared making her feel rejected and inadequate simply because he had once loved a man. As he gently held her hand, his voice trembled with the desire to reassure her of his love. She listened, her expression showing a mixture of understanding and pain, and at that moment, she said she truly understood.

Their conversation flowed with an honesty that neither had ever experienced before. Then Emily, with a voice full of guilt, confessed about the man she had helped to die. Together, they wept for her lost friend, and Joe assured her that the angels in heaven would see what she had done as an act of profound love and compassion.

As they continued to share their innermost fears and sorrows, the barriers that had stood between them for so long began to crumble. Their love, once shadowed by secrets and unspoken truths, now shone brightly. With this newfound clarity, they recognised that their life story was written in the stars with a timeless love.

Bryony's secret, however, was revealed more gradually. Piece by piece, she allowed her vulnerability to surface. This woman, who had devoted her entire life to caring for others and shouldering her parents' grief for Grace, was now ready to be supported herself. Joe, the man she had once deemed useless, emerged as her confidante and grew to be as cherished as a beloved son.

It seemed as though a valve had finally been released, allowing the boiling steam of long-concealed truths to escape into the fresh air. Each secret unveiled acted as a powerful catalyst, revealing other hidden truths in the brilliant light of day. The raw honesty of these revelations transformed their relationships, uniting them in a profound, shared understanding.

As Joe went back into the house, it embraced him with familiar warmth and comfort. He smiled to himself, so happy this was his home with his cherished family. He passed Bryony in the hall. She held the car keys in one hand and a bunch of cut flowers from the garden in the other.

'Are you off to visit the graveyard?' he enquired.

'Yes. I've picked these for Florence,' she smiled and walked out towards the car.

Bryony visited her sister in Brookwood twice a week after their reunion. It was a long overdue pilgrimage, which she willingly made. Maybe there would be some peace in atoning for the family's heinous sins. Each time she went, she asked Florence to try to find forgiveness, not for the sake of their mother and father but for her own redemption. Bryony wanted to take her home, but in her fragile state, the Doctors advised against the move.

Although her sister could barely communicate, an occasional squeeze of the hand or the faintest flicker of a smile reassured Bryony, Florence finally knew she was loved and not abandoned. On one visit, her sister managed to whisper, 'Bryony.'

When Andy called to say Florence had passed away in her sleep, Bryony felt an immense loss for all the years that had been stolen from them and for the years to come, which would never happen.

Florence was buried in a nearby churchyard, where the family had gone to church on Sundays in times that now seemed a millennia ago. Bryony replaced her trips to Brookwood with regular visits to her sister's grave.

On this glorious summer's day, she went alone, carrying the bunch of flowers she picked from the garden. She walked slowly through the tilted old gravestones with their fading inscriptions. Each one had its own story to tell if the passer-by took their time to dwell on them. The loves, the lives lived, the losses. Along one side of the graveyard was a high, mellow brick wall covered in a thick layer of fragrant honeysuckle, host to a myriad of bees. Bryony paused here for a few minutes and rested on a bench. The smell of the flowers was divine and the sound of the bees going about their business, a lovely chorus to accompany her thoughts.

She arrived at Florence's grave. The newly installed headstone was clear of moss, and the letters of the inscription, sharp and unfaded by frost and the passage of time.

Florence Rose Thomson
1926-1990
Much loved and missed

Bryony smiled, remembering a long-ago conversation when Florence had said to her.

'When I'm twenty-one and have handsome, wealthy boyfriends and glamorous clothes, I think I'll start using "Rose" - it's much more sophisticated than Florence. Having the right name's so important to attract attention.'

Bryony had then jumped on her sister and tickled her until Florence begged her to stop. The two girls giggled for hours, deciding the pros and cons of different names and then deciding exactly what their husbands would be like.

Bryony knelt and placed the flowers on the grave; waves of emotion and loss surged through her, and tears poured down her face. She said out loud.

'Florence, I'm so sorry I couldn't be there when you needed me most. I always took care of you when we were girls, didn't I? I miss you so very much and will always love you. We'll meet again one day, and then we can make up for all the years we've lost.' She pulled Ekatarina Zagorski's book from her pocket and opened it at another section Andy had marked. She read the passage out loud.

'In the loving embrace of the infinite, where time is a concept which does not exist, lies a golden realm of eternal forgiveness. Here the onerous burdens of mortal life, the scars of pain and regret, the harsh words of blame and judgment, and the dark shadows of past wrongdoings are healed by the hands of divine grace. In this celestial haven, the soul finds healing and renewal, bathed in the purifying light of the most glorious love.'

Later, when Bryony walked back to the car, she thought.

'Ekaterina's words are beautiful. I hope in heaven Florence will be able to find forgiveness for Mother and Father. If anyone could discover it within themselves, it would be Florence. She had the purest of hearts, more than anyone I have ever met.'

Printed in Great Britain
by Amazon